the SECRETS of ATTRACTION

Also by Robin Constantine
The Promise of Amazing

the
SECRETS
of
ATTRACTION

ROBIN
CONSTANTINE

BALZER + BRAY

An Imprint of HarperCollins*Publishers*

For Jim

Balzer + Bray is an imprint of HarperCollins Publishers.

The Secrets of Attraction
Copyright © 2015 by Robin Constantine
All rights reserved. Printed in the United States of America.
www.epicreads.com

Library of Congress Control Number: 2014952619
ISBN 978-0-06-227951-4

Typography by Erin Fitzsimmons
15 16 17 18 19   PC/RRDH   10 9 8 7 6 5 4 3 2 1

First Edition

ONE

"BREATHE," LEIF COMMANDED.

I reached out from my waist, hips aligned, then leading with my right hand, tilted toward the ground, forming a perfect triangle. Trikonasana was *my* pose. I was a statue. A rock. My feet firmly planted on my sticky mat.

Leif, a.k.a. Hot Yogi, stalked the room with his hands clasped behind his back. Slouchy black pants, gray tank, dark eyes looking at everyone and no one.

It was hard not to picture him naked.

"Trikonasana is a full-body opener. Spiral the femur bone inward, feel the stretch across the front of your chest, same as cobra. Imagine yourself between two panes of glass." His gravelly voice echoed all the way down to my root chakra.

Between two panes of glass.

With you, Leif.

Wren looked over her shoulder and wiggled her fingers in greeting as she reached toward the ceiling. We'd been taking class on Thursday nights at Namaste Yoga along with my mom since November. Mom took it to stave off her midforties. When she asked me to join her, I begged Wren to come along so at least I'd have someone to snicker with. Turned out, we both enjoyed the chill feeling we had after class. I also liked it because I was height-challenged, but after an hour of stretching, I felt about six feet tall. (Okay, maybe more like five foot six—still, taller.) For the first month a pear-shaped, aging hippie named Lena taught the class. Her ample booty defied gravity but halfway through January she herniated a disc in her lower back and took a leave of absence.

In walked Leif.

The class had started out with fifteen women. After word of the Adonis in yoga pants, it doubled in size. Wren and I were the token high schoolers. The majority of the class was made up of moms and twentysomethings. There were a handful of guys who either came to class with their wives or seemed to know Leif from the other studio where he taught. I'd never wished for an hour to feel longer in my whole life. He made Sanskrit sexy.

Leif stopped beside Wren and touched the spot between her shoulder blades, then leaned down and whispered something to her. She lengthened into the pose, reaching upward with her outstretched arm. Her fishtail braid slipped from her shoulder as she looked toward the ceiling. The side of her mouth curled in an almost imperceptible grin.

"Nice," he said, before walking over to the next mat.

The thought of royally screwing up so Leif would come over and adjust me crossed my mind. On the other hand, I wanted him to notice how effortless I made every pose. I was beginning to defy gravity myself. I took a breath and settled into stillness. Leif moved past me. For the barest of seconds, my eyes met his.

"This is an active pose. Feel the energy shooting out from your fingertips."

In that sip of a moment, energy shot through more places than my fingertips. *Zowee.* I wobbled.

In our next downward dog, Wren peered at me from under her armpits.

Omigod, she mouthed.

Bitch, I mouthed back, but smiled.

We'd had a bet on which one of us Hot Yogi would adjust first. I owed her an after-class chai latte. She shook her head and smiled as we moved forward into warrior one.

"Breathe."

All the reminders to *breathe* used to get on my nerves; as if breathing was some airy-fairy cure-all and not something you did automatically. One little pause, though, was sometimes all it took for me to refocus—even off the mat. *Breathe.* When I wondered how I'd scrape up the money to go to the summer arts program at the NJ Design Institute. *Breathe.* When Zach kept bringing up the subject of getting serious. *Breathe.* When sometimes it felt like it would be years before my life really began.

I dreamed of building something beautiful. A tree house. A home. Hell, a skyscraper that glowed purple at night. And the journey of a thousand steps toward my dream was a summer program to gain some practical experience so my résumé would stand out. I'd wanted to go to Pratt's summer program, but NJDI was more in my price range. And if I kept my GPA over 3.8, killed it on the SATs, and had a portfolio to die for—Pratt could be my future. Whenever anyone tells you to shoot for your dreams, though, they never mention the *cashish* involved. Buzzkill.

We moved down to the floor series, ending with happy baby, a pose that required you to grab the outside of your feet and pull downward so your knees opened wide and your vadge was presented to the world like a cookie tray. So okay, I got the baby thing, but doing this pose felt far from innocent to me.

"Happy Grayson," I whispered to Wren.

That was all it took. She snorted. Her belly convulsed and she lost her grip in the pose. She rolled to her side, hands over her face, body rocking with laughter. One of my greatest pleasures was making her lose it. She scurried from the room and didn't make it back for savasana. As the final "Om" sounded, Wren crept back in to roll up her mat.

"Mads, I'm freakin' mortified."

"Come on," I said, folding my mat. "That was pretty good."

Hot Yogi was suddenly in front of us. Wren's face flushed.

"I'm, um, I'm so sorry, for um, laughing like that, it wasn't—" she stammered, her hands gripping her rolled-up sticky mat.

"Hey, that's what yoga is for. Release. Laughter. Tears. No judgment," he said, looking from Wren to me.

The two of us were mute, but I swear I could hear Wren swallow as the word *release* crossed his lips. The kind of release that came to mind had nothing to do with laughter or tears. *Whoa, breathe.*

"I hope you two are comfortable in the class. You know they have one with music for teens on Sunday nights?"

"This fits better in our schedule," I said, bummed that he noticed how young we were. Up close there were fine lines around his eyes, but he couldn't have been more than, say, twenty-six was my guess. That would make us ten years apart. Maybe a world apart at this stage, but someday . . . hmm.

"I think it's awesome you're here. If I had practiced in high school, I might have had an easier go of it," he said as my mother sidled up to us.

"Thank you, Leif. I'm always ready for a good night's sleep after this class," she said as she ran a hand through her sweaty bob. Even my mother was not immune to Hot Yogi's charms. Every week, she freshened up her pedicure and put on tinted antiaging moisturizer before leaving the house for class. Seeing them together I realized that she actually could go for it, if she really wanted to, but that would have been so, um, ew, to be crushing on the same guy as my mother.

Leif smiled, clasped his hands at heart center, and gave us a small nod. "Glad to oblige."

He turned away and was approached by two women who gushed about how their shoulders had never felt better since coming to this class. Right. Their shoulders felt better. The subliminal undertone of this whole exchange was almost too much to bear.

Wren pinched me. "You owe me a chai."

Mugshot was the coffee shop next to the yoga studio. It was a little place that was always jam-packed after class—whether it was because of the tool behind the coffee bar messing up orders or that it was the one place aside from the diner where you could hang out for the price of a cup of coffee, I wasn't sure. The line was slowly strangling my yoga buzz.

"So, details, what was it like?" I asked, stepping closer to the counter.

Wren's eyes grew wide. "What do you mean?"

"When Hot Yogi touched you."

A glow rose in her cheeks, and she looked over her shoulder

to inspect the line. She stepped to her other foot.

"He didn't *touch* me, it was an adjustment. I was focusing on my ocean breath."

"Wait, there was a touch and a whisper. What did he say? C'mon, something worth a chai."

Wren bit back a smile, leaned toward me, and said in a breathy voice by my ear, "'Tighten your core.'"

"O . . . em . . . gee."

She laughed. "And then when he put his hand on my back? There was nothing, you know, *sexy* about it, but damn, I sort of felt it . . . *everywhere*."

I thought of the jolt of insta-lust I felt when my eyes met Leif's. I'd probably just melt into a puddle if he ever gave me an adjustment.

"Everywhere?"

"Well, for a split second. Then it was just weird. My mind went into overdrive, like, Did I remember to put on deodorant? Would Gray be pissed? I couldn't concentrate after that. Yoga's supposed to leave you calm, right? I miss Lena."

"Are you insane? Lena was awesome, but really, no comparison."

"I didn't feel like I had to put on lip gloss for Lena."

"Amen," said the girl behind us. We both turned. I recognized her from class; she always practiced in the front row, near the corner, and could do sick arm balances for what seemed like hours. She leaned toward us and whispered,

"When he demonstrated scorpion last week—"

"And his shirt kind of fell up?" I said.

"Stop," Wren said, smiling as she checked out the texts on her phone.

"I swear, even the walls sighed," the girl finished.

"We need to drag Jazz here next week," Wren said.

"Whatcanigetcha?" asked Broody Barista, fingers poised on the cash register to ring up our order. I was tempted to say, "The usual," but it would have crushed me the tiniest bit if he'd been clueless as to what that was.

He was a tall, lanky guy whose name tag read *JessE*. I couldn't tell if his last name began with an *E* or if he was trying to make a statement; either way, he didn't seem approachable enough to call him that, so he was Broody Barista in my head. Even though I was sort of involved with Zach, flirt was my natural language. It wasn't necessarily about getting with someone, more like making friends. Week after week, I tried my best, but this guy, the rim of his baseball cap pulled low over his light brown bedhead, never got into it. He wasn't snobby or anything; more aloof, or maybe just perpetually bummed.

"Two medium nonfat chai lattes, and a chamomile tea," I answered.

He chewed his full lower lip as he rung us up, eyes on the register until the total lit up on the display.

"Seven twenty-five." He knocked on the counter and threw

a glimpse at the growing line behind us. I reached into my backpack and pulled out a ten. I laid it onto his outstretched palm, my fingertips grazing the top of the wide leather cuff bracelet he wore. He didn't strike me as the jewelry type but there it was, along with several smaller bands, including one with a brass infinity symbol, on his left wrist.

He took the bill and called the order to the guy behind the coffee bar who was too busy staring at Wren to pay attention. I followed his gaze to see exactly what he was looking at. Her deep-green tie-dye exercise tank fit her like a glove. In class she looked like everyone else; in here, with her warm-up jacket zipped only halfway, she—or more precisely, her assets—stood out. Wren was bent over her phone, scrolling through her messages, oblivious to what effect that particular view was having on this creeper. I stepped in front of her and glared at him. He raised his eyebrows at me and shrugged.

Broody Barista cleared his throat to get my attention.

"Don't mind him, he only comes out at night," he said as he dropped the change into my hand. One corner of his mouth turned up. A tiny ripple in a mysterious sea, but it was *something*. I ran with it.

"Hmm, a nocturnal perv, the creepiest kind."

He laughed as he wrote in Sharpie on the to-go cups. "Tanner, you're scaring the customers again."

"Then my job is done." Tanner flashed me a megawatt grin that was irritatingly charming. Wren finally looked up from her phone and smiled at him. When faced with his object of lust, he got flustered and turned away. All stare, no bite, apparently. Wren furrowed her brow. We moved to the end of the counter to wait for our drinks.

"What was that about?"

"*That* was about *this*," I said, tugging up her zipper. "You don't realize the power of a little cleave, do you?"

She grimaced. "Ick, really? I'm sweaty and gross."

"No, you're dewy and flexible," I said, nudging her.

The door opened, sending a gust of cold air into the café. Leif stepped in, my mother right behind him, a plastic Quick Chek shopping bag swinging from her wrist. "Mom!" I waved her over. She acknowledged me with a nod, but then turned back to Leif and another woman from class. I wanted to tell her I'd already ordered for her, but she seemed completely engrossed in conversation.

"My mom is picking me up," Wren said, finally shutting down her phone and putting it into her yoga bag.

"Too sweaty and gross for Gray?" I asked.

She chuckled. "No, we're going to the mall to pick up a Kate Spade diaper bag for Brooke's baby shower. Can't be shown up by the in-laws. They're getting some stroller called a Bugaboo or something—it's, like, a bazillion dollars, so we have to, you know, up our game."

"Kate Spade for crappy diapers? Leave it to your sister. I thought your mom didn't believe in the baby-shower thing."

"She doesn't, but Pete's mom and sisters do, so they're throwing them a his-and-hers baby shower over George-town's spring break. Tropical theme. Can you imagine? My mother's making Josh go too. He said only if there are drinks with umbrellas. At least I get to drag Gray with me. Feel like taking a ride to the mall?"

"As lovely as that sounds, I should probably get some work done on my portfolio for the summer program application. It's due in mid-April and there's nothing impressive about it yet."

"That's doubtful. Even your stick figures are impressive," she said.

"Two nonfat chais," Tanner announced, pushing the cups toward us.

"We need a chamomile tea, too."

"Oh, right." He stole a glance at Wren before turning back. She was too nice to glare at him, but she averted her eyes and busied herself by rifling through the pocket of her yoga bag. More people began to gather around the tiny pickup area.

I reached for our cups and handed Wren her drink. They had *Thursday Girls* scrawled in Sharpie across the front. Broody Barista had given us a nickname. Maybe he had noticed more than I thought.

As my lips touched the rim of the cup, I anticipated the spicy sweetness of warm chai but got a gulpful of bitter. My taste buds recoiled.

"Don't drink that," I said, a second too late. Wren's wrinkled nose told me her drink was off too.

"Hey, yo, dude. There's coffee in these drinks."

"No there's not," Tanner said. He placed another to-go cup on the counter. The tag read CHAMOMILE; at least he hadn't screwed that up.

"Yes, there is, I can taste it," I said, putting it on the counter. I took off the lid to show him—the usual creamy tan was a darkish brown. He brought the cup up to his nose and sniffed.

"Ah, so there is. My bad." He slid the drink back to me. I had the sudden urge to pour it over his head, no matter how strangely endearing his awkward and pervy attempt at macking on Wren had been.

"Dude, we're backed up on drinks. What's the holdup?" Broody Barista joined in. The line that had been near the door now surrounded the pickup area.

"There's coffee in our chais," I said, meeting his gaze. "Maybe if your coworker wasn't busy checking out my friend's rack, he would have realized he was screwing up our drinks."

I'd meant it to be funny, but annoyance seeped through. Wren coughed and slunk back. Tanner paled. Some of the people waiting around us shifted. I was aware that Leif and my mother were beside me, still carrying on what must have been the world's most interesting conversation. My nerves sizzled, but I felt vindicated.

"Sorry," he said. "I'll take care of this."

He grabbed our cups and whispered something to Tanner,

who suddenly lost the clueless glint in his eye. They both worked quickly on the drinks, hammering them out one by one, until Wren, my mother, Leif, and I were the only ones left from the original line. Leif's matcha involved some special brewing method and a whisk. I wasn't sure what was taking so long with our lattes, but standing near Leif was enough to make me forget about the whole thing. He smelled like sandalwood incense.

Wren checked her phone.

"My mom's outside."

"Here's your chai, Thursday Girls—my apologies, next week is on me." Broody Barista slid the cups toward us. Wren grabbed her drink and hoisted her yoga bag over her shoulder.

"Sure you don't want to hit the mall?" she asked.

"Nah, have fun perusing the diaper bags," I said.

"Yeah, right. Thanks for the chai." She wiggled her fingers at me as she hightailed it out of the café. For a split second, I wanted to change my mind and go with her. Wren complained about her family sometimes, but in the end it was usually with a smile. The Caswells were awesome—always something going on, so different from my own family. Not that I had anything to complain about either. My mother and I were a tight unit of two. Small but fierce.

Broody Barista's eyes were on me. Waiting. I took a sip of the much-improved chai.

"It's great," I said. "Thanks."

"Anytime you have a drink emergency, please, consider it handled." He put a hand over his heart and bowed. Ice broken.

"I'm Madison," I said.

"Jesse," he answered.

"So now you don't have to call us Thursday Girls."

"I came up with that." Tanner poked his head out from behind Jesse as he put Leif's tea on the counter. Leif broke away from my mom to get his drink. I turned to see her take out her phone and *tap, tap, tap* something into it. What in the world were they talking about?

Tanner touched my shoulder. "So your friend . . ."

I swallowed back a grumble. *Really?* "Is very involved," I replied.

"How involved?" he asked. For a moment I felt bad for him; his eyes were so hopeful. He was sort of cute, in that messy, guy-who-doesn't-know-how-to-take-care-of-himself kind of a way. Sort of a fixer-upper.

"Like, soul mate–involved."

At this Jesse let out a derisive pop of a laugh.

"Ah, soul mates. I guess that means she'll be available in a month," he said, resuming his post at the register to help someone who'd just wandered in. It might have been funny if there hadn't been an edge to his voice. Maybe *soul mates* was overstating it, but did he have to be so freaking dismissive? Tanner put both hands on the counter and leaned toward me. His nails were bitten to the quick.

"Okay, well, um, what about you?"

I stepped back. "Dude, you did not just ask me that."

His face got twitchy. "Wait, no, I didn't mean—"

"Look, I can still tolerate you at this point, so before you say anything else, let's forget about this convo, 'kay?" I grabbed my mother's tea and turned my back to him.

"I hope you wanted this iced," I said. My mother smiled, and tucked her phone into her bag.

"Oh, Mads, I forgot, thanks," she said, taking it from me.

"I'll meet you out front."

"No, wait, we're done here." She wrangled her black hole of a purse open again, and took out her keys. "Leif, thanks, I'll be sure to check those out."

"Let me know if you need anything else, Dana."

They're on a first-name basis now?

I walked toward the front door, willing myself not to turn around, but in the reflection of the glass I could see Tanner making exaggerated hand motions at Jesse, who just shook his head and smiled. Like, a real one, teeth and all. I was too irked by what had gone down to say good-bye. As I pushed out through the front door, I wondered if he'd remember his offer to buy our chai lattes next week. My money was on *probably not*.

"So what were you and Hot Yogi talking about?" I asked my mother as she cut the wheel yet another time before finally

15

pulling out of the parking spot. Parallel parking had never been her strong suit, and it took her almost as long to get out of the space as it had to negotiate getting into it in the first place. Once she straightened out the car, she sped down the side street.

"Madison. *Hot Yogi?* His name is Leif." There was an amused lilt in her voice.

"C'mon, he knew your name. You guys were chatting; just wondering, you know—if you're into him."

She made a sound somewhere between a gasp and a laugh. "Into him? I'm old enough to be his mother."

My mom was going through a major dating dry spell. The better word was probably *drought*. The last more-than-one-date boyfriend/man-friend/suitor I remember her having was when I was ten. *You and me against the world, Mads*, she'd say, whenever I joked about it. Mom prided herself on being self-made, and it was great, but sometimes I wondered if she was waiting for me to go off to school before really hooking up with someone. Not that she needed anyone, but didn't everyone need a little fun now and then?

"But you can't deny his hotness."

We stopped at the red light and she raised her hands in surrender. "Fine, you win, I can't deny his hotness, but I can forget about it when I'm talking to him."

"Okay—how? Because I can't."

"Simple," she said, reaching for her chamomile. "I can

compartmentalize. Leif's not dating material but he's got more experience than me in yoga, so I'm attracted to his brain."

I snorted. "His brain? Why?"

She sipped her tea as we sat at the light.

"I'm ... well ... I'm thinking of becoming a yoga instructor."

I couldn't hide my surprise. "Wow, instead of hair?"

"No, mostly as a supplement, but I don't want to be in the salon forever. Standing up all day, crouched over customers, is taking its toll on me. Once we started practicing yoga, I felt better, had more energy. My nerves aren't as frazzled at the end of the day—you know, I feel *even*."

"And Leif is going to help you?"

My mother fiddled with her cup until it was back in the holder. The light turned green. She eased through the intersection, absentmindedly playing with her hair as she drove the five blocks home.

"We were talking about programs, turns out the studio is starting up a teacher training session in a few weeks. He gave me some book titles, websites—I'm still just thinking about it. With classes and materials . . . it's not cheap."

"Oh." Money. The Grim Reaper of dreams.

"But it's not *un*doable, either. I can take on some clients at home again, if necessary. You know, we'll see. I have some time to think about it," she said, pulling into our steep, narrow driveway and cutting the engine.

It made me think of my own plans for summer design camp

at NJDI. I was working toward the scholarship, but Mom had been putting money aside as a backup plan. There had to be a good five hundred; it might not cover the yoga training, but it was something.

"I think you should go for it. You can use the money set aside for my design camp."

"Absolutely not. That's your backup plan." She collected her bags and cup. I grabbed my latte and slung my yoga bag over my arm as I stepped out of the car.

"I won't need a backup plan—I'm getting that scholarship, or I could always get a job," I said.

"You know how I feel about that. High school . . ." she said, coming around to my side of the car.

". . . is my job," I finished. "But it doesn't pay very well."

She put her arm around me. "Ah, someday it will."

We walked up the stoop. My mother paused.

"Did you forget to turn out the lights?"

I shook my head. "I didn't leave music on, either."

As we got to the top step, the door opened.

"Paul," my mother said, grinning.

He filled the doorway, arms outstretched as he sang along to "Rosalita," which was blaring in the background. Smells of ginger and something peppery wafted through the open door. Paul stood there, wearing a cook's apron over dark jeans and a forest-green polo. He ensnared my mother in a bear hug before letting her pass.

"Ah, Mademoiselle Pryce," he said to me, kissing me on one cheek and then the other like he always did when I first saw him, before closing the door behind us. "You look more like your mother every day."

"Really?"

"Hey, would that be a bad thing?" my mother asked as she kicked off her clogs and put her cup down on the hall table. I plopped my yoga stuff next to the door.

"I guess not," I teased.

She unwound the scarf from her neck and tossed it over the coatrack, then walked across the parlor to turn down the music. "You said Friday."

"You should check your messages," Paul called over his shoulder as he went back into the kitchen. "I had the opportunity to grab a flight from Houston today, so I took it. Hungry?"

Paul Saylor was one of my mother's oldest friends from high school and pretty much the only steady male presence in our lives. He was a captain for a commercial airline and whenever he had a layover in the New York metro area, we were his own private hub. In exchange for a place to rest his head, he cooked and brought baked goods from his various travels. We occasionally got to fly places. Not a bad deal.

There were times I caught them looking at each other a certain way, which made me think that at one time they might have been more than just pals, but neither of them ever divulged more, even when I prodded them for information.

They hugged and stuff, but it was strictly platonic. After the conversation I had with Mom about Leif, it made me wonder what compartment she kept Paul in—*nice man-friend with occasional travel benefit; makes a mean omelet?*

"Not really," my mother yelled back. "But it smells delish."

"Vegetarian stir-fry." He returned with two open long-necked Heinekens dangling between his fingers. He held out one to my mother but she shook her head.

"Hey, I'll take it," I joked, balancing my cup and fishing through my jacket pockets for my phone. My mother shot me a look. I checked my messages. There were three from Zach.

"I think you should reconsider the beer," Paul said.

I stopped checking my messages. My mother raised her eyebrows. Paul looked at me, then back to my mother.

"You should reconsider because in a few hours it will be Friday," he said, holding it out again. "Hey, Mads, I brought the good doughnuts—they're on the kitchen table."

I took that as my not-so-subtle cue to exit stage left, which suited me fine. I had more pressing plans on my mind, which consisted of a hot shower, some sketching, a call to Zach, and now a good doughnut. This particular delectable delight was from our own lovely hamlet of Bayonne. I found the telltale white bag on the table, and reached in for a purple sprinkled doughnut. When I went back into the parlor my mother had the beer in her hand.

"Later," I said, brushing past them and climbing the stairs.

"You're welcome," Paul said.

"Thanks," I called down, before taking a massive bite of the doughnut. The chocolate and sprinkles melted in sweet perfection in my mouth. Maybe not as healthy as yoga, but equally as blissful. I went into the bathroom, pulled back the shower curtain, and turned on the water. I scarfed the rest of the doughnut waiting for the water to get hot, and checked my messages.

Hey Sexy
Waiting.

And then a selfie headshot of Zach, lying on his bed, hair splayed on his pillow, one arm carelessly flung over his head.

My heart did a disturbing little hiccup.

Yum.

Breathe.

TWO

"VERY SUBTLE BEFORE, T," I SAID, WIPING DOWN the coffee bar. "You should have Thursday Girl's digits in no time."

"Dude, don't remind me," he said, sweeping the floor in front of the counter with broad strokes. "You know how long it took me to work up the nerve to talk to her?"

It was seven thirty. The Mugshot dead zone. The after-yoga crowd had subsided and the café was dotted with the usual suspects: Hipster MacBook guy gripping his organic house blend while he stared at his screen; Homework Girls and their hot chocolates, although it seemed they were doing more laughing at me and Tanner than studying tonight. And Leif, feet up on the chair across from him, bowl of bright green pond water in one hand, a book titled *Wherever You Go,*

There You Are propped open in the other.

There'd be one more rush after the last yoga class of the night but then my shift would be over. Strange as it sounded, I dreaded it. Being alone with my thoughts was a dark place these days. At least at work, there was always some distraction. New customers. A difficult order. The douchey Top 40 station that my manager, Grace, insisted we play, which spewed corny sentiment 24-7. It all kept me from descending into my own private pity party. I focused on the task at hand, which at this moment happened to be ribbing Tanner about his latest infatuation.

"But you didn't actually talk to her; you pulled your serial-killer stare," I said, mean-muggin' to demonstrate. He stopped and rested his chin on the broom handle.

"C'mon, I wasn't that bad, was I?"

"No comment," I said, scrubbing a nonexistent spot on the counter.

"Damn, I can't help it," he said, sweeping again, although all he was doing was moving dust from one part of the floor to the other. I didn't have it in me to lecture him on the proper use of a dustpan. "I even screwed up talking to her friend. What was her name?"

"Madison."

"See, man, you got her name without any effort."

"We had a normal conversation. I wasn't angling for her name. You're trying too hard, dude. Just, you know. Smile now and then. Make their drinks right."

"She's with someone, anyway."

"Right. What did Madison call it . . . *soul mate*–involved? Bide your time, T, cuz once words like *soul mate* start getting tossed around, things turn to shit," I said, taking my best three-point shot with the mop cloth to the sink and missing by a foot. I crouched down to pick it up. Homework Girls giggled.

"How do you do it?"

"Do what?" I popped up to face him but Tanner was standing in front of Leif. When he realized Tanner was talking to him, Leif placed his book down.

"How do I do what?" he asked. Leif seemed like a pretty stand-up guy who could talk about Buddhism or the latest Joss Whedon flick with equal enthusiasm, but this was the first time Tanner had ever posed what sounded like a personal question. I tossed the mop cloth into the sink for real and leaned across the pickup counter to listen.

"You know . . . not get distracted when you teach?"

Leif looked at me. I shrugged.

"I'm not sure I'm getting you," he said to Tanner.

Tanner gestured with the broom handle to punctuate his words. "All that bending and stretching and yoga pants . . . I'd be walking around with a constant—"

"Whoa," Leif said, laughing and putting up his hand.

I shook my head. Tanner Smith was a great bass player

and a passable barista, but a puerile cretin when it came to the opposite sex. He had a point about the yoga pants, though. They'd been banned at school.

"Do you have some yogi voodoo shit that gives you special powers? C'mon, you've never wanted to, you know, get with someone?"

"It doesn't work that way, Tanner." Leif picked up his book again.

"Never been tempted?" I asked, fiddling with my infinity bracelet. The thin leather band had conformed to my wrist. I wasn't sure why I still wore it, a reminder of what might have been—even if . . . *Jess, just break ties already.*

Something always stopped me.

"Temptation is part of life, isn't it?"

"So you *have* wanted to bone a student," Tanner said, pointing the broom handle at Leif.

Hipster MacBook's gaze broke away from his screen for this answer.

Leif chuckled and turned a page. "No. When I'm in class, I'm a teacher, not looking to score. You do realize there is more to life than boning someone."

Tanner looked at me, shook his head, and resumed sweeping.

"Guess I can strike 'yoga dude' off my career short list."

The entrance bell chimed to announce customers. I glanced at the clock. A little early for the after-class rush, but

I turned to man the register anyway.

And walked straight into a brick wall.

At least that's what it felt like.

Hadn't we set limits with this place?

Hannah. *My* Hannah.

Arm in arm.

With Duncan. My friend. My drummer.

Ex-drummer.

Ex-friend.

Together.

Still.

My feet moved in slo-mo, slogging through mud. Every step was calculated, as if the moment I stopped thinking about getting to the counter, I'd snap and go ape-shit instead. I knew odds were that I'd run into them as a couple at some point. I just never thought they'd come to *me*. My hands found the register. Numbers.

You can do this, Jess.

Avoiding Hannah had been impossible, since we lived on the same block, but I was able to get away with a nod or a wave and then duck into my house or car. Duncan had been easier to lose, a limb I'd simply cut off and ignored in the hallways at school. All those nights in my room, imagining what I would do when confronted with the reality of HannahDunk, never included the scenario where I was mute behind the coffee counter, ready to take their order. If they were waiting for me to ask them, "How may I help you?" we'd be waiting for a very long time. What could they possibly want?

"Hi, Jess," Hannah said, looking up at me with wide, unblinking eyes that still made my stomach feel like a chipmunk was clawing its way out. Duncan's hand was planted on the curve of Hannah's hip, the corner of his mouth upturned. She noticed me notice and shifted, putting a whopping inch between them.

"You should know we have a strict no-douchebag policy on Thursdays," Tanner said.

"Nice to see you too, T," Duncan said.

"What do you want?" I asked.

"Blueberry mango bubble tea," Hannah said, biting her lip. "Nonfat milk."

"Blueberry mango bubble tea." The words hardly felt like my own. I was playing the role of dipshit cashier monkey, and if it would get them out of Mugshot faster, I could handle it.

"And . . ." I looked squarely at Duncan. His hair was longer and the beard he'd been trying to grow since the summer had finally filled in instead of looking scraggly, his Dave Grohl–wannabe transformation complete. He took a breath as if to say something, then clammed up and shook his head.

"I'm good."

That's it? Screw with Hannah, break up the band, ruin my life, and the first words you say to me are "I'm good"?

"Three fifty-two," Jesse, the dipshit cashier monkey, said. Duncan pulled a five out of his pocket. *One dollar, four dimes, a nickel, three pennies.* I deposited the change in his open hand and clapped Tanner on the shoulder.

"Got this?" I asked. He nodded. I walked to the back room.

"Jess, wait."

I ignored Duncan and shoved through the doors into the back. Grace was in her office at the computer, her fingers flying across the keyboard as she worked on an Excel spreadsheet. I knocked on the doorjamb. She startled, took off her glasses, and rubbed her eyes.

"Hey, what's up?" she asked, smiling.

"Would you mind if I left? The yoga rush is over and I have this killer physics test tomorrow and—"

"And leave Tanner here . . . alone? It's only about another hour or two, do you really need to leave?"

Tanner had been at Mugshot for three months and had come up short twice on the register due to errors. And he was *still* learning the drinks. I knew he'd be up to speed soon enough, but leaving him here alone wouldn't be doing any of us any favors.

"Can I at least grab my book out of my car, catch some study time during the lull?" I lied.

"Yep, great, Jess. Thanks," she said, readjusting her glasses.

I grabbed my jacket and keys and headed out the back door. Cold air smacked me in the face, but it didn't sting as much as . . . *I'd seen them*. Spoken to them. The earth was still on its axis. No sinkhole opened to swallow me up. Still. It felt as shitty as I thought it would. They'd have to take their order to go, right? I'd just sit in my car until they left.

I slid into the driver's seat of my Beetle and reclined it, closing my eyes. Flash. *Duncan's hand on Hannah's hip. His smug look.* The image was burned into my eyelids. I fiddled with the bracelet, rubbing the curved infinity symbol between my thumb and forefinger. Why couldn't I take this fucking thing off? *Infinity. Forever, Jess.* Bullshit. Was there even a chance she was still wearing hers?

Tap. Tap. Tap.

I jumped. Duncan's face filled my window.

"We need to talk."

Know what's worse than seeing your ex-girlfriend with your ex–best friend? Getting caught trying to avoid them.

Duncan stepped away from the door to let me out. I jacked up the seat, pretended to look for something, anything, even though we were both painfully aware of the awkward situation. I found a stray straw wrapper and shoved it into my pocket before finally getting out and leaning against the door.

We stood in silence, glaring in opposite directions, which probably looked like a killer album cover. We could call it *Betrayal*.

"Get a new drummer yet?" he asked.

"Nah, still looking."

Duncan and I had never officially talked about him leaving the band. I'd put up a sign on the message board at school and in the local rehearsal place to announce that Yellow #5 was looking for a drummer, even though I had no intention of finding someone new at that point. It was more of a passive-aggressive *fuck you* to Duncan, the quickest way to cut him as deep as he'd cut me. Four guys in two months had expressed interest. Tanner had collected the names, but we never had any auditions. Maybe I thought it would all blow over and HannahDunk would come crawling back to apologize. Maybe that was what was about to happen. A long-overdue apology.

"I joined Plasma."

Fuck me.

"Kenny Ashe's band? Cool."

"I guess. He couldn't believe I left Yellow Number Five. I couldn't either. Thanks for the heads-up."

I glared at him.

"That's your doing. Don't even start with me."

"You couldn't call me? We couldn't talk about this?"

"What's to talk about, Duncan? You made your choice."

"We could have worked this out, bro."

"That's where you're wrong."

"C'mon, Jesse. It's been two months."

"What do you expect from me, Duncan? To say, 'No hard feelings, come back to the band. Hell, maybe Hannah can play tambourine now.' We'll all be one big, happy family, until maybe Tanner tries to hook up with her."

He squared his jaw, nodded. "Don't."

"Or what?" I asked, standing up straight. I never thought of myself as a violent person, but all I wanted to do was punch him in the throat. I'd been sick. Like, *sick*-sick, with some apocalyptic flu over Thanksgiving break, when they accidentally hooked up at a party. Acci-fucking-dentally. That's how they played it.

Something happened, Jesse, Hannah had said.

I'd never in a million years thought that the something that had happened was Duncan. I still couldn't believe it.

"You had a choice," I said. "At some point, one of you had a choice."

Duncan growled and walked away, then turned sharp and got in my face.

"That's so typical of you, Jess," he said. "That this is something we did to *you*."

"It's not? What is it, then?"

"Maybe you should talk to her about it."

"I'm talking to you."

"I dig her, okay? She digs me. It has nothing to do with you. It happened."

"Have a nice life digging each other," I said, shoulder-bumping him hard as I walked past him to go back into the café.

"Jesse, I want the song."

I spun back. "What?"

"You know what I'm talking about. The song. The one we were writing before . . ."

"You screwed my girlfriend."

"Dude, stop already."

"Duncan," a soft voice called.

Hannah stood about three feet away from us, clutching her bubble tea in two gloved hands. Her shoulders hunched, she bounced on her toes, bracing against the cold.

"I'll be there in a minute, babe."

Babe. Knifepoint. Gut.

Hannah wouldn't look at me. Had she heard the "screw" remark?

She turned and walked toward the corner to wait. She pulled off a glove with her teeth and took out her phone; the light from the small screen illuminated her features. Shivering, she brought the straw up to her lips. *Who the fuck drinks bubble tea in February, anyway?* Hannah. That's who. I wanted to pull her toward me, wrap my arms around her to stop her shivering. Ask her how she could enjoy a drink that was like sucking fish eyes through a straw. The way I used to ask her. *Used to.*

"So—the song, Jesse."

I sighed. "What about it."

"If you're not using it, I'd like it. We plan on doing an original for the battle."

"What makes you think I'd hand over our song to Smegma?"

Duncan couldn't help but laugh at the nickname we'd given Kenny Ashe's band. He recovered quickly. "Because we wrote it together. It's part mine."

"It's not finished."

"You're not using it."

"Not at the moment, but soon, yeah, I will be."

"I thought you said—"

"I lied, Duncan. You're easy to replace. Drummers are a fucking dime a dozen. I already have a guy in mind, just have to make the call. Maybe *we'll* do the original for the battle."

"So you've applied already? Deadline is Monday, you know."

"That's why you came here? To get the song?"

Duncan shoved his hands in his pockets and looked up at the sky.

"Pretty much."

"Not to apologize?"

He turned to look at Hannah and raised his hand to signal that he needed another minute.

"If I apologize will I get the song?"

"Sure," I lied.

He squared his jaw again, narrowed his eyes, and then smiled, or more correctly, bared his teeth.

"I'm sorry I'm in love with Hannah. Sorry she's in love with me. Sorry this happened right under your nose and you were too full of yourself to even notice that you treated her like shit. Sorry I didn't give you or your feelings a second thought when I kissed her the first time. Sorry I still don't. Wait, no, I'm not sorry for that."

He stepped back, eyes hard.

"Just keep the fucking song, Jess. I'll write a better one."

With that, he turned and joined Hannah at the corner.

Neither of them looked back as they walked away.

I stormed into Mugshot and tore through the back room, knocking paper cups off a shelf in my wake.

"Jesse?"

I heard Grace's voice but my rage was a wave; I pushed through the doors into the café with such force they slammed into the wall. Tanner and Leif stared at me.

Get a grip, Jess.

I took a few deep breaths and grabbed the nearest thing I could find to clean.

"You need to rinse these after you use them, T," I said, grabbing the stainless steel container we used for frothing.

I turned on the hot water and started scrubbing the milk crust from the sides.

Tanner sidled up to me.

"Hey, um, everything okay, Jesse?"

"Fucking peachy."

He grabbed another of the containers and started scrubbing alongside me.

"You still have those names? The ones who called from the flier?" I asked.

He stopped mid-scrub. "Does this mean—"

"We need to find a drummer."

"JEEEEEEEESSSEEEEEEE," my sister, Daisy, yelled up the stairs for the fourth time. From the decibel of her screech, I knew we were at Defcon Two. Next it would be Dad, threatening to take away the keys to the Beetle or . . . well, there wasn't much else he could punish me with at that point. I'd become too skilled at punishing myself.

Stay in my room? If I wasn't at work, my ass was in bed anyway.

Take away the Fender for a week? I hadn't touched it since HannahDunk.

Put half my paycheck in the swearing jar? Fuck that.

I pawed around my desk for my phone and blinked the morning grit out of my eyes. 10:00 a.m. My tongue had been replaced with a bloated, hairy caterpillar.

Lemonade and vodka had seemed like such a good idea after our Friday-night Mugshot shift.

Saturday was McMann family breakfast day. The only time we were all under the same roof at the same time. Weekdays my mom crunched numbers for long hours. Sundays my dad would go off into his writing cave with strict orders not to be bothered. I worked most nights at Mugshot and spent afternoons practicing—or now, staring at the ceiling. Saturday-morning breakfast was my parents' attempt to create a perfect family moment.

For the most part, I was okay with enforced family time. I offered up just enough details to satisfy my parents, laughed at Daisy's lame knock-knock jokes, and made funny faces with baby Ty. Half the kids I knew had parents who were divorced. Mine still groped each other and "never let the sun go down on an argument." And while I didn't add much to the conversation since my breakup with Hannah, at least there was always bacon, well done, the way I liked it.

I tugged on the first pair of jeans I found on my floor, and ran a hand through my hair. *Yee-ouch.* My temples throbbed as I teetered downstairs. The morning was bright. Too bright. The pale-yellow walls of the kitchen burned my eyes like neon. I swallowed back a dry heave.

Friday after work, I'd gone over to Tanner's house with the plan to talk band strategy, which we did for all of two minutes. *Yep, still need a drummer. Will call those guys. Find audition space next week.* That was the extent of it. Then the vodka flowed and the poor dude had to listen, once again, while I analyzed the fuck out of my breakup.

"Could you get the juice glasses, Jess?" my father asked. He stood behind the griddle, flipping pancakes in the air, performing for Ty, who sat grinning in his high chair.

It was a daunting task, but I gathered the glasses from the cabinet and placed them on the center of the table next to the juice carton. My ass was an inch above my seat when Daisy blurted:

"Jesse's half-naaaaaaaayked." She stuck out her tongue for emphasis. Proving, once again, that ten-year-olds are minions of the devil. It had only gotten worse after my breakup with Hannah. Daisy loved her. My mother looked up from the newspaper.

"Shirt, Jess," she said.

I stumbled to the laundry room and grabbed the first white tee I put my hands on. My pocket vibrated. It was Hannah.

Oh hell no.

I leaned against the laundry room wall and slid down, as a memory from last night exploded in my brain. The drunk text. Three little words. If I didn't answer the call, maybe that vodka-fueled moment of weakness would cease to exist.

"The cakes are getting co—hey, you okay?" My father peered behind the laundry room door. "You're looking a little green around the gills."

With great effort, I pushed my back against the wall and rose to standing, ignoring the dizziness I felt from getting up too fast.

"Yeah, fine, I'll be right there," I said. My phone buzzed, alerting me to the missed call and a voice mail. *Great.* This had to be bad. I listened to the message.

Hey, you. Meet me at the swings. Noonish. Please. We really need to talk, Jess.

After breakfast and a long, hot shower that finally made me feel human again, I pulled on a gray hoodie and headed out to the playground at the corner. The afternoon was even brighter than the morning. I squinted to block the sun. Normally I would have raced down the street, but I was in no rush. The message had put my brain into overdrive. As I walked, my mind reeled with scenarios of what exactly Hannah had meant by *We really need to talk*.

Of course, I knew what she meant. We did need to talk, because we hadn't talked since the breakup. Or talked civilly, at least. I'd become an avoidance ninja, always ducking and disappearing, knowing the moment I locked eyes with her I'd be a goner. Hell, I couldn't even get rid of the stupid fucking infinity thing on my wrist because that would mean we actually were finite.

Hannah was on a swing, spinning in a slow circle to twist the chain above her head. My mouth betrayed my feelings with a smile. I ran my fingers across the chain-link fence as I headed to the entrance. She picked up her feet, leaned back, and spun around. A grin that made my flatlined heart feel the tiniest spark of hope spread across her face. Maybe the *We really need to talk* would actually be a confession that *Duncan is an ass-weasel, it's you I love, Jess* brought about by my innocent *I miss you* text.

Hope was snuffed out moments later when she saw me. She stomped her feet onto the padding below the swing and came to an abrupt stop, jerking forward with the momentum. The grin faded. She tried to stand up, but quickly sat back down.

"Ow," she said, putting a hand to the back of her head.

I trotted over to her. Her hair was wound up in the chain.

"Wait, don't move," I said, crouching down and trying to get it loose without scalping her.

"Jess, be gentle."

"Don't worry, I've done this before," I said, chuckling and tugging gently at the strands of her hair until they unwound from the chain. My hand lingered, raking through the bottom of her hair for a moment past friendly. She gathered her hair in a ponytail, pulling it away from me and then letting it drop again. I shoved my hand into my pocket. Her cheeks and nose were pink from the cold.

Did she have to look so damn adorable?

I sat in the swing next to her, facing the opposite direction, and I straightened my legs and pushed back, gripping the chains, but standing still.

"I miss you too, Jess. It doesn't have to be this way, you can say hello to me now and then, it wouldn't kill you."

"Ah, but it would," I said, swinging. Big mistake. My head whirled. I dug my feet back into the worn rubber mat under the swing and stopped.

"Jesse."

"Why him?" I asked.

The question stunned her. She looked down, rocking gently.

"I don't know, it just . . . happened."

"Things don't just happen, Hannah."

"You're not being fair, Jesse."

"Fair? Why am I the one who needs to be fair?"

"Do you want to talk or do you want to fight?" she asked.

I thought of all the times we'd sat, just like this, before we were officially together. Hannah was a friend, a crush, and then the best of both. At the yearly block party on our street, our parents always joked about how we were destined for each other. Her mother had even said once, "They'd make beautiful babies together," long before either of us even understood what that meant. When we were younger, it was a source of embarrassment. In recent years, not so much. Jesse and Hannah forever. I'd never really thought about it, the "Jesse and Hannah forever" thing, but I never thought of our ending, either. I swung again, this time slowly.

"Did I really treat you that bad?" I asked. Duncan's words had stalked me since our conversation.

"What?"

"Duncan said—"

"You pissed him off the other night, Jess."

"Is it true?"

She sniffled, reached into her jacket pocket, and pulled out a crumpled tissue. She always needed tissues when the weather got below seventy degrees. If you looked in any of her pockets there'd be one, rumpled and close to disintegrating. Feeling mushy over snot rags. I'd reached a new low.

"The timing of it all sucked, you know?"

"Because I was sick?"

She looked at me and pressed her lips together like she wanted to say more but didn't know how. *Oh, fuck.* This had happened before I got sick over Thanksgiving break. I wasn't sure I wanted to know. But I did, of course, want to know, being a masochist and all.

"It happened before then."

"Way before?"

"You're okay with this?" she asked.

"Sure," I lied. "If we're going to do the friends bit, we have to be able to talk, right?"

She looked at me skeptically.

"My birthday, Jess."

Her birthday. Of course. I'd been a total jackass because I knew how much she'd been looking forward to her party. *I lost track of time* was a lame excuse, even though it had been the truth. It was hard to explain, and probably even harder for anyone to understand what happened to me when I got lost in music. I'd been working on Slash's solo from "Sweet Child O' Mine," and I was killing it, just wanted to play it *one more time.* Time had no meaning as my fingers moved across the frets, burning the memory of the song into my muscles.

41

I'd only gone into my garage to fool around with it for a little while, but a little while had turned into three hours, and I was late, like *late*-late, to Hannah's sweet sixteen.

"And then the card."

I dropped my chin to my chest, staring down at my feet. "It was personalized."

"In crayon," she laughed.

Hearing it now, I couldn't deny it had been an idiot move. Why hadn't I just stopped at Walgreens on the way? Or why hadn't I bought one weeks before the party? Hannah loved cards. I knew that. Big, glittery, sparkly ones, ones that played music, even the cheap ninety-nine-cent ones for "just because." I had a shoe box filled with them from her.

"Daisy helped me, cut me a break, huh," I said, shouldering my swing into hers gently. Our knees brushed against each other.

"It was more than the card," she whispered, sniffling and swiping again.

"Hannah, I . . ."

"I love that you love music, Jesse. You're good—no, better than good, and I know how you get when you practice but . . . I go to all your band stuff: the fall concert, the block party, the time you guys played at the pool. But how many of my volleyball games have you been to? How many times do I give you a pass for being late to something before I look like a complete doormat?"

"I get it, okay, stop."

"Do you, really? Remember in the fall when we took a ride over to the city, I kept thinking, 'Wow, this is it, we're finally doing something,' and we ended up at Sam Ash for two hours. I stared at guitars while you talked to that guy with the dreads about the death of guitar solo and how you wanted to bring it back and—"

"We went for bubble tea after that. Walked around Times Square."

"It's all about the band. I want something different."

"But you're dating Duncan. He's in a band."

"Duncan plays the drums, Jess, he's not a *drummer*. There's a difference."

"And you'd rather be with someone like that?"

"I'd rather be with someone who wants to spend time with *me*."

"Hannah, I do."

She sighed, twisting up the swing again.

"You just think you do, because you can't." She let go and spun around.

I grabbed the chain of the swing and stopped her, pulled her close to me. Our foreheads touched. I tried to look her in the eyes but it was a distorted, too-close cyclops eye. She didn't pull away; she leaned into me. A sign. I moved my face toward hers, her mouth a few sweet seconds away.

"Hannah," I whispered.

She turned her head, my lips stranded there in midair.

"Please, don't."

I leaned away, staring at my feet again.

"So is this what we needed to talk about?"

"No, Jesse, I wanted to ask you for a favor."

This was getting better and better. I gripped the chains on the swing and pulled myself back to standing. It was fucking freezing out, but suddenly my pits were damp. I put my hood up and turned to her. Waiting.

"Please, give Duncan the song. He's really put—"

"WHAT?" I yelled, arms outstretched. A lady pushing a jogger stroller along the sidewalk in front of the park startled and eyed us through the chain-link face. I shoved my hands into my pockets. "This is what you meant by 'We need to talk.'"

"No. Yes. Not exactly. Look, what I just said about Duncan playing the drums . . . this Battle of the Bands thing, it's important to him. Just, reconsider. You could probably write another song in your sleep."

"Did he ask you to do this?"

"No."

Somehow that made me feel worse.

"I have to go do a few things before work. I'll catch you around," I said, walking away.

"Jesse, the song? Please."

I turned toward her. She hopped off the swing.

"I just—I know this is a mess and I hurt you and I'm sorry," she said, coming closer, "but I really hope we can be friends. That we all can be friends. He makes me happy."

This was it. The end. In a crazy, backward movie reel, our relationship swirled through my head. I'd never be the one to make her laugh so hard, soda shot out of her nose. Or pry her hands from her eyes during *The Blair Witch Project*. We'd never go on the Zipper at the St. Mary's carnival so many times in a row we'd want to hurl. Memories. Packed up tight in a little box, shoved away like the cards. Done.

"I want you to be happy, Hannah. I just don't want to see it," I said, backing away. I saw in her eyes this was a direct hit. They sharpened, lost just a bit of their light.

I resisted the urge to apologize, and left.

THREE

MADISON

YEARBOOK WAS MOSTLY PAINLESS, EXCEPT WHEN
we had our bimonthly deadline meetings. Piper Murray, editor in chief, liked to call them "socials" to make them sound
more fun, but they were really just deadline check-ins with
Chips Ahoy! and Red Bull. The yearbook office was a forgotten room in the basement of Sacred Heart. On any given day,
the heat either blasted or was nonexistent, and the awful fluorescent lighting made everyone look like zombie apocalypse
survivors. At least we didn't have to share it with another club.

We sat around a long table, noshing on cookies and waiting for Piper, who was busy staring at her bulletin board of
multicolored Post-its with the same concentration you would
expect from a warlord devising a plan of attack. I entertained
myself by continuing a mehndi-inspired floral design I'd

started earlier in the day on the back of my hand with a dark brown Koh-I-Noor pen.

I was officially on design staff and didn't need to be at both monthly editorial meetings, but it was cool hanging out with Jazz and Wren. The three of us were in the running for editor positions next year when we were seniors. Aside from looking excellent on my college app, being in charge of design was something I couldn't wait to sink my teeth into. I figured an interest in every facet of production would help my cause.

Piper grabbed a neon-blue Post-it and planted it on the desk next to me.

It had *Sadie Hawkins Dance* written in bold letters.

"What's this?" I finished the vine on my hand with a spiral and looked up.

"Marissa Teller was originally supposed to handle the Sadie Hawkins Dance section, but she's going on a ski trip with her family. I need you to take photos for the layout."

Wren covered her mouth but failed to conceal a quickly growing grin.

"This is your doing," I said, pointing at her. She had already tried to rally both Jazz and me to go to the dance since she was working it for Spirit Club.

"No, swear," she said, raising her right hand. "I'm writing the copy for the section. Although, I thought Jazz could help too—there should be a sidebar with the history of the dance, don't you think?"

Jazz glared at Wren over her laptop. Once something was said in front of Piper, there was no turning back.

"When is this?" I asked.

"Next Friday." A chorus of voices around the table answered.

"I don't get the whole Sadie Hawkins thing; I mean, technically, since we're an all-girls school, isn't every dance a Sadie Hawkins dance?" Jazz asked.

"True, but still—we need this. Between winter and midterms, this dance is the only social event until prom. It's way better than some Valentine's BS with balloon hearts," Piper said. "Maybe you could somehow work that angle in the copy. Wren, how were you thinking of incorporating the theme?"

Wren shuffled through a couple of the pages in her notebook, stopped at one and put her finger on it. "I was thinking 'On the Edge of . . . Romance'?"

"Too banal," Piper said, waving her hand. "Dig deeper, what were you going to write about? I want it to be more than just the basic 'There was a band and cupcakes.'"

"Of course. I planned on interviewing couples to see how they felt about the dance, if a girl asking a guy to a dance was even that big of a core-shaker anymore. And I know some girls are making it a girls' night, so that would be interesting to include too."

Core-shaker? I mouthed to her across the table. Wren pretended not to notice so she wouldn't lose face with Piper, who took the yearbook's theme, "On the Edge," seriously. The faculty had given us some trouble, thinking it sounded neurotic or like some veiled drug reference. Piper assured them "On the Edge" was positive and meant being on the forefront. I didn't always understand Piper's vision, but the challenge of figuring it out was kind of fun.

"Cool. I like it. Have it to me the following Wednesday after the dance, right? Jazz, where are we on the Fathers' Club layout?"

"Um, well . . . we're . . . Piper, I have no clue what I'm doing with it yet. Not sure how to make the Fathers' Club edgy. All I have so far is the fall bowl-a-thon and sponsoring Toys for Tots."

Piper knocked on the table. "Anyone have any ideas?"

Silence. I went back to working on my mehndi design—brainstorming about fathers was something I could thankfully be excluded from. There was a time when it might have made me feel awkward, but I'd grown out of it. When I was in third grade, my mother had explained it very matter-of-factly—my biological father was far out of the picture by the time she realized she was pregnant with me. He hadn't been the right person, but it was the right time and there was never a doubt in her mind that she wanted *me*.

It's not like I never wondered if he was out there, somewhere . . . but it's not like I had a gaping hole in my life either. Mom and I were fine; besides, when Wren had sleepovers I lived vicariously with Mr. Caswell doling out Sunday-morning banana pancakes or dousing us with the hose when we sunbathed in the yard. I mean, who wanted to go to some lame-ass fall bowl-a-thon anyhow? Puh-lease.

"Well, we have time to figure out how to make bowling edgy," she said, smiling and moving on to another Post-it.

"So you guys are really going to Sadie Hawkins, right?" Wren asked as we walked to our lockers after the meeting.

"If it involves me asking someone, then no," Jazz said.

"Come on, Zach can—" I began.

"You don't need to find me anyone, okay?" She dropped her chem book to the floor and muttered under her breath. Wren and I exchanged puzzled looks.

"What's wrong?" I asked, crouching down to pick up the book.

Jazz took the book from my hand and slid it onto the top shelf of her locker. "Nothing, I just hate being put on the spot like that. This 'On the Edge' thing is hard."

"Yes, but one more year, and then we'll be running the book. And we can come up with a normal theme but nothing *banal*," Wren said, mimicking a Piper hair flip with a smile.

"You don't usually get so upset at this stuff," I said.

"The meeting ran late and I was supposed to . . . I just missed my run, that's all," she said, grabbing her coat.

"Don't you usually run with your dad at night?" Wren asked.

50

Jazz leaned against her locker and frowned. She looked between us.

"I really didn't want to talk about it yet. It's so new and—"

"Omigod, just spit it out, Jazzy," I said.

"There *is* someone I wanted to ask to the dance."

"Great!" Wren said.

"No, not great—he's already going with someone."

"Who?"

"Darby Greene."

"No, who were *you* going to ask?" I was not about to let her off the hook. This was too juicy a development on an otherwise completely boring Wednesday afternoon.

"This guy I've been running with."

I motioned for her to go on but she clammed up. "Do you want us to play twenty questions to get it out of you?"

She laughed, then took a breath. "His name is Logan, remember the guy from—"

"Andy Foley's party?" Wren asked. Jazz nodded.

"What party?"

"In December, you were puking your brains out and couldn't go. We went to see Gray in Sticky Wicket. Logan played kings cup with Jazz," Wren explained.

"Oh, right. This has been going on since then?"

"No—I mean, we met that night, but it turns out he runs. I saw him at the park a few weeks back, we got to talking, and, well, we've been training together. He says I keep him on pace—we're both trying to get down to a seven-minute mile."

"How romantic," I said.

"So, yeah, I'm kind of bummed about it."

"No—you need to go to the dance," Wren said.

"Absolutely. So he can see you there, realize that his amazing running partner is also scorching, and he will fall head-over-Nikes for you."

"Mizunos."

"Huh?"

"He trains in Mizunos."

"Whatever—he won't be wearing running shoes when you train to do something else in seven minutes."

Jazz blushed. "Madison, geez."

"I'm loving this idea. Come on, Jazz—it'll be fun." Wren batted her eyelashes. I put my hands together in prayer. We stared Jazz down until she gave in.

"Okay, okay, fine—but where will I find a date?"

"Consider Zach your hookup source."

"Who's the guy who went to the movies with us the last time we all went as a group? Zach's friend . . . the blond, not the one who smelled like pepperoni."

Wren laughed. "The one you sat next to?"

"Um, Kyle, maybe?" I said.

"Yeah, we had a great conversation about history mash-ups and movies. He was pretty cool. I could handle, um, being fixed up with him."

"I'm seeing Zach later," I said.

"No, wait. Just ask Zach if you think Kyle would be into it. Then, I don't know, get me his number, I'll call him. That's how this works, right? Have to get over my nerves somehow."

"Consider it done," I said.

It was hard to focus on homework across from Zach O'Keefe. We sat at my dining room table—well, I sat; Zach took up two chairs, his legs draped over the seat of one, his body slunk down in the other, the tip of a pencil grazing his bottom lip as he read from his history textbook. Dark curls fell over his forehead. His hair had been short when we first met, close-cropped to keep out of his eyes during fall soccer. I loved the length now, the wildness of it. The way he owned the space around him was distracting.

While he studied history, I studied him—his angles and edges, the gentle swirls and waves of his hair. How his orange tee fit him just right, not too tight but showed off his chest, his arms. I could spend hours drawing his arms alone, the way his biceps and triceps curved into each other. As a subject, he was captivating.

I was supposed to be working on a dwelling design for the scholarship portfolio. I'd chosen to put an addition on my house—well, at least to draw the floor plans for it. Something functional and beautiful and congruent with the original house design. Right now, all of those words described Zach.

Except, I couldn't get his nose right. He had a small bump near the bridge that I kept turning into a beak. Noses always gave me trouble.

Without warning he snatched the sketchbook from me.

"Hey," I said. A long, jagged line now went through the picture where my pencil had still been in contact with the paper as he pulled it away. I squirmed in my seat while he looked at the drawing. Zach's idea of art was the Manchester United flag he had hanging above his bed. I knew he would never say my drawing was total crap—it was of him, after all—but showing it to him made me fidgety.

"Nice floor plan," he said, smirking and sliding it back to me.

"You're distracting." I opened up to a fresh page.

I knew art was a process; trial and error and failing and growing, but anything that came out through my pencil lately looked *nothing* like the vision in my head. Not being able to translate what was in my brain to paper made me want to hurl my sketchbook across the room.

"You need to chill, like that little shirtless dude over there," he said, referring to the new resident of our mantelpiece: a Laughing Buddha statue my mom picked up to help her focus on all the abundance in her life while she meditated.

"That little shirtless dude is enlightened, so happiness is his natural state—he doesn't need to earn a scholarship anywhere."

"No, I think he's happy because he's half-naked." Zach pulled his shirt off to prove his point. If I thought I could draw his arms for hours, Zach's torso could keep me occupied for weeks.

"See, you're smiling already," he said. "Stop worrying, it'll get done."

That was Zach. SAT scores? He'd get an athletic scholarship. Backup schools? Without a doubt in his mind he was going to Rutgers. He'd play soccer for four years, and be in TKE like his older brother. And if none of that worked out? Something else would come along. Nothing fazed him. He was spectacularly uncomplicated, a living, breathing chill pill.

"Please, you have to put your shirt back on. Want a water or something?" I asked, getting up to go to the kitchen. He reached for my hand as I brushed past him, and pulled me onto his lap.

"I think we can do better than water."

My muscles tensed to spring up, but he was so warm . . . and half-naked. Maybe he was right. I needed to loosen up, although the moment his lips grazed my neck every cell in my body snapped to attention. Chillin' was the last thing on my mind.

His curls brushed my cheek, then my chin, as he kissed my neck. I traced the curves of his arms with my fingertips, buried my face in his hair. *God, he smelled so good.* Like mint. Some sulfate-free organic shampoo his mother insisted he use. The day dissolved. *What floor plans? What dance?*

"Oh, hey, Zach," I said, my voice sounding far away to me.

"Mmmhmm."

He lifted his face to mine, planting a kiss on my mouth. He looked sleepy, unconcerned.

"Yes," he said, kissing my cheek.

"What's Kyle doing next Friday?"

He stopped, stiffened. "What?"

I pulled back from him. "There's this dance at school and—"

He laughed. "You want to go with Kyle?"

"No, but . . . is he seeing anyone?"

"No."

"Think you could hook me up with his number? For Jazz."

"For Jasmine, yeah, sure," he said, grabbing his phone off the table.

"Wait, do you think . . . He'll go, right?"

He scrolled through his contacts, copied Kyle's number, and sent it to me in a text. My phone dinged from across the room.

"Dunno, I guess. Am *I* going?" he asked, placing his phone back down.

I walked my fingers up his chest. "Maybe."

"Maybe?" He put his hands on my waist and poked his fingers into my ribs—my absolute worst ticklish spot. There was a dare in his eyes. I wriggled in anticipation.

"Okay, okay. Sure," I said.

"Sure what? Are you asking me?" His fingers poised to dig deeper.

"Zach O'Keefe, will you go to this silly dance thing with me next Friday?"

He stared me down, then all-out tickled me until I howled.

"Zach . . . okay . . . okay . . ." I begged. Just before it got more painful than fun, he stopped. I wrapped my arms around him, laughing. It took a few seconds to catch my breath. I rested my chin on his bare shoulder, resisting the urge to give him a nibble.

"Why wouldn't you ask me first?"

"Huh?" I sat up to look at him.

"Why would you ask for Kyle's number first? It's just weird."

"Your noticing is even weirder," I said, running my fingers into his hair, gently nudging him to look at me. Zach was a warrior on the soccer field and had that quiet sort of confidence that made people take notice when he walked into a room. But here, in this moment, his brown eyes searching mine, he looked lost. Did not officially being asked really bother Mr. Chill Pill?

"Zach," I said, kissing the corner of his mouth.

"Would you go . . ." I kissed the other corner.

"To the Sadie Hawkins Dance with me next Friday?" I ended by running my bottom lip across his. He took it between his teeth and nibbled, eyes still on mine. His jaw softened, our mouths dropping open. My tongue found his. Zach's hands wandered along my waist, my hip, my thigh. His kiss made me want to be somewhere soft. He stopped a moment to look at me.

"You make me—"

"Shh," I whispered, touching my lips to his again. He gathered me in his arms and stood up, stumbling for a moment before getting his footing. I laughed underneath his kiss.

"Madison."

Our mouths pulled apart, and the realization that neither of us had said my name made us both go wide-eyed. Zach looked up and gently tipped me to standing.

"Mom, I thought it was your late night," I said, smoothing my skirt. Even though I was fully clothed I felt completely naked. But Zach . . . oh fudge. He stood there shirtless and stunned. How had we missed the door being opened?

"I got off at six tonight, I thought I told you that," she said, her face flushed as she looked at Zach. He finally grabbed his shirt and put it on. Was she blushing or was it from the cold? Paul was behind her, trying his hardest not to grin and losing. They both held bags of groceries. Long, leafy sprouts and a baguette poked out of the top of my mother's brown paper bag.

Zach brushed past me.

"Here, let me help you, Ms. Pryce," he said, taking her bag.

"Thank you, Zach," she said. Paul closed the door and followed Zach out to the kitchen. I busied myself with pushing Zach's chair into the table. Straightening up papers. Anything but looking at my mother. The thought of what they might have walked in on had they arrived five minutes later made me cringe.

"Why was he shirtless?" she asked.

"He, um, was inspired by the Laughing Buddha." I pointed to the mantle and tried not to succumb to the fit of giggles that was building in my stomach. *Wow, that sounded ridiculous.* My mother put a finger to her lips to stifle a laugh herself.

"You really expect me to believe—"

"Mom, you can ask him, I swear, he was doing it to make me smile."

"You weren't going upstairs, were you?"

Mom was always candid with me about sex. Not that she was okay with me having any, just that she let me know it was cool to talk to her. We'd had the discussion on house limits when I was old enough to have friends over unattended. She was okay with boys in the house when she wasn't home but she had a strict no-bedroom policy that, even though I'd thought about it, I'd never dream of breaking. We'd done plenty of damage on the couch, though, but it was different knowing someone could walk in on you at any second.

"No."

She shrugged off her gray coat. "Good."

Zach came back to the dining room and collected his books from the table.

"You're more than welcome to stay for dinner, Zach," my mother said.

He looked up as he stashed his notepad into his backpack. The way his hair framed his face, the light in his eyes, made my fingers itch to sketch him. He pulled his jacket off the back of the chair.

"Thanks, but I have a scrimmage tonight for my indoor league," he said, telling what I knew to be a bald-faced lie. He slung his backpack over his shoulder. My body still ached from kissing him.

"Dinner will be ready in thirty, Mads, so clean up." She disappeared into the kitchen.

I walked Zach to the door.

"Scrimmage," I whispered, laughing.

"Call me later, we'll pick up where we left off," he said, kissing me.

I nodded, and stepped onto the porch, folding my arms against the chill.

"And Maddie . . ." Zach said, stopping at the top step.

"Yes."

"I'll go to that dance with you," he said, before trotting down the steps to the sidewalk. He walked up the block, looking back once to grin. I waved and went inside, jogging upstairs to my room to change out of my school uniform.

I should have been thrilled, and I was, I guess—a dance together would be a new experience for us. I'd get to hang with Wren and Jazz. Buy a new dress. And I suppose it was sort of cute the way he wanted to be asked. What guy does that? There was something about it, though—maybe the fact that I knew he wouldn't say no because that's who he was in my life. He was in the *hot boy who makes me laugh, turns girl-bits nuclear* compartment. I wasn't sure I wanted any more from him than that or if he could even give it to me.

I stayed up in my room, starting pre-calc until the smell of onions frying became too much to resist. I wandered back downstairs to find that our dining room had been transformed into a place where people could actually have a meal.

The table, half of which usually served as a catchall for junk mail and miscellaneous random crap, was completely cleared from when Zach and I were there earlier. It was set with a wrinkly green tablecloth from some Christmas past and the good china, the flowery stuff that my grandparents left when they bequeathed us the house and moved to Cocoa Beach twelve years ago. There was even a crystal pitcher of ice water on the table.

My mother breezed in with a basket of bread in her hand.

"Wow, what's the occasion?" I asked.

"Nothing, just dinner. We thought it would be nice to eat

in the dining room, with real plates for a change."

"We have real plates?" I joked. On an average night, mom and I were the takeout queens, even had our favorite, Tandoori West, on speed dial. I followed her out into the kitchen, where the delicious, onion-y aroma was even stronger.

"Can I help?" I asked, peering over Paul's shoulder into the skillet.

"Hey," he said, blocking me from seeing anything. "You must wait for *zee masterpiece*."

"Here," my mother said, handing me some silverware. I finished setting the table, then took a seat.

The fabulous meal turned out to be tortilla Española—which had nothing to do with flour tortillas and everything to do with eggs, potatoes, onions, and olive oil. Paul claimed it was a little something he'd picked up when he lived in Spain, basically a fancy omelet, or from that moment on, my new favorite food. I ran my last piece of crusty bread over my dish to sop up the olive oil that remained, and slunk into my seat.

"That was amazing," I said, scarfing it.

"Well, I try," Paul said.

My mother's plate was still half-full. She traced the rim of her wineglass with her forefinger. Her auburn bob was freshly sleek and angular and drew attention to her eyes. *Bangs.* She had bangs now.

"You cut your hair," I said to her, wondering why I hadn't

noticed before. Getting caught with Zach must have nullified my observational skills.

"Yes, finally, I was getting tired of it always in my eyes," she said, running her fingers through her new fringe.

"They make you look hot," I said.

"Ha, funny."

"No, she's right, Dana," Paul said, lifting a glass to her.

She shook her head and waved her hand, dismissing the flattery.

Wait, had Paul just called her hot? Maybe they wanted to be alone.

I inched away from the table.

"I'll clean this up, you guys hang out," I said, stacking Paul's empty plate onto mine.

"I'm still working on it," my mother said. I carried the pile out to the kitchen.

The sink was almost full with warm, sudsy water when she walked up behind me and squeezed my shoulder.

"Mads, could you come sit with us? There's something we need to talk to you about," she said. *We?* My stomach dropped to my feet. Was I about to get a lecture on being alone in the house with Zach? *With Paul right there?*

"What's up?" I asked, sitting down. I didn't know what to do with my hands, so I folded them in front of me, then I unfolded them because, duh, what am I? Five? I wished I had my pen so I could distract myself with some more mehndi design on my hand. This had to be about Zach.

"So I guess you've noticed that Paul has been here for a few days," my mother said.

"Um, yeah, I guess."

"He's here because . . . Well, do you want to tell her?" My mother took a sip of wine. I looked at Paul.

"I had a bit of a falling-out with the airline. And I'm jobless right now."

"Is that a fancy way of saying you were fired?" I asked.

"Madison."

Paul laughed. "No. They're doing a lot of restructuring and I'm not too happy about some of the new policies, so I decided to jump ship before things got too ugly. I'm through with the politics of the big guys."

"But, don't you love to fly?"

"Oh, I'd never give up flying—just doing it on a smaller scale. I have a connection at a smaller, private company and thought I'd give it a shot. It's based here in New Jersey. So if it works out, you might be seeing more of me."

"Cool," I said, looking at Mom.

"There's something else," she said.

"While I get settled, I'm going to need a place to hang out—not a permanent thing or anything but—"

"Paul wants to stay with us for a while."

They both looked at me, searching for a reaction, which on my end felt like something between shock/relief and confusion. This wasn't about Zach. At all.

"Are you *asking* me?"

"Of course," my mother said. "This involves you, obviously; some of your freedoms won't quite be the same with someone here after school."

So maybe it was a little about Zach.

"But Paul will be paying rent, so that will help with some expenses."

"It's not like I'm going to be here all the time," Paul added. "This is just home base, until I figure out if I want the job. Consider me a tenant who cooks and brings the good doughnuts. Does that sound okay?"

It felt nice sitting there with them. They say you can't choose your family . . . but what if I could? What if part of Paul figuring things out included him and Mom getting together? It wouldn't be the worst thing that could happen.

I smiled.

"It sounds fantastic."

FOUR

JESSE

"WHAT WAS WRONG WITH THAT DUDE?" TANNER asked as soon as the fourth audition victim was out of earshot.

I sat with my feet propped up on a music stand, arms crossed, doing my best impression of taking this selection seriously. Tanner had talked Ms. Shultz, the music teacher, into letting us use the orchestra rehearsal room for our auditions. It was too large a space for the measly six prospects we had, but it was convenient and came with a drum set. The possible spurned-psycho factor was what made me bail on holding them in my garage. School was the safe option. *Safe* and *rock and roll* didn't quite fit together, though. Maybe that was my problem.

"*Dude?* That kid probably has a killer Pokémon collection."

"So what if he's a freshman, he could play."

"We need someone with 'nads, T. Can you picture that kid in a bar?"

He shook his head as he crossed the kid's name off the list. *Four down, two to go.*

It had never been this hard.

Yellow #5 pretty much fell together when Tanner, Duncan, and I were in eighth grade. At first it had been more of a school club—an offshoot of orchestra. After the obligatory "Hot Cross Buns" and school Christmas pageant stuff, we'd get together and work out some of our favorite songs. Both Duncan and I could play by ear. Tanner was clumsy at first, but he had grown into a player who could hold his own. By sophomore year we were tight—a Christmas party here, a block party there, we even came in second to Plasma in Bergen Point's Battle of the Bands last spring, mostly because Kenny Ashe's neighbor had been on the judging panel. We had planned on winning this time around.

Until HannahDunk completely stole that future.

"Why aren't we playing along with them? Wouldn't it be easier to tell?"

"We're weeding. Besides, I can just feel it," I said, pounding my chest for effect.

"The first guy was fine."

"Sloppy playing. I didn't like his teeth."

Tanner sprang up from his chair and threw up his hands. "His teeth? Why are you acting like such a dick? Maybe if you took off the fucking Ray-Bans and pretended to care."

I slid the sunglasses up into my hair. "It was also obvious he had no band experience."

"We just need a body."

The more upset T got, the more calm it made me. He was getting pissed enough for the both of us.

"Why? We missed the deadline for the battle. What does it matter if we find someone today or two weeks from today?" I asked.

"Don't you miss it?"

My mouth opened but the words got stuck in my brain. Did I miss it? Aren't musicians supposed to work through their pain in music? My breakup had the opposite effect. As if playing my guitar opened a wound. I didn't want to feel it. I just wanted to forget it. And that, more than anything, scared me.

But the other night when Duncan asked for the song, I had felt something. Rage, maybe, but it was better than the facedown-in-a-mud-puddle feeling I'd been living in post-breakup. I had to keep reminding myself—I wanted this. A new drummer. A fresh start. No matter how long it took.

And I had to stop comparing everyone to Duncan. As much as I wanted to hammer the guy into the ground, he was still . . . We'd been tight. Friends and bandmates. Finding another person felt like auditioning a new family member, but that was making this damn near impossible. Maybe approaching it like Tanner had said—that all we needed was a body—was the right way to go.

The classroom door creaked open.

"Just, give it a chance, okay?" Tanner whispered.

A tall dude wearing a T-shirt with Animal the Muppet and the word *BEAST* below the picture strolled over to us with his drumsticks in hand. Whether he was trying to be ironic or just a douchebag was anyone's guess. He may as well have been wearing a tee with the word *Drummer* across it. Poser. I had the urge to yell, "Next!" just for the hell of it. I slid my Ray-Bans over my eyes.

"Hey, this is the audition for Yellow Number Five?"

"Yeah, drum kit's over there," Tanner said.

Animal dude's brows bunched together.

"I'm just . . . I thought— It's just me?"

"Yes," I said, resuming dick mode.

"Your flyer said to pick a song from either—"

I held up my hand. "Don't tell us. Just play."

His face was blank a moment, but then he stood up straight, shoulders back, corner of his mouth curling up. "Cool."

After a moment of adjusting the drum kit to fit his height, he stretched his wrists, bending one back, then the other. Tanner looked over his shoulder at me and crossed his eyes. Animal dude dropped one of his sticks, and picked it up with a laugh. I braced myself for some overplaying. Closed my eyes.

He started out hard, the beat familiar—"Smells Like Teen Spirit." Not an especially intricate drum piece, but a solid choice. I kept waiting for him to screw up, quicken the pace, miss a beat, but his timing was insane. He played soft, then explosive at the chorus, even putting his own spin on the fills. I slid my shades into my hair, sat up straight. Tanner was plucking a phantom bass line on his leg, nodding with the beat. It was the longest we'd let anyone play during an audition.

And the look on this guy's face as he pounded away was, like, *Okay, fuckers, now show me what* you *got.*

Don't compare. Don't compare.

It was hard not to—he reminded me of Duncan even if he did blow him away—at least in this audition. It was only one song—he'd probably practiced the hell out of it. Jamming with us could be different, I knew that, but for the first time all afternoon this guy made me regret not bringing my Fender. There was just one weird thing.

I stood up as he finished.

"Why don't I know you?"

"Huh?"

"The scene in this town is so small. Everyone knows everyone, and well, that was . . . You can play. Why haven't I seen you before? Were you in a band?"

He laughed. "If you can call it that. Sticky Wicket."

"Cool name," Tanner said, sidling up to me. He was practically foaming at the mouth to get this guy. I still wasn't sold, but the Animal shirt was growing on me.

"Doesn't sound familiar."

"Well, it wouldn't," he said. "We only ever did house parties, and that was when we felt like it. Guitarist was a major stoner. The band split a few months ago. Cool guy, just not as serious as I wanted to be. Do you guys play out?"

"That's the goal, we've done a few parties. We were in the battle last year. We have some prospects, a few CDs making rounds," I said, embellishing. We had one CD. That I'd sent before it all went to shit.

"That sounds cool," he said, standing up. "If you don't mind me asking . . . why are you looking for a new drummer?"

"Dude's a dou—"

"Creative stuff, you know how it is," I said, cutting off Mr. Truth. No need to spill anything until we knew this guy was in; we did have one more person to see. "Are you willing to do originals?"

"Hell yeah."

"Great, well, round two is seeing how we fit."

"Yeah, thought you'd be playing today."

"What's your name?"

"Grayson Barrett."

"I'm Jesse, this is Tanner. I'll send you a set list, but it's mostly the bands from the flyer. We have your number. Maybe next Friday?"

"Um, Friday's no good, but the rest of the week is cool."

Tanner waited until Grayson was out of the room before speaking.

"Round two? Dude, what the hell are you talking about? We'd be insane not to take this guy on."

"Can't let him know that. And what if this was a fluke? At least we have an out. Don't want to look desperate."

He laughed. "Nice to have you back."

"What?"

"Now if we can only get rid of that dorky infinity bracelet, you'll be yourself."

"It's a *wristband*, not a bracelet."

"Whatever, bring it in," Tanner said, raising his hand.

"The high five is dead, T."

"But Yellow Number Five isn't."

Duncan sat at his drum kit in the middle of Mugshot. There was a party going on around him, but he kept pounding away. I yelled over to him, but my mouth was gummy; the words wouldn't come out. Why was he auditioning? I searched over the sea of heads to find Tanner, who was busy wiping down tables . . . with Hannah. Where was my Mugshot shirt? Why wasn't I behind the counter? *We don't need you!* I wanted to yell to Duncan. Then I felt a tug on my jacket. That girl with the short hair who came in after yoga . . . *Madison* . . . stood there, smiling at me. *You should give him the song*, she said. Her eyes were so blue; I'd never noticed that before. She kept tugging at my jacket.

"Wake up, Jesse."

I could feel myself being pulled from the dream, I wanted to stay there, like I was on the cusp of understanding something important, but there really was someone shaking me . . . small hands on my shoulders.

"Jess, someone's at the door!"

Daisy stood next to my bed, dressed in her unicorn pajamas, her eyes puffy from tears. I sat up.

"Whyareyatellinme?" I yawned, propping myself up on my elbows. "Where's Dad?"

"He and Ty went out to get bagels. It's Mom's Saturday at the office. The doorbell is freaking me out. I let it ring like Dad said to when I'm by myself, but they won't go away."

I ran a hand across my face. The bell rang again. And again.

And again.

I grabbed my phone off the charger. Twenty messages from Tanner. And it was 8:30 a.m. WTF?

"It's gotta be Tanner," I said, ignoring the messages. "I'll be down in a minute."

"What if it's those guys who always talk about the end of the world?"

I rubbed my eyes. "They wouldn't be this rude. Wait in the hall, I'll be right there."

Daisy waited outside my room until I was dressed and followed me down the stairs, holding on to the back of my hoodie. As if there was anything I could do in the face of a maniac at the door. Every so often it was nice to be the big brother, I guess.

"There'd better be a meteor headed straight for the planet, T," I mumbled as I got to the landing. Sure enough, when I opened the door, Tanner was there, finger poised on the bell. The moment he saw me he rushed in.

"Smegma's got a gig."

"Come in," I said, closing the door behind him.

"Didn't you see your messages? Freakin' Smegma—already."

"Smegma?" Daisy asked as Tanner nearly steamrolled her.

"You mean Plasma, right?" I asked, motioning with my eyes toward Daisy, who did not need to learn any new words from Tanner.

"Oh, yeah, Plasma," he said, turning toward me.

"Duncan's new band?" Daisy asked.

T and I did synchronized head-whips toward her.

"What?" I asked.

"Hannah broke up with you, not me," she said, smirking. "We talk."

In Tanner's presence she turned from lil' sis back to devil's minion. I glared at her. She grabbed her tablet from the coffee table and slumped on the couch.

"What else do you talk about?" I asked.

She shrugged as she searched out yet another Minecraft video to watch.

"Oh, and Dad said if you got up before he got back, you should start the coffee."

Does Hannah say anything about me? was on the tip of my tongue but Daisy was already lost in YouTube Land and well, Tanner, my Forget-about-Hannah sponsor, was there, watching. I walked into the kitchen, motioning for Tanner to follow me.

"What is this about Plasma now?" I asked, filling up the coffeepot with water.

Tanner leaned against the counter, pulled off his toboggan hat. "They're playing a dance at Sacred Heart next Friday. I think we should go."

I put a filter in the coffeemaker and popped the lid off the ginormous can of cheap coffee Dad insisted on buying from Costco. At least it was still fresh, the familiar robust aroma releasing into the air. Nothing like the smell of our Mugshot brews, but it made me think of Madison. Madison? She drinks chai. Why would I dream about her telling me to give Duncan the song? Why would I dream about her at all?

"Aww, Tanner, I'm touched. Are you asking me to the dance?"

"We're hoooome," my dad announced, followed by quick little steps galloping into the kitchen.

"Teeeee!"

"Tyyyyy!" Tanner said, opening his arms to my little brother. He crouched down and held up his hand.

"Slap me high, little man."

Tyler reached up and whacked Tanner's outstretched palm.

"Slap me low, too slow," T said, lowering his hand and then pulling it out before Tyler could slap it, sending Ty into a fit of hysterical laughter. In my little brother's eyes, Tanner was the bomb. Same mentality. Tyler wrestled out of his coat and left it on the kitchen floor as he ran out to haunt Daisy.

"To what do we owe this pleasure?" my dad asked T.

"Tanner asked Jesse to a dance," Daisy yelled from the couch.

"Well, good to see you two getting along," my father said, crouching down to pick up Tyler's coat. He put the bag of bagels on the table, and walked off to the closet.

"For a recon mission, Mr. McMann," Tanner called after him. "Duncan is going to be playing with the new band." He pulled out a chair from the table and rummaged through the bag, taking out a salt bagel. I grabbed some silverware and the cream cheese and slid it over to him.

"Butter?" he said.

"You did not come here to mooch a bagel," I said, taking the butter out of the fridge and sitting across from him. "Is Plasma playing a dance something you couldn't tell me at noon?

"Ah, checking out the competition, classic move." Dad walked back into the kitchen, Tyler in tow. He settled Ty into his high chair and took the seat next to him.

"I couldn't sleep. I think we need to choose a drummer, today."

"We've got time," I said, cutting into my own salt bagel.

"How are the prospects?" Dad asked.

"Two guys . . . hard to choose . . ." Tanner said between bites.

The guy who'd come in after Grayson was good too but he'd been the *first* drummer for Plasma, not the one that Duncan replaced—Kenny Ashe went through drummers pretty quickly. There was something that didn't feel right about him, though. Technically he was incredible, and he had more experience than Grayson, but choosing him . . . I don't know, it felt like it would just drag us down into weird band politics, which I hated. Like if we picked him we'd be saying: *You have our drummer, now we have yours.* I wanted to start something new, not recycle. On the other hand, if we went with him we might be able to play out sooner.

"You know who you want," my father said, lifting his chin to me.

"You do?" Tanner asked, as if I was keeping a secret from him.

I shook my head.

"Sure you do, it's in the gut. Whenever we needed some fresh blood for Backtalk, it always ended up being a gut decision," Dad said, spreading his sesame bagel with butter and tearing off a piece for Ty.

"The sooner we pick someone, the sooner we can play out. We could be doing dances and stuff—"

"Screw dances, I want to play for people who want to hear a band, not slow dance," I said.

"Croooo dance," Tyler said, raising his fistful of bagel.

"It's basically money for practicing," Tanner said.

"He has a point," Dad said.

"I'd rather play the Whiskey."

"You want to be your best for Declan." Declan was Dad's old bandmate and the only one of them who had ended up doing anything remotely related to music. His bar, Whiskey Business, had been the place where Electric Hookah, a thrash band from Manalapan, had been discovered by a small indie label. Now it was every band's wet dream to be plucked from obscurity, and dates were booked far out. I'd dropped our CD off right before HannahDunk. It was cover songs, but that's what they focused on for the eighteen-and-over nights. I was pretty sure Dad could call in a favor. Maybe if we took on the second guy and had some intense practice, we'd be ready soon. But did I want a favor? Wouldn't it be better to earn it?

"I don't know, T . . ."

"Procrastination is really fear of the future," my father said, full-on college-professor mode.

Tanner nodded. "Wow, um, what he said. C'mon, Jess, we can jam with them this week, make a decision, and start practicing."

What if we chose the wrong guy? What if we were never as good as we were before? But what if we were better? Wondering about it was safe . . . and stupid.

"Okay, let's do it. Guess we're going to a dance next Friday."

FIVE

MADISON

ON SATURDAY MORNING, MOM DROVE ME, JAZZ, and Wren to the mall to hunt for something to wear for the Sadie Hawkins thing. Wren had already purchased the perfect little black dress weeks ago so she was there to help us get our glam on—and maybe hit the food court for lunch afterward.

"What do you think?" I asked, checking myself out in the three-way mirror. The lacy cream-colored dress draped perfectly over one shoulder and came to a flirty but chaste stop right above my knees, perfect for a Sacred Heart event.

And something a granny might wear.

A hip granny with rockin' shoulders, but still.

"It's pretty; you just don't look like *you*," she said.

"You should talk, where would you wear *that*?"

Wren was on tiptoe, pivoting to see the back view of a tiny

black miniskirt with zipper pockets and barely there halter top she was modeling.

"You don't think it's appropriate for Brooke's baby shower?"

"Have they changed the theme from tropical to S&M? Wait, that would probably be more fun for you," I laughed, doing a twirl of my own. *Nope, still not me.*

"No, Gray might . . . *might*," she said, knocking on the wall for luck, "actually make it into this band he auditioned for yesterday. Just trying the rocker-chick look on for size in case, you know, we get to see them play out. Think he could handle my edgy side?"

"The bigger question is, can you handle him handling your edgy side? Because I think he'd handle it fine."

"Hmm, exactly what I was going for," she said, pivoting one last time, a sly grin crossing her face.

"Okay, how about this one," Jazz said, slinking out of the dressing room in a red cocktail dress with an A-line skirt.

"Jasmine Ka-Day-am—that is . . ."

"Stunning," Wren finished.

"No, come on, better than the white one?"

She stood before the mirror, lifting out the skirt a bit and then letting it swish back into place. The color complemented her bronze skin and dark hair in a way that made her look lit-up. Not sure how she pulled it off, but she looked sexy and modest at the same time.

"The other one was nice, but this is, wow," I said, stepping back to take in the dress again.

"That's just it, I think it might be too special," she said, turning to the side. "It's not like it's prom or anything. Just a dance with someone I barely know."

"No, this is the dress that Logan is going to see you in and forget why he's there with Darby," Wren said.

"Are you bummed that you're going with Kyle?" I asked.

She crossed her arms and leaned against the wall. "No, I'm happy I'm going with him, I guess. He's cute, nice, can carry on a conversation, but he's, well, I already know I don't want to, like, hook up with him, and shouldn't that be part of a dance? Shouldn't you want to kiss your date? I mean, if it happens, great, but I'm thinking more about Logan. It doesn't feel right."

"You're putting too much importance on what things *should* be like," I said, popping back into my dressing room to try on my next choice—a strapless black-and-white brocade dress with a high/low illusion hemline. I fumbled with the zipper for a moment, then went back out to the mirror.

Wren clapped. "Now that is you."

"Absolutely." Jazz grinned.

"Yep, I think this is it," I said, twirling. The dress showed off my legs, which were seriously toned from months of crescent lunges and downward dogs. I pulled both Wren and Jazz next to me and we struck a vampy pose. The saleslady breezed in to collect the clothes off the reject rack.

"How are you girls— Ooh, so pretty," she said. "What's the occasion?"

We stepped away from each other, giggling.

"Oh, um—Sadie Hawkins Dance," I said.

"Fun. I have to say that red dress is lovely. Didn't seem like much on the hanger, but on you it's really smashing. Let me know if you girls need anything else." She darted out of the dressing room with clothes draped over her arm.

"See?" I said. "Even the saleslady thinks you look *smashing*."

"She's not exactly impartial." Jazz checked out the price tag near her armpit. "And hey, look, all of my birthday money and a month's worth of working for my mom just for what's pretty much a practice date."

"Okay, you've got to stop this—so what if you're not in love with this guy? We all can't be Wren and Gray."

They both gave me quizzical looks.

"Aren't you in love with Zach?" Jazz asked.

I laughed, but when neither of them joined in, I stopped.

"No, I'm not," I said. It felt strange to be declaring it out loud in front of a three-way mirror—endless images of me saying the same thing. "I mean, I like him a lot— we have fun and all, but do I think this is love? Hell-to-the-no, but I'm not hung up on it. Neither is he."

My little speech was met with an uncomfortable silence. Was it really so awful that I felt that way? Wren checked her butt out in the mirror again. Jazz looked at the floor.

"I just don't know if I can do that. Be all casual," she said.

"Omigod—lighten up. Consider it an experiment. You didn't ask the guy to marry you, it's a freakin' dance in a high school gym. You're not going to wreck your love life with one awkward date. There are worse ways to spend a Friday night."

"She's right, Jazz. Kyle's hot and you guys seemed to hit it off that night at the movies. I like the experiment idea."

"Buy the dress. Kiss the wrong boy. Flirt your butt off."

Jazz face-palmed, but laughed. "Guys . . . ugh . . . okay. Yes. You're right."

"Success," Wren said, waving her hand in the air as she returned to her dressing room.

After our purchases, we wandered over to the food court to meet Mom in front of Jamba Juice. My stomach growled. A berry smoothie would not cut it. What I really wanted was a honking plate of nachos from the Tex-Mex food stand.

"Hey, you guys want to split nach—"

The words stopped as my eyes landed on my mother.

Sitting in front of Jamba Juice.

"Is that Leif? With your mother?" Wren asked.

"Yes."

Was it him? He looked different in jeans, although I guess it was ridiculous to think he'd be roaming the mall in yoga pants and his mat strapped to his back. He had a life outside the yoga studio, of course. Damn, he wore it just as well. I could not for the life of me understand how my mother could compartmentalize Leif into yoga-information guy. There was a stack of books between them. My mother spoke using gestures that made her look like she was swirling the air around her.

"That's Hot Yogi?" Jazz asked.

"Are they on a date?"

"Nah," I said. "My mom's thinking of becoming a yoga teacher—Leif is, like, her young hot mentor."

Mom spotted us and waved us over. She was glowing—no, really—like the space around her was charged. Leif sat with one leg loosely crossed over the other, as if hanging with my mom was the way he spent every Saturday at the mall.

"Am I allowed to see the dress now?" she asked as we got closer.

"Hey," I said, folding the dress bag over the back of the chair. Wren and Jazz deposited their things next to mine. "Fancy seeing you here."

Leif laughed. "We bumped into each other in the bookstore."

"Yes, I was desperately lost in the self-help section when I realized the books I needed were somewhere else. He sort of saved me."

"Nice."

"Any change from the dress?" she asked.

"About forty. Oh, um, we were going to get some nachos, is that okay? We've got time, right?" I asked.

"Sure."

"Want anything?" I looked between them.

"No, I'm on my way out," Leif said, but he still sat there, sipping his drink.

Wren, Jazz, and I walked over toward the food stands.

"That's cool your mom is going to be an instructor," Wren said.

"You think?"

"Yes—she's amazing in class. Didn't you see her doing mermaid last week? She just sits there, in the pose; I can't even get my foot to stay in the crook of my elbow that long, I'm always wobbling, and she's there totally chill, like she could sit that way for hours."

"No, I didn't notice," I said, looking back at them as we waited on line.

Leif finally got up and gave my mother's shoulder a pat before walking away. Nothing sexy about that—except the smile on my mother's face was . . . well, it was obvious that seeing him made her happy. She opened one of the books. He came toward us, looking more college student than guru with his messy hair and his messenger bag slung over his shoulder.

"See you next week," he said as he walked by us.

"Bye," Wren said as our heads turned to follow his exit. There was a slight scent that followed him—some citrusy, spicy cologne that enveloped us as he passed.

"I need to get to one of those classes," Jazz said. "He even smells good."

"I think that's just the nachos," Wren said. "I'm seriously

starved, can we get the deluxe? You can have my share of the jalapeños."

"Yeah, sounds good," I said, looking back at Mom.

She was still smiling.

Once at home, Mom insisted I model my purchase for her and Paul. I tottered down the stairs, holding the bottom part of the dress up so I wouldn't trip to my death.

"Ready?" I called.

"Yep," my mother said.

"Okay, I'm turning the corner now." I reached the landing and pivoted toward the dining room, where my mother and Paul sat. Paul had his hands over his eyes. My mother gasped.

"Mads . . . that's gorgeous," she said, getting up from her seat. Paul uncovered his eyes.

"Va-va-voom," he said, grinning. I shook my head at the corny compliment, but it did feel kind of good. It was a great dress. And I happened to rock it pretty hard.

My mom grabbed my hands and held them out to the side to get a better view. "You sure Sister Teresa is going to let you get away with so much skin?"

"It's not that bad, is it?"

"I'm just teasing. You look lovely." She put her hands on each cheek, played with the ends of my hair, pulling some strands toward my face. I knew my hair was in desperate need of serious shaping. It was starting to look shaggy instead of pixie.

"We should lighten up the color around your face before next Friday. Were you thinking of going a little spiky and edgy or kind of soft?"

"I can't decide—maybe softer, but messy? And I was thinking big earrings, but keeping the rest bare, no necklace or anything. Lighter makeup—bright-red lip, maybe?"

"I love it," she said.

"You two are speaking a different language," Paul said, standing next to Mom. He did a quick once-over and shook his head. "Our little Mads all grown up."

My mother looked at him, and a faint smile crossed her face, then she took my cheeks in her hands again, tilted her head to the side.

"My beautiful girl," she said. "You guys are stopping here for pictures, right?"

"I guess," I said, pulling away. For some reason the moment was overwhelming—the way my mom looked at me. What Paul said. I liked it, the little rush of happiness I felt when he said *Our little Mads*, but I wasn't sure why. It all felt familiar. And comforting.

"I'm gonna get changed. Are we ordering from the Indian place for dinner?"

"Order out? No way, shrimp scampi is on the menu tonight—will you be joining us?" Paul asked.

"Sounds good," I said, heading back up to my room.

It was nice having Paul in the house. My mother seemed lighter, mellower around him. And I certainly appreciated the home-cooked meals, even liked hearing him whistle Springsteen songs as he worked in the kitchen. But why didn't my mother smile at him the way she smiled at Leif this afternoon? Was Paul too boxed up in the friend compartment for her to ever consider he could be more? It was hard to believe that in all the years they'd been friends, they never once looked at each other that way. I mean, Paul was kind of dashing, for an older guy.

My wheels turned.

If I didn't join them for dinner, they'd be alone.

And if they were alone . . . shrimp scampi, bottle of wine . . .

What if the reason Paul wanted to call New Jersey home was Mom? Maybe that was the bigger reason he was here—even if he didn't know it yet. They could use a nudge in the right direction.

I called Wren. She picked up on the third ring.

"Hey, can I still come over tonight?"

"Yes, please, I only have to put a bazillion mint lentils into these little starfish-shaped boxes for Brooke's shower. Want to help?"

I wasn't sure what a mint lentil was, but if it got me out of the house for a while . . .

"Can we order a pizza?"

She laughed. "Yeah."

"I'm in, see you soon." I hung up. I grabbed my coat and went down to the kitchen. Mom sat at the café table, a glass of wine in front of her as she helped Paul devein the shrimp. They were laughing about something as I walked in.

"Hey, you know what, I forgot I told Wren I was going to help her with something, so I'm going to have to bail on the shrimp. Is that okay?"

"Yes—do you need a ride?" Mom asked, probably desperate to stop working with shrimp guts. My mom, knives, and the kitchen were not a happy combination. The fact that she was even doing this with Paul, well, spoke volumes. At least I thought so.

"No, I should walk off those nachos from before."

"You don't know what you're missing," Paul said as I went out the front door.

Funny . . . I could say the same thing.

TANNER AND I LURKED IN FRONT OF SACRED
Heart, watching as groups of couples walked up the steps into
the building. For such a small school, it fit an endless mass of
people. All dressed up. As in, not in jeans, like us. Every so
often we'd get a look that made me feel like I should be holding out a donation cup or something.

"This doesn't look like the sort of dance you can just show
up to, T," I said.

He craned his head to get a better look into the vestibule.
There was a table with two girls sitting behind it. Two very
dressed-up girls.

"There's a sign that says it's fifteen at the door," he said.

"Per couple, which we are not," I said. "Let's just get outta
here, hit a movie or the diner." I started walking toward the

VW, which I'd parked about a block away, but slowed when I realized Tanner wasn't following me.

"Dude, we're here," he said, waving his arms around. "We might as well figure out a way to get in, or stand by the gym door."

"I'm not standing by the gym door to hear Smegma," I said, walking back to him. I'd felt pathetic enough the night Duncan caught me sitting in the Beetle trying to avoid him and Hannah. No matter how curious I was to hear their sound, I wasn't going to freeze my 'nads off and risk the humiliation of getting caught lurking.

What the hell were we doing here?

"When the crowd thins out, I'll go in and chat up the ladies," Tanner said. I laughed but his face was determined.

"Oh, you're serious?"

"Why not? I'm sick of waiting for shit to happen," he said.

He'd made an effort—his usual white-boy 'fro tamed and combed to the side. And he reeked of some shower gel stuff that he claimed was supposed to smell "exotic and spicy." I'm sure whatever that was supposed to smell like wasn't something you needed to brace yourself against. Tanner was surrounded in a formidable cloud.

"Fine," I said.

We waited a good five minutes until the front door was dead. Tanner loped up the steps and opened the glass doors to go inside. He shoved his hands into his pockets as he stood there, and both girls looked up at him. There was no way they were letting us in.

The one girl whispered in the other's ear. She gave Tanner a once-over. He gestured toward the door—toward me, I realized in horror—and shrugged, arms out to the side, hands up. They kind of squinted, one girl shielding her eyes from the overhead light like she was saluting someone, and looked right at me. I wasn't sure if they could see me in the shadows, but I slunk back behind the fence. One of the girls shook her head and smiled. Tanner walked out.

"Not an open dance. We need a Sacred Heart chick," he said, trotting down the steps.

"Well, that settles it, then," I said, turning. He grabbed my sleeve.

"I think you should talk to them," he said.

"And say what?"

"I dunno, something that will get us in."

"Why would they listen to me?"

"I didn't really try that hard. Jess, come on, you're a front man, start acting like one. These girls would be pressed against the stage for you. I've seen it. Just, you know—"

"What? Sing to them? This is a stupid idea."

"Sure, a stupid idea, like finding a drummer or taking off that fucking wristband, or anything that means leaving her behind."

Every so often, T would cut to the chase. You'd think he

was clueless and goofy and then, there it was—a spot-on revelation. But the drummer thing—both guys were good. It felt like choosing one over the other would be shutting down a world of possibility. Although in my gut I thought I knew which choice would be the best for us.

"That's not what this is about."

"Really? So if Hannah came up to you right now and told you it was all a mistake and she wanted to hook up again, you wouldn't crawl right back to her."

"No."

"Bullshit."

Before I could think about it any more, I tore up the stairs and opened the door. *Jesse the front man can handle this. Own it*, I thought, even though I generally believed anyone who talked about himself in the third person, even in his head, was a complete nimrod. The girls looked ready to be challenged. No backing down now.

"Hey," I said, sauntering up to the table. I hooked my thumb in my belt loop, taking the laid-back, I-don't-really-need-to-get-in, caj approach.

"Hi," the girl with the dark hair said.

"This dance—you really have to know someone to get in?"

"It's a Sadie Hawkins dance, you have to be asked," the other girl said with a smile. The smile was key. Genuine. Cute. An endless stream of girls in dresses and guys following them flowed into the gym. The doors were only about ten feet away and wide open. I could see the stage. Plasma wasn't on yet.

"I'm just here for the band, is there any way you could look the other way for, like, five minutes? I'll even pay the fifteen dollars. I swear I won't stay long."

"Why do you want to see the band?" the dark-haired girl said, putting her chin in her hand.

"I hear they're really good."

"Liar," the other girl said.

"Okay, maybe I want to see how good they are. Kind of friendly competition."

They looked at each other. There was a cheer from the gym. The band walked out onto the stage. Kenny Ashe pulled his guitar strap over his head. Duncan settled down behind the drums. When the rest of the guys were in place, Kenny counted off the song. The sound exploded into the gym, "Dance, Dance"—*really?* Duncan was a little fast on the beat.

"Please," I said.

There was a slow second, a moment I knew they were wavering. Then a tall girl in a short black dress with legs for miles walked over to us.

"Hey, ten more minutes and we can officially close the door," she said. Her cool green eyes darted over me—my Vans, leather jacket, the frayed pocket of my jeans. Whatever progress I'd made had just gone back to square one.

"Can I help you?" she asked, looking at me like I was

something she'd flick off a friend's sweater.

Front man, Jess.

"He just wants to see the band, Ava."

She crossed her arms. "You can't."

"Look, I'm friends with them, I'll just stay for one song, two tops," I said. "I'll even stand at the doors, how's that?"

"We're at capacity."

"But . . ."

"Do I need to get someone more persuasive to walk you out?"

Who? The Sadie Hawkins police? I wanted to say, but I didn't need to call more attention to myself. I shook my head and went back outside. Tanner waited at the foot of the steps.

"So?"

"They opened with Fall Out Boy, can you believe that? Then some girl kicked me out."

"Damn."

"Wait," I said, checking out the fence around the property. From the top stair the fence looked easy to get over. "There must be another way in—a back door or something. If I get in, I can let you in one of the gym doors. Give me a boost."

"Huh?"

"Do we want to see Plasma or stand out here like numb-nuts waiting for shit to happen?" I asked, checking out the area to make sure we were alone.

He grinned and interlocked his fingers, then hoisted me

up. I teetered on the top of the fence for a split second before grabbing a tree limb and dropping down onto the lawn.

"Wait, what should I do?" Tanner whisper-yelled.

"I'll text you when I find a way in," I said, heading toward the side of the school, although what I was going to do after I got past the shrubbery and statues of stern-looking angels, I wasn't sure. Tanner's "waiting for shit to happen" got to me. Is that what I was doing? Would I really let Hannah walk back into my life if she wanted? And if she did . . . would it make everything better?

Past the shrubs was a wide, tree-dotted lawn that ran the length of the building. I crouch-walked toward the classroom windows, hoping to find even the tiniest breach. Sacred Heart was ancient. My mother had told me once that she and her friends would climb out the window in the spring to catch some rays during study hall. I couldn't imagine my mother being that ballsy, but if she could climb out a window, I could climb in. I only hoped they hadn't updated their security system to more than the stone angels that guarded out front.

Each set of windows I tried was locked. Shit. Then I spied one toward the end of the building that was cracked open slightly. The lengthwise window opened outward. There were two panes in it, but it was one solid piece. I slid my fingers in and pulled. Nothing. I tried again, widening my grip. It gave a tiny bit. My fingers ached from the cold. I shook out the numbness, adjusted my grip, and pulled again, working it for a good minute until it opened enough for me to slip through. I took a last look outside for any telltale security lights or cameras in corners of the building, and wriggled my way in.

A thick drape covered the window. There was a moment when both feet dangled on either side of the windowsill, until my left foot finally found the floor. I gripped the sides of the frame and backed in. My fingers slipped and I toppled down, the drape fanning out around me as my ass hit the floor. I groaned and propped myself up on my elbows, letting my eyes adjust to the dark.

The only light in the room came from the dimly lit hallway. I pushed myself up to standing and brushed myself off before shutting the window. Desks were arranged in a semicircle—and on the chalkboard—*they still had chalkboards here?*—was the quote "To be or not to be, that is the question." Ha. Well played, universe.

When I opened my messages to text Tanner, I already had two from him.

I'm in.

Side door to caf open.

For fucking real? I laughed. I felt stupid. Reckless. Alive.

I stepped into the hall. The sound of the band—Kenny Ashe's muffled voice screaming out a song I couldn't decipher—echoed through the empty corridor. Farther down, people milled around in front of two open doors. *Cafeteria, maybe?* I hugged the wall as I moved toward the action. As I got closer, I noticed a leggy silhouette turn the corner at the end of the hallway. *The girl from the front who shut me down.* My heart shot into my throat. No fucking way was I getting kicked out after this. I ducked into the cafeteria, crouching a bit to get lost in a throng of kids.

I worked my way over to a vending machine and studied it as if my life depended on finding a healthy snack. In the reflection of the glass I could see that I was unnoticed, at least for the moment. I peered over my shoulder, scanning the room for Tanner. My eyes landed on a familiar-looking girl in a black dress standing behind a long table covered in water bottles and several trays of cupcakes. Where did I know her from?

"Jesse?"

Someone tugged my jacket. I flinched and turned toward the voice.

There was a girl next to me. The short-haired one from yoga.

"Madison." I could not hide my surprise as I checked her out. There wasn't a word to describe how she looked. Only sounds, syllables. She was cute after class, but damn.

"Wow." *Smooth, Jess, why don't you just grunt?*

She lowered her eyes and smiled.

"Thanks," she said. "Who are you here with?"

"I—um . . ." I stuttered as she gave me a once-over. I could see it was dawning on her that I wasn't exactly dressed for the occasion. Her grin got wider. I knew it was okay to tell her the truth. I wasn't sure why, maybe it was that smile—man, it was the kind of smile that gave you an adrenaline rush from just being on the receiving end. I had to smile back.

"I'm not here with anyone, just snuck in to see the band," I said. Her eyes got round. *Had I made the wrong call?* She leaned toward me.

"Then why are you staring into the vending machine?" she whispered. "Especially this one—seriously, who would actively choose papaya fruit leather over peanut M&Ms?"

I laughed. "Well, I kind of got hassled at the door, so I'm, um, flying under the radar."

"C'mon." She motioned for me to follow her. I looked down, careful not to step on the back of her dress. We walked up to the table. The girl in the black dress handed Madison a camera on a long strap. *Ah, the other Thursday Girl from yoga.*

"Thanks for watching it," Madison said as she put the camera over her head. "Look who I found wandering around the cafeteria."

"Hey, Mugshot," the girl said.

"It's Jesse," I said.

"Wren," she said, smiling. "Your friend just wandered through here a little while ago."

"Really? No one hassled him?"

"Not that I saw."

"Where's the ball-and-chain? He bailed on cupcake detail already?" Madison asked her, fiddling with the camera and pointing it at Wren.

Wren put her hand over her face and waved the camera away. "The band played some Nirvana song he wanted to check out. No reason the two of us should miss out. If you see him, tell him my shift is done in about ten minutes."

"I'm off to be roving photographer—don't forget we need to get a picture of the three of us later," Madison said, sneaking in a few fast clicks of Wren, who finally smiled for the camera. *The three of us?* She tugged my sleeve again and I followed her through the side doors of the cafeteria and right into . . . Legs. Who *immediately* recognized me.

"I thought I told you—"

Madison grabbed my arm. "Ava, he's with me."

Legs/Ava blinked fast a few times and looked between us. Madison moved even closer to me.

"Wait, I thought you were with Zach O'Keefe."

"I am, and I'm also with Jess. It's ladies' choice, right? I can have two dates, there's no weird Sadie Hawkins bylaw I'm not aware of, is there?"

This stunned her speechless.

"Ava, come on, stop being a dance Nazi. It's a success. Enjoy it," Madison said, pulling me along. "And Wren wants to dance with her boyfriend, no one cares about cupcakes!"

Ava opened her mouth to say something but then just shook her head and almost, *almost* smiled before walking into the cafeteria. *Did that mean . . . ?* I was in the clear. Madison held on to my hand, leading me down a narrow, darkened hallway toward the pounding thrum of the band. People were coming and going, like an ant tunnel, but she held on to me, looking over her shoulder once and saying something I couldn't hear. It was hot and loud; I gripped her hand a little tighter. We finally made it to a door that opened to the gym.

The gym floor was thick with people in front of the stage dancing to a craptastic version of "What I Like About You." Kenny was breathless as he sang—probably from jumping around the stage like an idiot. We wove our way through the mob, stage lights flashing red and green and purple over the crowd. Madison stopped to chat with a few people, then held the camera in one hand over the mass of heads and started snapping random pictures. The flash made my vision spotty. We made it to the far wall, where she finally let go of my hand.

"So are they friends of yours?" she yelled, gesturing to the band and rocking a little to the beat.

"Not really—that's our old drummer. Just checking out the competition," I yelled back. She nodded. The gym was less crowded than it appeared from up front. Most of the people were toward the stage, with a few stragglers hanging around the perimeter of the room. Tanner was still MIA. I checked my phone. Nothing.

"Hey, I'm going to find my date. You okay?" Madison asked.

I wouldn't have minded hanging out with her some more, but yelling at each other over the music wasn't exactly the perfect situation to get to know someone. Oh yeah, and the fact that she was here with someone made the whole thing a bit inconvenient.

"Yeah, thanks for helping me."

"You still owe me that chai." She waved as she walked off into the crowd. What guy would be idiot enough to let her out of his sight at a dance?

I leaned against the wall and finally spotted Tanner. He was dancing with Tori Ashe and her friends. I guess he threw the lying-low plan out the window. I laughed. He looked a little spastic, but it worked for him. I'd forgotten that Kenny's sister went to Sacred Heart, which probably helped with them getting the gig. One thing Kenny had was connections. I tried to be objective—just a dude listening to a band. They weren't that bad and the crowd seemed to like them.

Then I saw her.

Hannah. She was in a dark dress, hair down, and moving to the music, her face lit up red. Green. Purple. I hadn't thought about seeing her or if the band could bring dates. Anytime I thought I was over it, that she hadn't crossed my mind in a few hours—*zap*. This awful jolt Tased me. Maybe it hurt a little less.

Or not.

I fiddled absentmindedly with the infinity band—okay, bracelet—that I still wore . . . for her. For us. Hoping.

"Come on, Jess, just get them. One for me, one for you," she'd said. We'd been walking around the street fair for a while, browsing the table of, like, the tenth jewelry vendor we'd seen.

"Guys don't wear bracelets," I'd said, even though I knew I was going to cave.

"What's that big-ass ugly thing you've already got on?"

"That's a wristband. There's a difference."

"So call it a wristband—pretty please, sugar on top, and all that stuff."

The look in her eyes was worth the forty bucks. Worth a million.

I hadn't taken it off since that day. Even at my worst moments, when I hated HannahDunk more than I thought I could hate anything, it was still on my wrist. I tugged at it and looked away.

The band finished the song with a crash. Kenny breathed into the mic—*Back in ten!*—and the guys walked off. I sent Tanner a text where to find me; I didn't want to walk over there to his dance circle. I'd seen enough. We could pick the shittiest drummer and still be better than Smegma. Booming dance music blared out of the speakers and the crowd swelled as some rapper sang about talking dirty. My head pounded with the beat. My jacket felt tight. The edges of the room

103

blurred. Madison was suddenly in front of me.

"Couldn't find him," she said. "Hey, you okay?"

"Yeah, fine. I just hate this music."

"I know, right?"

"Mads! I'm free!" Wren scurried across the dance floor to us. "Where's Jazz? I haven't seen her since we got here."

Madison shrugged.

"Duuuuude, did you get a load of . . . Hey, Thursday Girls," Tanner said, joining us. His stunt on the dance floor must have given him some swagger because I'd never seen him so laid-back in front of these girls. "So what'd you think, they suck, right?"

"Pretty much," I said.

"Who, the band?" Wren asked.

"Yeah," T said.

A tall guy crept up behind Wren, putting his finger to his lips. Madison pretended not to notice him. Wren jumped as he wrapped his arms around her, then laughed. The "ball-and-chain" . . . Wait. He looked at me.

"Grayson?"

"No effing way," Tanner said, realizing his number-one drummer choice was wrapped around the girl he'd drooled over for a month.

"Hey, how do you know—" Grayson said.

"Jess works at Mugshot, we go there after yoga." Madison motioned back and forth between us.

The five of us stood there, kind of nodding to the over-powering beat and just looking at one another, searching for something to talk about. I knew what was coming, could feel the subject swirling there in the center of us, building up energy. Grayson spoke first.

"So did you ever, um, you know, find anyone?" His eyes darted from me to Tanner.

Grayson was not my first choice; the other dude, Plasma's old drummer, was technically better and more experienced. Tanner, on the other hand, thought he'd want to come in and take over, whereas Grayson would be a better fit for *us*. We were at a stalemate, but standing there, having Grayson ask me point-blank, my gut told me a different story. It craved action. Forward motion. I looked at Tanner.

"Um, yeah, you, well . . . you saved us a phone call," I said.

"What?"

"Can you practice with us tomorrow?" I asked.

"Yeah, definitely."

"What do you think?" I asked Tanner.

"Great."

"So you can vouch for this guy," I said to Madison.

"Me? Um, I guess he's all right. His car is awful, though."

"Thanks, Mads," Grayson said, grinning.

I looked at Grayson. "Guess you're in."

"The band for this sort of sucks, don't they?" he said.

"Yeah." I already liked him. This was the right decision.

He gave us each an enthusiastic handshake to seal the deal.

The music changed to a slower groove. The crowd split apart, some people pairing off like magnets, a few leaving the floor or awkwardly standing there. Madison searched the dance floor, looking for her idiot date no doubt. She fumbled with the camera.

"No more interviews or cookies, right? We can dance?" Grayson asked, holding out his hand to Wren. She grinned, took his hand, and it was like they were already dancing. He brought his forehead down to hers, her hands clasped behind his neck, up into his hair as they curled into each other, eyes open.

"Sickening, isn't it?" Madison said, tilting her chin toward Grayson and Wren. She said it with a smile, like she didn't really think it was sickening at all but felt like she needed to say something since we were just there gawking at them. They kissed. She walked out to the center of the floor and took some snapshots of them. I looked away.

Bam.

Duncan and Hannah swayed into my view. They weren't pressed together like Grayson and Wren, but their arms were around each other and Duncan was talking, a smile on his face. Hannah leaned into him and whispered something in his ear. He laughed and then brought her in closer. She put her head on his shoulder and closed her eyes. I could not look away. There was no jolt this time. More like an empty ache, pressure, like someone was slowly pushing the air out of my lungs. They were happy. They didn't even know or care if I was there. Their relationship had nothing—*nothing*—to do with me.

Madison walked back over to me.

"I think we should go," Tanner said.

"You're leaving already?" Madison asked.

A chestnut husk stuck in my throat; the room was hot again.

"Yeah, we've seen enough, right, T?"

"Yep."

"Well if you need to sneak into Sacred Heart anytime, I'm your girl," she said.

I pushed open the side door, and a cold gust shot in. Madison shivered.

"I'll keep that in mind, thanks."

We walked out into the night, silent as we went back to the car. My ears still thrummed with the sound of the gym, my mind still numb from the reality of what I'd seen. I yanked off the infinity bracelet, stopped short of tossing it to the curb, and shoved it into my pocket. No more pining, for fuck's sake.

"You're okay we went with Grayson?" I asked Tanner.

He nodded. "Why, because he's with Thursday Girl? We have a drummer. I'm on top of the world."

"Because if you had a problem with it, we could—"

"I like the dude, Jess. He's a good fit. Plenty of fish in the sea. Did you see me dancing with Tori Ashe?"

I laughed. "Yep, but isn't that a conflict of interest?"

"Or sleeping with the enemy. That sounds hotter. What changed your mind about Grayson?" he asked as we reached the VW.

"Dunno. Game-time decision, I guess."

"So it had nothing to do with him being six degrees of separation from the little blonde?"

"Nah."

We got into the car and sat a moment while it warmed up. Was Madison the reason I suddenly thought Grayson was a good match? Of course not—he was good, and we'd grow as a band, on common ground. I knew that's why T wanted him—the other guy was *too* good, as ridiculous as it sounded. There was something I had to admit, though.

"I mean, it wouldn't suck if she came to see us."

Tanner smiled and looked out the passenger's-side window. "I knew it."

"I'LL KEEP THAT IN MIND, THANKS," JESSE SAID before exiting.

I crossed my arms for warmth, watching him leave after his friend. I had the weird urge to follow and see what Broody Barista did in his free time. Running into him had been such an unexpected surprise in an otherwise meh kind of a night. The door closed with a clunk. I walked over to it, running my hand along the cold push bar—one swift motion and I'd be out. Not that I really wanted to leave—the night had barely started. And this dress was far too fabulous to just roam the streets in, plus I still hadn't gotten any decent photos or slow-danced with Zach.

Why was I making a list of reasons to stay at the dance?

School dances always sounded better than they actually

were. Why not call it what it really was: Friday night all dressed up trying to be something it wasn't. No matter how much balloon art filled the gym, it still boiled down to a room with blue padded walls, retracted basketball hoops, and the faint smell of rubber and Simple Green where we'd be slapping around a hockey puck in class on Monday. Seeing it as a romantic place was hard, even with the mood lighting.

Except watching Wren and Grayson—the building could have come crashing down around them and I doubt they'd have noticed. They really were *that sickening couple*—annoying and sweet and in their own world. I took a few pictures of them, then wandered deeper into the crowd, ignoring the disappointment that threatened to bring down my already precarious good mood. There was nothing that sucked more than searching for your date during a John Legend song. Where was Zach?

I made my way to the front of the gym to see if there were any interesting shots—I'd been wary of the dance assignment at first but realized it could be a great opportunity to build my portfolio. Photography was not my thing but my art teacher had said a diverse portfolio showed that you weren't afraid to take risks. That what these art programs wanted to see most was your potential.

Earlier in the year, I'd taken some artsy shots between the spokes of a Ferris wheel at the Sacred Heart Founders Festival that had won a ribbon in the fall art show. Granted, there wasn't much competition. I looked around for something out of the ordinary, anything I could see with a different perspective. As I brought the camera up to my face, Zach's grin appeared in the frame.

"Where have you been?" he asked, grabbing my hand and leading me toward the dance floor.

"Zach," I said, taking quick little steps to keep up with him. "Slow down."

I adjusted the strap so the camera was to my back, like a purse—it had really become the clunkiest of accessories. We found an empty space in the center of the gym. He drew me close, hands sliding up my arms, his fingers tracing my shoulders and trailing down my bare back. I clasped my hands behind his neck, keeping my eyes on his.

"Where was *I*? Where were you?"

He leaned down.

"Let's just dance," he whispered, lips brushing my ear. My breath stopped. Maybe I was too quick to dismiss the dance, because his mouth on my skin made me forget we were even on planet Earth. I snuggled into him as he caressed my back and we swayed to the music.

For all of ten seconds.

Until the beat got fast, and Pitbull echoed through the gym, sending up some loud whoops as the crowd got crazy again. A few of the teacher chaperones darted onto the dance floor as a precaution. Sacred Heart was a no-grinding zone—but it didn't stop people from trying. Zach lifted his arms up in the air and rocked his hips, with the sort of fearlessness that canceled out the goofy moves. He moved closer to me, so serious I had to laugh. I wondered if he'd practiced in a mirror.

"C'mon," he said.

He screwed up his face like he was in pain and continued to dance around me. I finally relented until Miss Preston, the driver's-ed teacher, gave us an *I'm watching you* glare and we parted. I took the moment to search the floor for Jazz or Wren but it was impossible to see anyone through the thick mass of bodies.

"I need some air," I yelled at Zach, and pointed out to the hallway. He led the way toward the door. Once outside the gym I felt cooler. Zach draped his arm over my shoulders as we walked down the hall.

"Have I told you how smokin' you look?"

"Yes, twice, but you can keep telling me." I snaked my arm around his and leaned into him.

"We should do something after this," he said.

"Like what?"

"Your couch, maybe?"

"This is not a couch dress."

"Who said you had to be wearing it?" He nuzzled my hair.

I stopped short. "Zach, really?"

"What?"

His brow bunched up in confusion. I wasn't sure why what

he'd said bothered me. Zach's pervy side normally made me swoony, especially the thought of being skin to skin. Somehow, in the hallway of school, it pissed me off. Maybe it was from watching Wren and Gray slow-dance and realizing that it might not be so bad to have a main squeeze I kind of adored. Someone who would seek me out during a slow song instead of grinding against my leg. Not that that wasn't fun. Why wasn't spending time with me *in* the dress enough for him? Couldn't he think of anything else for a moment? He brushed some hair away from my face.

"Madison, what did I do?"

"Nothing."

"It's not just tonight, you know, you've been . . . weird lately. I feel like I'm always one step away from annoying the hell out of you."

He frowned, his eyes soft, uncertain, making me feel like such a hard-ass. How he could go from howling on the dance floor to this vulnerable mush in a few short minutes was part of the reason that whenever I thought about untangling myself from him, I couldn't. I couldn't stand this look being directed at me or thinking that I was the cause of it.

"No, you're not," I said, tugging on his tie.

He leaned down and I brushed my lips across his, getting lost in the heat of the kiss. This was where we were perfect, the lovely liquid place when our eyes were closed and our mouths touched. Was this how Wren felt with Gray on the dance floor? My whole body relaxed as his arms surrounded me. We stepped back until I bumped the wall behind me; the cold tile made me tremble. Or maybe it was Zach and the way his tongue wrapped around mine.

You couldn't build a relationship with someone simply because you got off kissing them, I knew that, but it wasn't exactly a shitty way to start.

The urgent click of heels in the hallway coming in our direction made us part. Miss Preston walked by, smiling as she made her way to the cafeteria. I ran my thumb along the corner of Zach's mouth, to wipe off where my lipstick had smeared. He took my thumb in his mouth and nibbled before I pulled away, laughing.

"Why don't you help me with these pictures I'm supposed to take—it'll go faster, then we can just enjoy this thing. Sound like a plan?"

"Sure," he said. "What should I do?"

"Let me know if you see anything interesting."

He lifted the strap over my head, and holding the camera at arm's length, put his cheek to mine and said, "Say whiskey." He held down the button so the camera clicked multiple times. A group of girls walked by us and giggled.

"Zach! You left without saying good-bye," a girl with long blond hair and a sparkly purple dress said.

"Hey, smile for the camera," he said. They pulled together, three of them hiking up their dresses to show some leg, and grinned.

"Got it! Official yearbook business," he said, which caused the girl in purple to laugh a little too loud at him. She . . . was flirting? Zach looked back at me, goofy-ass grin on his face.

"What?"

"You left *where* without saying good-bye?"

"Oh, the caf—Kyle and me were talking to them. They're sophomores—come to our indoor matches sometimes. Why? Jealous?"

I shook my head. "Nope."

Slight disappointment flashed across his face, but then he kissed me.

"Why don't you just pass the camera around to different people, make your job easier," he said.

"Because it's, like, a three-hundred-dollar camera, and it's my job, come on." I tried to get it from him but he held it out of my reach.

"You said you wanted me to help you," he said. "Chill, trust me."

I swallowed a groan. I didn't want to chill or trust him. I just wanted the freakin' camera. "Zach."

He wandered farther down the hall, stopping to take a picture of a statue of the Blessed Mother, which, considering he'd just had his tongue down my throat, seemed slightly inappropriate.

"Zach."

He was a good five feet ahead of me, when he stopped, looking down the annex hallway that led to the two newer classrooms in the building. His mouth opened slightly as he raised the camera to his face. "Cool."

"Please give it—" I said, then looked at what he'd deemed "cool."

It *was* pretty cool.

The hallway was decorated with bunches of pink and purple glowing balloons. The ribbons trailed down into the hallway and were gathered with ties made of tulle; each bunch had a large rectangular card attached to it.

"Hey, um, babe," I cooed. "Could I have the camera, please?"

He handed it off to me and I went to work. When I got closer to the balloons I saw that each card had a different word on it. I stopped at one that read *CHOICE* and snapped a picture—trying to get different angles, looking up at the balloons, focusing on the word and the glow of the hallway. Another bunch had the word *BOUNDLESS* attached to it, another had the word *UNSTOPPABLE*. For dance decorations they were pretty esoteric. Zach followed behind. The last one had the word *INSPIRE*.

"You know how this dark hallway inspires me?" he whispered in my ear.

"Shh." I crouched down to get a more interesting perspective.

That's when we heard it.

A high-pitched sound, not exactly a squeak, more like

a sigh. Zach's eyes grew wide and he grinned. There was breathing and a soft smacking noise. I froze, the sinking realization in the pit of my stomach that we had happened upon someone doing something in the small alcove of senior lockers that were now about two feet away. Zach shrunk back against the wall, sliding along it, doing his best impression of an undercover agent about to catch the criminal. I motioned for him to stop.

No, I mouthed.

He shrugged and kept moving. Whoever was in the alcove, ugh, I cringed at the thought of them being discovered. I coughed. Loud. Purposeful. Zach put his hands up, like he was angry, but he smiled. Foiled.

I grabbed Zach's hand and we backed down the hallway, the balloon ribbons swaying in our wake. Once we were out in the main hall he spoke.

"Why'd you do that?"

"Would you really have wanted to surprise someone in the middle of something?" In the middle of what I wasn't sure, but I could use my imagination, and it was quite steamy.

"No. I don't know—you told me to look for interesting things," he said, raising his eyebrows.

"Fine. Let's stand here for a few minutes and see if they come out."

I might not have wanted to catch someone in the act of whatever, but I was curious to see who was horny enough to hook up in the senior alcove. We waited for a good five minutes. Drums echoed down the hallway—the band was back on. Finally a guy with longish sandy hair emerged. Alone.

His tie was loosened, part of his shirttail hanging out in back. He barely glanced in our direction as he tucked his shirt back in, then walked toward the gym. I looked at Zach and stifled a giggle, then we heard the telltale click of heels strolling down the hallway. I lifted the camera up to our faces, taking selfies like Zach had done, so we'd look inconspicuous, just there goofing off. We mugged a few times as the footsteps came closer. In my peripheral vision I saw a figure, heard the swish of a skirt. I saw the dress first, the A-line shape swaying with her movement.

"Jazz?!"

Her eyes went from the camera to me, Zach's face, and then she looked down the hallway—her thought process in motion.

"That wasn't Kyle," Zach said.

The sight of Jazz emerging from a clandestine hookup necessitated an emergency confab in the bathroom. I'd dispatched Zach to find Wren while Jazz and I waited.

"Please tell me you did not get any pictures of that."

"Nope, no evidence," I said, crouch-walking along and peering under the bathroom stalls to make sure we were truly alone so we could get the dirt.

Wren arrived, positively glowing. I felt a stab of envy that I wasn't having a better time; that I didn't feel the way about Zach that she did about Grayson. Would I ever feel that way about anyone? Did I even want to? She did a quick mirror check, running her hand through her hair, and came over.

"What happened?" she asked.

"Jazzabelle happened," I said.

Jazz grinned and chuckled to herself.

"Huh?"

"Jazz hooked up with someone," I said.

"Not Kyle?"

"No," Jazz said. "Logan."

Wren and I squealed and high-fived.

"So wait, what happened with Kyle?" Wren asked.

"And what about Darby?" I asked.

Jazz motioned for us to come closer. "The other day after the mall, I called Kyle to talk. I really felt bad about, you know, using him as a date for the dance."

I groaned.

"No, no, really, it was cool. Awkward at first, but then we talked and he said he was fine going as friends. Turns out Darby and Logan just came as friends too—they're here with a group of people. We bumped into each other in the cafeteria, and talked and—"

"And you got friendly down the glowing hallway," I finished.

"Ooh, my glowing hallway? Cool," Wren said.

"You did that?" I asked.

"Yeah, they were going to spread those out in the gym, and they looked so sad in such a big space so I thought, why not? People would be passing through the hall all night."

"Apparently," I said.

Two of the girls Zach had taken a picture of earlier walked into the bathroom. One was the girl in purple who had flirted with him. She gave me a sharp look before disappearing into the first stall.

"Did you just see that?" I whispered.

Wren nodded. "What's that about?"

"I don't even know who she is," I said.

"She was one of the girls that Kyle and Zach were talking to in the cafeteria before. She was pretty much hanging on Zach's every word. He wasn't doing anything, though—you know, just talking."

When he should have been dancing with me.

"He can talk to whoever he wants," I said, shrugging it off.

"So where did you leave it with Logan?"

"Not really sure. We didn't do much talking." She smiled, dimples and all. Jazzy was a fade-to-black girl so this was about the only detail we were going to get out of her. The boy must have been good.

"We exchanged numbers—but for now, I'm just enjoying this *experiment* like you told me to. We'll probably run this week too."

The sophomore in the purple dress came out of the stall to wash her hands.

"C'mon, let's get out of here," I said, tossing my shoulders back. "We need to get a picture of our gorgeous selves so we can put it in the yearbook spread."

As the three of us left the bathroom I gave Purple Dress a wave and a smile. No need to be bitchy.

The rest of the night was a blur. I commissioned Grayson to take a picture of me, Jazz, and Wren because I trusted his ability to click and shoot. Logan asked Jazz to dance. I got some more artistic shots for the yearbook and ended the night with three full slow dances with Zach that more than made up for his ditching me earlier. We helped Wren with some of her Spirit Club clean-up duties before heading out. Kyle dropped off Jazz first then swung by my house.

Zach walked me up to the stoop.

"You don't have to wait until I get in," I said.

"I want to."

I tugged on his coat to bring his lips to mine. As I was about to pull away, he deepened the kiss, both arms wrapped around me so tightly he lifted me off the ground.

"Whoa," I said, laughing as we parted.

"Madison, I . . ." he said.

My stomach dropped. He had this earnest look about him, and I suddenly got the feeling that he was about to say something I wasn't prepared to deal with.

I stepped away from him, walking toward my stairs. "I had

a great time tonight, Zach. I'm happy we went."

"Wait," he said.

"I'm freezing," I said. "I really have to get in."

Don't say it. Don't say it.

He nodded. "Okay. I'll, um, call you, maybe we can do something tomorrow after my game."

"Sounds great." I started up the stairs.

"Madison?"

I turned, still holding on to the railing. He ran up to me, his lips brushing my cheek as he brought his mouth to my ear. I shivered.

"I love you," he whispered.

He backed away before I could say anything, which I was grateful for, because I'd stopped breathing.

"Just, you know, think about it," he said, getting into the car.

Why did he have to go and ruin everything?

The yelling woke me up.

I rolled over and looked at my clock. Ten a.m. I thought for a moment it could have been something on TV, but it was coming from downstairs, and we didn't have a television on the first floor. I sat up, rubbed the sleep from my eyes. Listened.

"How could you do this?"

Paul. *Paul?*

"Please stop yelling."

"Dana . . . why? Why would you keep something like this from me?"

It felt weird to eavesdrop, even though it wasn't like they were doing much to keep it down. My bedroom was directly above the dining room, so I hopped to standing, making sure they heard my footfall in case they were there. I took exaggerated steps toward the door, swung it open, and whistled as I walked into my bathroom. Silence. Paul had said something about making Nutella crepes for Saturday breakfast, but there were no delicious aromas wafting up from the kitchen.

I padded downstairs in my slipper socks and jammies and rounded the corner to the dining room. It was empty. I looked toward the kitchen. Paul was leaning against the counter. The expression on his face was odd. Intense. His features hardened. When he looked over at me I startled.

"Hey," I said. A chair scratched across the linoleum and my mother appeared in the doorframe. She was in her yoga gear, flushed as if she'd just gotten back from a class.

"Madison," she said, walking out to me. "Good morning."

She gave me a hug. I squeezed her back. Not that my mom didn't hug me, but it was a little out of sorts for first thing in the morning.

"What's up?" I asked as she pulled away. Something about the way they both looked freaked me out.

"Sleep well?"

"Like a baby," I lied. I'd tossed and turned all night thinking about Zach. I'd even turned off my phone for fear he'd want to text or talk, neither of which I was up for after what he'd said to me. I wasn't exactly sure what I was going to do. He had told me to think about it. If I loved him—would this be how I reacted?

"Let's sit down." She gestured to the living room we rarely sat in, especially now that it had become her meditation spot. Dread snaked up my spine. She was acting odd, stiff. They both were. I perched on the couch. Paul sat in the wingback chair; my mother was next to me but on the far end of the couch.

"What's wrong?"

My mother played with a phantom thread on her yoga pants, making small circles with her index finger.

"Dana, please," Paul said.

"Madison, you know how much I want to integrate yoga in my life, right?"

"Um, yeah," I said. Paul ran a hand across his face then fixed his eyes on me. I shifted in my seat.

"Well, it changes you, makes you reevaluate your life and your beliefs. And one of the first things you learn about is the principles of yoga."

"Mom—what are you talking about?"

She took a deep breath and looked at me.

"Satya. Truth. It's about living an authentic life."

"Is this about Leif?"

It snapped her out of whatever yogi-wisdom trance she was headed into. Her face scrunched up. "No."

"Who's Leif?" Paul asked.

"Our instructor. Mom, you're seriously freaking me out, please just spill it," I said.

"I want you to understand, I've always done what I thought was right for us. And I knew there would come a time when, well, we'd have to face this at some point."

"Face what?"

"Oh hell, Dana." Paul stood up. "I'm your father, Madison."

I repeated the words in my head while looking between them, waiting for more of an explanation. My mother was on the edge of the couch, lips pressed together, her brows practically up in her hairline. Paul had his hands on his hips. I looked between them, unsure of what to say, letting the words sink in, trying hard to understand.

Paul is my father.

My eyes landed on the Laughing Buddha statue—his mouth frozen in a perpetual smile. A reminder of abundance. Of Zach with his shirt off. I started laughing, low at first, but then I couldn't help it and covered my mouth in a fit of silent giggles. I finally caught my breath.

"Yeah, right."

"Madison, it's true," my mother said, reaching for my hands. I pulled away and moved from the couch.

"But he's been here. He's been in our lives forever. You . . . How . . . I don't understand. Did you know?" I looked at Paul, his eyes pained. He shook his head.

"Mads, you have to—"

"I don't have to do anything, Mom."

I paced back and forth, my hands clutched together.

"I know you're—"

"Why would you do something like this?" I asked.

"Madison," Paul said. "It's a lot to take in, I know, but we'll figure it out."

Did I have to listen to him now? Did his words carry more weight because he was my father?

"I . . ." Words were meaningless. My mind could not wrap around what had just happened. The only thing I knew was that I didn't want to be with either of them at that moment. I ran up the stairs to my room and slammed the door.

EIGHT

THE MORNING AFTER THE DANCE, I WOKE UP WITH a mission. It was as if seeing Hannah and Duncan happy together had kicked my ass into time-to-get-on-with-my-life mode. For the first time since our breakup, I couldn't wait to get out to the garage. Dad's Saturday-morning omelet-fest was a blur; I scarfed enough for fuel, then went out to warm up. The garage was cold, but that would change soon enough.

My Fender had actual cobwebs between the tuning keys. I wiped them off, pulled the strap over my head, and plugged in. Practice was at eleven; I had a full hour before Tanner and Gray were supposed to show. For all my bullshit about picking the perfect drummer—if I'd auditioned for a band at the moment, I'd have a hard time making the cut. The calluses on my hand had even gone soft.

The guitar growled to life as I ran my pick across the strings. I hit a couple of sour notes, tuned and strummed again, over and over until the sound was perfect. Then I launched into the beginning notes of "Sweet Child O' Mine." Fumbled, really. Three months of not playing and my fingers were rubbery. I ran through it a few more times, until it finally began to come back.

The song was Hannah. It wasn't our song or anything, and I hadn't been learning it to impress her—she would have been like, *Guns and Roses who?* She always joked about my love for classic rock that I'd picked up from my father. This was for me, music to disappear into. The lyrics reminded me of her. Playing it felt like connecting to some real, raw part of *us*. The couple we were when we were together and it was good.

This was as close as possible to saying good-bye without physically saying it to her.

Each note was a memory, a fight, a smile, a kiss. All of the anger, remorse, sadness, and desire came out through my fingers as the guitar screeched and wailed. I hit that sweet spot where I didn't need to think about what I was doing, just closed my eyes and felt it. Music washed over me, through me. Flowed electric from my animal brain.

I wasn't sure how much time had passed but next thing I knew, my shirt was soaked and my father was standing there, arms crossed, leaning against an amp.

"Hey," I said.

"Sounds good."

"You weren't listening closely," I said. "Was it too loud?"

My dad and I had turned the garage into a practice space—a couple of posters on the wall, and some of his old amps. It wasn't soundproof, so we had to keep our sessions to a minimum, or until one of the neighbors complained—but at least it was a place we could use and store our stuff.

"It should be loud." He pulled the cover off one of the amps for me. "How long do you think it will take with this new drummer to sound like you did when you gave your CD to Declan?"

"Grayson's good but, I dunno, a month maybe, maybe less."

"I talked to Deck the other day—"

"And?"

"He liked your sound, wants to talk to you."

"Really?"

"Yep, said if you had any free time this week to stop in."

"Just stop in? And what?"

My father laughed. "Deck's always been a face-to-face guy, just wants to meet you. Feel you out, see if you speak the same language."

"But I thought you said we should be at our best."

"I didn't mention your drummer trouble. See how things go today, it's not like he'll book you in the next month—he said he usually goes three months out. A date to play can get things going."

"Mr. M—you jammin' today too?" Tanner and Grayson had come in the side door of the garage. Tanner's face was lit up, huge grin framed by the off-kilter toboggan hat he insisted on wearing when he played. He placed his case down.

"Not today, T," Dad said, laughing. He held out his hand. "You must be Grayson."

Gray shook Dad's hand. "Is it okay that I'm parked in the driveway? I just wanted to unload—"

"Yep. Need help?"

"Nah, Dad, we're cool," I said. I felt bad for answering so quickly, but I just wanted to play, to start this fragile thing of forming a band.

"I'll leave you to it, then."

It took us a good ten minutes to set up. As Grayson was assembling the final part of his drum kit, I grabbed a fresh shirt from the laundry room and changed from the sweat-soaked one I'd been wearing.

"Hey guys, we might—"

The news about Declan and Whiskey Business came close to spilling out of my mouth but the words caught in my throat. Letting Tanner and Gray know before we practiced seemed like a setup for failure—after, when we were warmed up, would be better.

"We might what?" Tanner asked, stomping along with the bass line he warmed up with.

"We might want to start with the Arctic Monkeys song."

"Sounds cool," Grayson said.

Yellow #5 take two was officially official.

The streets of Hoboken were crazy busy for a Wednesday afternoon. I had exactly two hours between school and work and was pushing it, but Wednesday was the only day Declan had an opening to see me. Tanner had wanted to come but I was more relaxed knowing at least one of us would be on time for the Mugshot evening shift. And Tanner . . . he was overenthusiastic about the whole thing, and when he was that way, he tended to speak before thinking. Then there was the hat, which he was convinced brought him luck when he played. Not ready to fly that freak flag quite yet.

I finally found a spot about four blocks away from Whiskey Business. We weren't anywhere near ready to play out, but the more I thought about it, the more I realized my father was right—a date looming would be great incentive for us to get our shit together. Practice hadn't sucked. Completely. The first time we went through our set, we'd each been doing our own thing; Grayson was too loud, Tanner was rushed, and even I missed coming in on the right beat a few times, but by the end of practice, we at least sounded like a band. Not a great one, but on our way. Declan didn't need to know that.

Walking through the front door of Whiskey Business was like walking into a different realm. I blinked as my eyes adjusted to the darkness. The building was an old firehouse, complete with a brass pole and high ceilings. Along the one wall were venue posters from every band imaginable, with spotlights on some of the more prominent ones like the Stones and U2. The front area looked like someone's living room. There were couches and chairs, and a few low tables between them. The bar took up the rest of the front, while in the far back was a smaller room with a stage. One guy sat hunched over a beer mug at the end. The bartender had his elbows on the bar, tip of a pen in his teeth, working on a newspaper crossword. I cleared my throat. He dropped the pen and looked up.

"ID."

"I'm here to see Declan. Jesse from Yellow Number Five."

He gave me a once-over as he texted someone.

"Who did you say you were?"

"Jesse McMann, I have an—" I stopped short of saying *appointment*, it sounded too formal. "I'm here to see Declan about a gig."

"He's free now—just head to the back, staff door, can't miss it," he said, going back to his crossword.

I navigated around tables and across the floor, pushing through the door marked STAFF into an even darker hallway. There was a sliver of light, and as I neared it, a door whooshed open and Declan appeared. I resisted the urge to jump and ignored my hammering heartbeat. I wanted to play in this place so bad it hurt.

"Jesse, come in." Deck grabbed my hand and pumped it as I walked into his inner sanctum. There were more posters and photos and graffiti on one wall, but at the same time it looked orderly, everything in place. It was hard imagining him knowing my dad—Deck wore tight black skinny jeans, combat boots, and a pinstriped vest over an Alice Cooper shirt. He looked like he could have been in one of my father's classes, not in a band with him twenty years ago.

"Last time I saw you, you were drooling on your father's shoulder. Man, you've grown."

"We met?"

"Oh god, years ago. How are the Prof and Mrs. McMann doing?" He motioned for me to take a seat, while he slid into one of those office chairs that look more like a throne, behind a huge black desk. The desk was spotless except for his laptop and a large glass jar of Charms Blow Pops, with a sign that read IF YOU'RE GONNA BLOW IT, BLOW IT BIG!! I sank down onto a couch across from him that was less comfortable than it looked.

"Oh, um, they're good."

Declan typed something into his keyboard. Yellow #5's cover of "Longview" played over the sound system. A grin fought its way onto my face. We hadn't sounded like that in practice this week. Declan leaned back in his chair, hands clasped behind his head, and grinned.

"This is good, you guys sound tight. So what have you been doing?" he asked.

Moping, brooding, making lattes. I did some creative elaborating—a.k.a. lying through my teeth.

"We played a Christmas party, street fair, stuff like that. We're gearing up for a Battle of the Bands," I said, imagining I was talking about Yellow #5 pre-breakup. Then it would have all been true.

"They still do those battles? Fun stuff." His tone was unimpressed.

"Yeah." My jacket felt heavy, my cheeks hot. If blushing was a lie detector I was screwed. I'd hit nuclear-meltdown mode.

"Cool, do you guys have a logo? Merchandise? Fan page?"

Nope. Nope. Nope.

"We're working on it."

"Your sound is perfect for the eighteen-and-over nights. They like recognizable stuff. When your dad called—"

"My dad called you?" Somehow I didn't think this was the way Green Day got started. How un-freaking-cool.

"A little healthy nepotism never hurt anyone. You have to deliver, though."

"Absolutely."

"So, here's the deal—the eighteen-and-overs are booked until September."

"September?"

"We only do them twice a month, and skip the summer."

"Oh." Why was I there? I was starting to feel like a supreme douche-nugget. And suddenly our cover of "Longview" sounded too fast. Amateurish.

"There's a few places in town that do the eighteen-and-over nights. I might be able to recommend you somewhere. In the meantime, do you want the September date?"

I wasn't sure what I was doing tomorrow, let alone September—Gray was a senior, would he even be around? *Forward motion, Jess.*

"Yes."

He typed again, took a card out of a drawer, and scribbled something down. He stood up and held it out to me.

September 18th. Yellow #5.

We had a gig. Far away, but we had one. And maybe he would recommend us to someone else. It was a start.

"Hey, is your contact info the same as on the CD?"

"Let me give you my cell," I said. He pulled out a pad of neon-orange Post-its and slid it across the desk. I jotted down my cell, and also the line at Mugshot. Putting down more than one number seemed to show I had places to be—that I wasn't necessarily waiting for a phone call. Even if that was the case. He peeled off the top of the pad and stuck it to his laptop screen.

"Great. You should start thinking about a logo; we put promotional flyers out in the local colleges and we like to include that. Do you do any originals?"

"Working on it," I said.

"Cool. You really do have a great sound."

"Thanks," I said, heading out the door. I didn't want to make a run for it, but I already knew I'd be late.

"See you in September," he called after me. The last thing I heard was his laugh echo down the hallway.

Getting out of Hoboken and back to Bayonne was a nightmare. I sweated it out, inching along with construction traffic until I finally hit the back roads, going as fast as I possibly could without wrapping my car around a utility pole. Miraculously there was a parking spot on the side street near Mugshot. I raced through the front door, muttering apologies as it shut behind me. Grace stood behind the register, scary-manager-face softening when she saw me.

"Jess, I've got to pick up Ella from day care," she said.

"I'm sorry, school thing, traffic," I spluttered, grabbing my apron from the back and tossing it over my neck.

"You two are okay with closing?"

"Gracie, baby, we got this," Tanner said.

She sighed and looked at me. "Are you sure?"

"Got it," I said.

"We're out of soy milk, but you should be set with singles for the register. If you have any trouble, call me. But, you know, don't call me, if you can help it."

"Yep."

She grabbed her bag and coat and raced out the front door.

My phone dinged.

"So how did it go?" Tanner asked.

A mom pushing a jogger stroller came up to the counter, her cheeks red from the cold. I ignored the text and rung up her order.

"Nonfat mocha latte," Tanner said, tossing the cup in the air. The toddler in the stroller clapped her hands as Tanner caught it. The mom handed me her money and I gave her the change along with the biscotti she'd ordered for the kid. My phone dinged again. I waited until Tanner gave the woman her drink before checking my messages.

"So . . . what's the deal, are we playing there are not?"

"Holy crap." I read the message again, just to make sure I was reading it properly. The bells announced another customer.

"Just read this out loud," I said, handing Tanner my phone.

"'Must be kismet. Band dropped date last weekend in March. Want?' Who's kismet?" he asked, handing the phone back to me.

"Kismet is fate," said a voice behind me. I whirled around. "Madison."

She wore one of those slouchy knit hats, her hair sticking out every which way from underneath. The tip of her nose was pink, her blue eyes bright. She was in her school uniform, with a backpack slung over one shoulder.

"Hey," she said, looking between Tanner and me.

"So what does that mean?" Tanner asked, nodding toward my phone.

"It means Declan wants us to play at the Whiskey at the end of March."

Tanner let out a whoop.

"That place in Hoboken?" Madison asked.

"Yeah," I said, reading the message again just to make sure. "Wait, don't tell me—a chai to go?"

137

"Actually, I'm staying awhile. I've got some stuff to work on, and I don't . . . It's a little distracting at my house. Can I have a Mexican hot chocolate?"

"Ooooh, spi-cee," Tanner said, throwing a cup in the air, but missing it this time. Entertaining toddlers was clearly more in his wheelhouse.

"She's having it here," I said. "Regular cup."

"Oh, right." He grabbed a large ceramic cup that looked more like a bowl with a handle. Madison reached into her backpack.

"Hey, I owe you, right?" I said. "I'll bring it over to you if you want to get a table."

She cocked her head sideways, slight smile crossing her lips. "Thanks."

I took the cup from Tanner. "Let me do it. Why don't you wipe down the tables and keep an eye on the register."

"Of course you'll do it," he said, puckering his lips and kissing the air. "Don't forget to purge the wand."

I glared at him.

"You know, after steaming the milk."

"Just make sure everything's clean," I answered, tossing the mop cloth to him.

Months ago Grace had hired a guy to come in to teach the staff how to pour steamed milk correctly to make fancy patterns in lattes. There was a barista who worked on weekends who could make Darth Vader and Yoda. I didn't get much daily practice but I could manage a decent-looking rosette and a heart. I debated on which one to pour as I prepped Madison's drink.

I watched the milk steam, making sure it was the right consistency—thick and smooth like paint. Tilting the cup, I poured until the drinking chocolate reached the top, then shook the pitcher back and forth to make the swirly lines of the rosette. Not perfect enough to make it look like I was trying too hard and not too sloppy, so that maybe she'd be slightly impressed. I grabbed a madeleine and set it on the saucer next to the hot chocolate, and walked it over to Madison.

She was sitting on one of the crushed-velvet chairs, close to the window. One leg curled underneath her, laptop on the table. She had a sketchpad on her lap, pencil poised as she stared out the window. When she saw me coming over, she slipped the pencil behind her ear and smiled.

"I'm freezing," she said, rubbing her hands together.

I placed the drink down next to her laptop. She reached for it, wrapped both hands around the cup, and brought it to her face. She paused before taking a sip, noticing the pattern in the milk.

"Pretty. Hey, I didn't order a madeleine."

"Oh, that's on me. You need something to go with hot chocolate; it's, like, a law, or it should be," I said as her lips touched the rim of the cup. With a gentle tilt she took a sip, then ran her tongue across her top lip to get the extra foam.

She was just enjoying her drink, but damn if it wasn't sexy. Almost involuntarily, my butt hit the seat across from her. A few moments away from the register wouldn't hurt.

"This is the best freakin' hot chocolate I've ever had," she said, putting the cup down on the saucer. "Did you melt a chocolate bar in there?"

"Pretty much." I puffed up like an idiot, giddy from her approval. *And guess what, Madison? I invented chocolate, and the wheel, and I can play "Eruption" on my Fender like Eddie Van Halen, do you know who that is?* I may as well have been sitting at Madison's feet, panting, waiting for her to pat my head.

"It's awesome."

"So you draw?" I asked. *Great, Jess, Captain Obvious, she's sitting there with a pencil behind her ear.*

She laughed, kind of a muffled giggle. "Today it doesn't feel like it, but yes, I draw."

The phone buzzed in my pocket again. Holy shit, I'd forgotten about Deck.

Want date or not?

YES!! I typed, and hit send. Three weeks to get our shit together. That was enough, right?

Cool. Get me logo + band photo next week

The photo would be easy.

A logo?

Madison.

"Hey, have you ever done anything like a logo?"

She shook her head before taking another sip of her drink. I looked away, feeling so damn pervy for staring at her mouth. *Focus.*

"Would you consider doing one? We need one, for Yellow Number Five, for promotional stuff. It doesn't have to be anything—"

Her eyes caught fire. "Omigod, yes! I'd love to do that. I'm, wow, you haven't even seen my work."

"You look like you know what you're doing. I trust you."

"So how did practice go? Is Grayson pulling his weight, 'cause if he's not, you know, we'll have to do something about it."

"Yeah, he's great."

"And you're really ready to play out somewhere?"

"Ready? Not sure, but this will just give us incentive."

"That's pretty brave."

"Or stupid," I said.

She grabbed her pad and pulled the pencil from behind her ear. "So who named the band Yellow Number Five?"

"Tanner. It was kind of a random thing, but he said since it's on the label of so many things we'd get a ton of free advertising. So it stuck."

"Ah, so he can do more than make drinks," she said, scribbling something down. "And what kind of music do you play? Is there anything in particular you want me to focus on? Color—or is that obvious?"

"Grunge . . . punk . . . Grunk." *I did not just say that, but if it made her smile . . .*

"Here," she said, handing me the pad. "Give me your number, in case you—I mean, I—have any questions."

I blanked for a moment before writing it on the sketchpad.

"Maybe you should take mine."

I took out my phone. My fingers were useless as she rattled off her number.

"Can you say it again?"

"Here." She took the phone out of my hand and typed her number into my contacts. My heart knocked on my ribs as she handed it back to me.

The hiss of the steam wand followed by a shout of *"Muy caliente!"* caused us both to turn. Tanner grimaced, waving his hand back and forth.

"I guess I better get back there before he gets third-degree burns."

She laughed. "When would you want the logo by?"

"Next week, maybe? You think you can—"

"No problem, I'm on it."

"So does this mean you'll come see us at Whiskey?"

She took another sip from her drink before answering. "I

guess if Wren is going . . . But isn't that, like, a bar? Not sure we'd be able to get in."

"It's eighteen and over."

"I'm not exactly eighteen."

Onstage, I forgot myself—the awkward guitar geek/barista who got tongue-tied and self-conscious. When I sang I could growl, spit, look into people's eyes and make them listen. Standing there, in front of Madison, I tried to tap into that onstage confidence. I could have let it drop but I got the feeling that Yellow #5, playing a real show, in Hoboken, had impressed her the tiniest bit.

"I bet that wouldn't be a problem for you. I think if you want to be somewhere, you definitely have a way of making it happen."

Her eyes lit up again. I walked away before I could say anything else, ignoring all impulses to look back at her.

"Did you melt her with your barista skills?" Tanner asked.

I stole a glance at her. She was shaking her head slightly, smile on her face.

She'd be there.

"Something like that," I said.

NINE

MADISON

BROODY BARISTA HAD CHANGED INTO FLIRTY Barista overnight. It was just the distraction I'd craved. After being in the light and chatter of our yearbook meeting that afternoon, the idea of being home brought me down. It's not like I wanted to sit and bond with the Mugshot regulars. I just didn't want to be alone with my thoughts, because my thoughts had become barbed wire on my brain. It physically hurt to think.

I'm your father, Madison.

What was I supposed to do with that?

Hanging with people who were just going about their lives, drinking coffee, faces in a book or computer, felt normal. And the Mexican hot chocolate was almost enough to make me forget everything, it was *that* good. The Aztecs were definitely onto something. Jesse would have been revered as a god. A cute god, who looked particularly scorching in his Levis and black tee that afternoon.

What was it about broody band guys?

I leaned back in the chair, my blank sketchpad begging me to create something, to get lost in the details of a drawing. A logo for a band? Hmm . . . I'd been thinking about something different for my portfolio, just one more piece that would round it out. This was perfect. Something pop culture–ish and fun. I closed my eyes, thought of the band name, trying to see it in some unique, fresh—

I'm your father, Madison.

There was no getting away from it. The moment I let myself get distracted or lost in something else, the phrase came floating across my mind's eye, like a storm ticker on the Weather Channel. Even though it still hadn't quite sunk in. Would it ever? I'd stayed in my room most of Saturday—ignoring my mother and Paul. He had left for a job on Monday and wasn't supposed to return from Martha's Vineyard until later in the week. My mother told me he was using the time to think. I envied him that. I hadn't sat down with my mother yet either. One of the benefits of her new yoga philosophy was giving me my space. I wasn't sure why I wasn't talking to her—I think I needed to protest somehow until I knew how I really felt about the situation, but that could take forever.

Paul was still Paul—that exciting guy who swooped in a few times a year with travel stories, and jokes and smiles and Springsteen songs. I should have been happy. This was a good thing. I knew I felt strongly about him, enjoyed the times when he was around. But did I love him like a person loves their father? Could he ever think of me as a daughter?

I hadn't told anyone yet. The words would not make it to my lips. I'd tried to call Wren and Jazz at different times over the weekend, but neither of them had been around. Wren had been at her sister's tropical baby shower. And Jazzabelle had been out, probably clandestinely kissing her running partner behind one of the oaks in the park. Monday on the Boulevard bus, sandwiched among the leering dockworkers, prim weekday church ladies, and Sacred Heart girls hardly seemed the appropriate place to spill my news. Everyone had been all abuzz about the dance anyway.

It had been the same way in yearbook earlier that afternoon, too. I'd almost blurted it out when Jazz finally pitched an idea about making the Father's Club layout "On the Edge." "You think that's edgy? Wait till you hear this!" I'd imagined saying, but of course, I swallowed it. Piper had been annoyed at me because while Wren and Jazz handed in their Sadie Hawkins copy, I still hadn't looked at the pictures from the dance. I rattled off some lame excuse and promised to look at them before Friday. The layout wasn't due until the end of the month. I knew I took some decent shots, I just hadn't had the time to really look at them yet.

A knock on the window startled me.

"Zach?"

He stood there and pointed to his phone, then shrugged.

Mom and Paul hadn't been the only people I'd avoided over the weekend. Zach's "I love you" was also on a ticker through my brain. And I still had no idea what to say to him. Maybe I could take it to the next step with him, but I wasn't sure if I was ready to be with just him and only him; he was easier to handle in the hot-guy-I-have-fun-with role. I gestured to the door, reaching into my bag for my phone. I'd kept it off in protest too. It had been nice being unreachable. My own version of *time to think*. When I turned it on, there were at least twenty texts and three missed calls. Ignoring them made me feel like I had some control over something.

"Are you ever going to pick up your phone?" The cold air had followed Zach in and I shivered, wrapping my hands around the hot-chocolate cup. Out of the corner of my eye I swore I could see Jesse watching. Or maybe I was just imagining it. I glanced at the counter, but he and Tanner seemed otherwise occupied. Jesse knew I'd had a date at the dance— why did I even care?

"Sorry," I said. "I needed to get some work done."

"So you came here?" he asked. He reached down and took the madeleine, mouth opened, teeth bared to wolf it.

"No," I said. It came out more forcefully than planned. A girl studying at the next table looked over at us. Zach's eyes sharpened, a jagged line of confusion forming between his brows. He placed the madeleine down and raised his hands.

"Okay, I'll get my own." He sauntered up to the counter without saying another word.

His tone made me feel like a first-class puppy-stomper. I shrugged off the feeling and settled back into my seat, but the desire to draw was gone.

What the hell was wrong with me? I should at least try with him, right? I wasn't ready to say anything back to him but maybe one day I could.

Zach came back a few minutes later with his own hot cup and a ginormous chocolate chip cookie. He put both on the table and wriggled off his jacket. My throat tightened—he wasn't expecting to have some love talk here, was he? Maybe if I didn't bring it up, he wouldn't either. He thumped into the chair and devoured half the cookie in one bite.

"How did you know where to find me?"

There were crumbs on his lips and lap, a blob of dark chocolate in the corner of his mouth. He finished chewing before he answered.

"I didn't," he said, tongue dabbing at the chocolate. "I stopped by to see you and your mom answered the door."

"Really? Today's usually her late day."

"Well, she was there. I was on my way home when I spotted you. Your mom told me to tell you to call her. So, call her."

"How did she seem?"

He shrugged. "Okay. Why? Something up?"

And there it was—the perfect entrance for me to tell him about Paul. I imagined hopping into Zach's lap, his strong arms around me. *That guy Paul? The one with my mother when they walked in on us? He's my father.* Could he be there for me? Or would he just say, *That's cool. Chill. Everything will work out.* I didn't want to hear that because right now, it felt like the equivalent of *Shut up.*

"No, I just haven't spoken to her all day," I answered.

"Oh."

He picked up my sketchpad from the table. My first instinct always was to snatch it back, because it felt like my soul was up for scrutiny. His eyes scanned the paper.

"Who's Jesse?"

I grabbed the pad, aware of its heaviness in my hands, Jesse's number like a beacon on the page. I wasn't sure why I was so flustered—it wasn't like I'd planned on keeping it a secret. I closed it and shoved it into my backpack.

"He's right there," I said, gesturing toward the counter. "He asked me to design a logo for his band. Cool, right?"

"A logo? Really? Why you?"

"What's that supposed to mean?"

"It's not like you advertise logo design. How did he know—"

"He saw me sketching and asked."

Zach gave me a deliberate and slow nod, while he lifted his drink to his mouth and looked out the window.

"What?"

He shook his head but remained silent, a small, annoying smile crossing his face.

"I think I need to go." I shut down my laptop, gulped the rest of my hot chocolate, which wasn't really meant to be gulped since the cayenne pepper made my throat raw, and gathered my stuff. A shadow crossed the table.

"Everything okay?"

Jesse. Zach sized him up, or at least that's the way it felt, and then peered at me over his to-go cup.

"Great. Hey, Jess—this is Zach. Zach, Jess. I'm designing the logo for his band." Neither of them made more of a move than a slight chin-jab in each other's direction. Jesse picked up the dirty cup. Zach chugged the rest of his drink, then held out his empty cup to him. Not awkward at all.

"They're playing in Hoboken this month."

"Yeah, Whiskey Business, you should come."

Zach seemed to relax a bit. "Sounds cool. What kind of music?"

I busied myself with my coat and hat as they spoke, telling myself that this was fine even though I felt slightly smothered. Jesse was becoming a friend, something separate from Zach, another life that included yoga and chai and sneaking around Sacred Heart. But why shouldn't they meet? I carefully wrapped the madeleine in a napkin and put it in my pocket.

"I can't wait to work on the sketches for this, I'll have something for you soon."

"Great, see ya," Jesse said, walking back behind the counter with our dirty dishes.

Zach's eyes were on me. *Why are you so uptight about giving him a chance?*

"I know you just came from there, but do you think you could walk me home?"

He smiled. "Sure."

He draped his arm around me as we walked outside. I nestled in closer to him, shielding myself from the cold.

"So why didn't you tell Band Guy I was your boyfriend?"

Band Guy.

I nudged him. "I didn't know I needed to, isn't it obvious we're together?"

He shrugged.

"Did you, um . . . About the other night, what I said . . ."

"Still thinking."

"What does that mean?"

"I'm not sure I'm ready to say it. Is that cool?"

He sighed.

"Oh, Zach, come on." I took the madeleine out of my pocket and put it in my mouth, tilting my face toward his.

"Nope."

"Mmmm-mm."

It was a food thing we did sometimes with Twizzlers at the movies, or his mom's chocolate chip cookies. I stopped until he looked at me, one corner of his mouth pulling up in a sexy side grin.

"Fine."

He leaned down and took the other half, biting down until

our lips met and it was all about tongues and crumbs and missing the light to cross the street. Gross and sexy, all at once. We both laughed, swallowing our respective pieces. I hated public displays of affection, but there I was, on the corner of Thirty-Fourth and Broadway, proving to Zach he had nothing to worry about.

Or maybe . . .

. . . I was just trying to prove that to myself.

The house was dark when I got home, except for the kitchen. The spicy smell of Indian takeout filled the rooms. I took my time, pulling off my hat and coat, hanging them on the coatrack, placing my backpack down. Creaky floorboards announced my entrance long before I reached the kitchen.

Mom was at the café table, takeout boxes from Tandoori West surrounding her barely touched plate of food. She looked up, her face pale, eyes devoid of makeup. She looked so small and fragile sitting there—so alone. My chest ached with guilt. I was finally ready to hear her side of it.

"Hey." I sat across from her.

"There's some bhel puri and tandoori chicken." She gestured at the open boxes.

"Thanks. I'm not hungry," I said, almost a whisper.

She dropped her fork onto her plate with a rattle. "You should have answered my phone calls."

"Mom, I'm sor—"

"No, I get it. You're punishing me, but this—*this*—is huge and I can't take that you're not talking to me about it."

"What do you want me to say? You dump this on me some random Saturday morning after you've decided to 'live your truth' or whatever it was you said and expect me to sit and chat about it? Especially about Paul, who's been in my life, like, forever? Did you ever think to tell us before? Why now, Mom? Why now?"

Her palms went up to her forehead, as if she suddenly had a killer migraine. I expected her to rage back at me. Instead she just breathed out hard, put her forearms on the table alongside her plate, forefinger and thumb on the right hand together in a yoga mudra we'd learned in class a few weeks ago.

"I don't know. I guess I'd thought about it before, but it's always been you and me ag—"

"Against the world," I finished her sentence. "That's great, Mom, but I didn't really have a choice in that, did I?"

"Madison, please. I wanted to tell Paul, I did, but I wasn't lying when I told you that it was the wrong guy, right time. I knew I wanted you, could handle raising you on my own, but I also wanted to keep Paul as a friend. I wasn't sure he would have been able to handle it and I didn't want to face that sort of rejection."

"Was he mad when you told him the other day? Is he . . . is he upset that—" I couldn't voice what I wanted to say because in all of it, the virtual Pandora's box of emotions this announcement had opened, the last thing, underneath it all was this—did he want this? Did he want . . . me?

My mother reached across and took my hand, and I didn't resist.

"He's angry at me, Madison. Not you. It's an adjustment for all of us, but the news was happy."

Relief blurred my eyes; tears I hadn't even known I was holding in rolled down my cheeks. I swiped them away, sniffled. That was why I hadn't told anyone. I wanted to be sure he was okay with it too. To go from not knowing who your father was to knowing that he didn't want you were two different things.

"Were you really worried about that?"

I nodded, swiped my cheek. My stomach growled—maybe I was hungry, or maybe letting go of such a heavy thing had emptied me out. I grabbed a plate from the cabinet and filled it with bhel puri and tandoori chicken. Mom handed me a fork as I sat down.

"He was surprised. And hurt. And—"

"What I don't understand is, if you're such great friends, why didn't you think he could handle you being pregnant?"

She exhaled slowly, staring out the small curtained window to the yard. "Paul was different then, Mads. I'm not sure he would have taken the news the same way. He got this dream job and his hub was based in Spain. We went to Atlantic

City to celebrate. We saw this indie band he'd been following, and played roulette and craps—we won—and it was . . ." She looked out the window again, but instead of being wistful or sad, she fought a smile, chuckled to herself. "One of those nights you never forget."

I nearly choked on my food.

"I know it's weird to talk about it like this, Madison, but I wasn't sure I'd see him again once he moved."

"So you asked him if he could . . ." I said, suddenly conscious of what an intimate question I was asking.

"No, it wasn't formal or anything, it just happened. It was—"

"Please stop, I think this is about all I can handle right now."

"Isn't it better to know we were friends who loved each other, instead of someone random who disappeared?"

"I'm not sure," I said. "It just— It would have been nice to know that he was my father."

"What do you think of when you think of Paul?"

"I don't know. Doughnuts? Airplanes? Loud Springsteen music?"

She laughed. "Exactly. Fun stuff. I was afraid that if you'd known, you'd pay more attention to the time he wasn't here than to the time he was, and it didn't seem fair to either of you."

Now *my* head hurt. I just wanted to stop thinking.

"I'm sorry I didn't answer my phone before; that was total douchebaggery on my part."

"You don't have to use that word—"

"It fits, though. I didn't answer on purpose. I wasn't ready to talk about it. Can we just eat now, Mom? Please? I just want to eat, take a hot shower, do my homework. Be normal. This is all I can handle for now. Is that okay?"

She picked up her fork. "Yes, but you know anytime you have any questions—"

"I know where you live," I said.

After dinner I holed up in my room with my computer and the memory card from the Sadie Hawkins Dance. For the first time since that night, I was excited to look through the pictures, to see if there was anything portfolio- or yearbook-worthy.

The first few were awful, blurry, random crowd shots that made me worry the whole night had been like that. What had I been thinking? Then I saw the one of Wren and Gray, which was . . . sweet, sexy. Their foreheads touching, Wren had a soft smile on her face; Gray, too—they were both in the same blissful, secret world behind their closed eyes.

I scanned through some more. The selfies Zach and I took made my heart ache—we leaned into each other, cheek to cheek and grinning. Before he'd said *that thing*. We made a pretty scorching couple. Why had I gotten so annoyed that he showed up at Mugshot? Why couldn't I just say what he wanted me to say?

The shots of the hallway with the glowing balloons were striking; I knew I could play them up with some effects and turn the photos into something special. A definite portfolio piece. The one of me, Wren, and Jazz was adorable, one that even Piper would approve of—we'd captured a perfect moment, the three of us smiling, arm in arm but in a casual way. Maybe I'd have to give Grayson photo credit. I went back to the beginning of the pictures, to the first one of Wren and Gray, ready to start editing.

I pulled up the cropping tool, selecting the space I wanted to focus in on, when my eyes fell upon something in the background. Not something . . . someone. Jesse. He was up against the far wall, staring into the crowd. A few clicks and I came in closer on his face. It wasn't crystal clear, but his features were plain as day. He was looking at something, or someone; his gaze seemed too fixated to be spaced-out. I studied the way his jacket hung on him, the line of his jaw, how his hair swept across his forehead. I got up from the bed to grab my sketchpad and a pencil off my desk.

You're supposed to be finding pictures for the layout.

My pencil scratched across the paper as I blocked out the dimensions of the sketch.

Jesse McMann was an intriguing subject.

TEN

JESSE

"TAKE IT FROM THE TOP," I SAID.

"Again, dude? Come on," Tanner said. "Can't we break for a minute? I'm spitting dust here."

"Two and a half weeks until we play, we have two songs down, last I checked that's not a set. We're outta here in twenty, T, you can make it. Maybe if you took off the hat."

"Nope."

Grayson wiped his brow along the sleeve of his Batman shirt. "It is kind of hot in here."

Practice had become too intense for my garage—twice a week was about all the neighborhood could handle before someone called to complain. We decided to pool some work cash and spring for space at Lot 23, a warehouse turned rehearsal studio between an oil refinery and a strip mall on the far end of town beyond the old rails. They had four rehearsal rooms, and Plasma was taking up one of them too. Small town, even smaller rehearsal space, we were bound to run into someone we knew. The competition made us work harder.

Tanner lifted his strap over his head. "I'm gonna pass out, Jess, just let me grab a water."

"Fine," I said. "Hurry."

I strummed the opening of the next song, turned to Grayson. He'd come prepared, at least—chugging from a water bottle he brought with him. After sipping he trickled some over his hair, shook it out, and laughed. I had to give him props—I'd never seen someone work so hard or make that much progress in such a short time. He attacked it.

"You really think we'll be ready?" he asked.

"Yeah." I kept thinking about that jar on Declan's desk —*If you're gonna blow it, blow it big!!* We sounded better—would we be our best by Whiskey? Probably not, but we'd go down trying. The door creaked open.

"Now we're down to fif—" I stopped. "Hannah?"

"Hey, Jess. I saw Tanner in the hallway." She smiled. Her presence lightened the room—a butterfly coming in through an open window. My knee-jerk reaction to seeing her pissed me off—my nerves turned to live wires. Would that ever stop?

"What are you doing . . . oh, I guess . . . Plasma," I said, answering my own question.

"Yep, getting ready for the battle," she said, peering behind me.

I turned. "Oh, Hannah, that's Grayson, our new drummer. Grayson, Hannah."

Grayson nodded at her and stood up. "I'm gonna see what's taking Tanner so long. Be right back."

She was silent, toeing the floor with the tip of her boot, until he left the room.

"You never came here for our practice," I said.

"You never asked me."

"I never thought I needed to."

"Don't start, Jess. I just wanted to say hi."

"And ask why I haven't contacted Duncan about the song."

"Maybe. I guess. But now I know why you haven't given it to him. You're doing the battle too."

"No, we're not. We didn't get the entry form in on time."

"But Tanner," she said. Just then someone shouted, "Douchebag!" through the hallway. We both turned as a cacophony of voices stormed closer and closer to the room. Tanner barreled in, followed by Duncan, Kenny Ashe, then Grayson, who lingered in the doorway, observing.

"So you are doing the battle," Duncan said. "Guess that's why you're still holding on to what's part mine."

Hannah stepped back, closer to Duncan. It was a small movement, but one that felt like she was letting me know where she stood. The live wires in my chest sizzled momentarily. I wanted to roar, to make them all spontaneously combust and splatter against the walls, but I had no idea what he was talking about.

"No, we're not. We're playing Whiskey Business in a couple of weeks," I said. Duncan flinched. He'd been so pumped to play there when we sent Deck our CD.

That's what you get for boffing my girlfriend.

"Then you're not doing the battle?" Kenny asked. In a parallel universe, I'm sure Kenny and I were great friends. I admired his playing, and he had this rasp in his voice when he sang that I envied, but he was all technique, methodical. I could play by ear and it pissed him off so much that the one time we tried to be together in a band, it didn't last after one practice.

"No." "Yes." Tanner and I said it together.

"Tanner?" I said.

He nibbled the side of his lip before speaking. "I put in the entry form."

The battle meant nothing to me anymore. We had a real gig, we didn't need this high school pissing contest where it always felt like it was more about who you knew than how you played. I was about to say as much, that we just wouldn't show up and I'd give Tanner the fifty bucks for the entry fee back, when I saw Hannah lean into Duncan. They stood there . . . waiting.

"Then I guess we're doing it," I said. "What's the big deal?" I could see plainly what the big deal was—they didn't want the competition. And Duncan wanted the song, but *part his*? Fuck that.

Tanner grinned and let out a *"Whoop!"*

"Stupid hat," Duncan said, pulling it off Tanner's head as he left. Kenny and Hannah followed him out. Hannah gave me one last lingering look, which I returned with a stony glare. Tanner was still grinning as they left.

"Why didn't you tell me?" I asked when they were gone.

Grayson bent down and picked up Tanner's hat.

"Geez, dude, this hat is rank," he said, tossing it to him and wiping his hand on his jeans. Tanner caught it and slipped it back onto his head.

"Because you were all depressed and shit, and I knew you would pull that tortured-artist crap. And I wanted to be sure this worked out."

"Am I *this*?" Grayson asked.

Tanner punched his shoulder and smiled. "Yup."

"Tortured-artist crap?" I said.

T's face contorted into an exaggerated grimace and he clutched his hands to his chest. *"I can't play, it's not fun anymore, Hannah ripped my balls off when she left me and the world has no meaning.* You know, all that stuff that spills out after a few vodka lemonades."

"Okay, okay," I said.

"When is it?" Grayson asked.

"After the Whiskey—first week in April."

"We don't have to do it. It's a stupid contest," I said. "I just couldn't back down when they were standing here."

"No, I'm in. That was hard-core," Grayson said. "I've only played in basements."

"Then we've got fifteen minutes, let's do it," I said.

"Why don't we stay longer? I don't think there's anyone coming in after us," Tanner said, pulling his bass strap over his head.

"Can't do it tonight."

"But dude, the battle? Whiskey Business? We need to practice," Tanner said. "You're not on tonight, what gives?"

"Have to go see a girl about a logo."

I stopped home to take a quick shower and wash the rehearsal-space funk away. Lot 23 may have been soundproof, but it stunk. Madison was expecting me at six and I had about fifteen minutes to get there. I shrugged on a tee and towel-dried my hair. I hadn't had a cut in months and the most I could say for it was that it covered my head. I ran a hand through it, pushing strands to the side so they wouldn't hang in my eyes. Maybe I'd swing by Vito's for a trim before I came home. My stomach growled. Mom had chili on the stove, but I didn't think it was the best thing to chow on before meeting a girl.

"Be back in an hour or so," I called as I bounded down the stairs and out the front door, ignoring the questions that were hollered at my departure.

I arrived at Madison's with five minutes to spare, taking my time, climbing the two sets of stairs to reach her porch. My finger was poised to touch the bell, when the door opened.

"Hey," I said.

"Come in, come in," she said, grinning. She held out her arms for my jacket.

"Oh." I shrugged off my jacket and she took it. I followed her into the dining room. The house was dim, her computer the only light source in the room. She snapped a switch on the wall, and the chandelier above the table slowly came to life.

"Sorry. You ever do that? Lose track of time and the next thing you realize, you're sitting in the dark? Seriously, if I hadn't heard you stomp onto the porch I'd still be staring at the computer, oblivious," she said, tossing my jacket over a highback chair.

"Yeah, totally," I said, looking around. "So whatcha got for me?"

She slid into the chair in front of her laptop. Her computer was pulled up to a page with a modern-looking house on it; it was all lines and angles and looked suspended in the midst of trees and a cascading waterfall, but made sense somehow. I knew I'd seen it before. She jiggled the mouse, trying to close down the page.

"What's that?" I asked.

"Oh, just the most amazing house design, like, ever. Frank Lloyd Wright designed it when he was in his late sixties. *His sixties*. There's hope for me yet."

"Wait, that's . . . What is it . . . water . . . something . . ."

"Fallingwater. You've heard of it?"

"My aunt lives in Pennsylvania, not too far from there. It's in the middle of Bumfuck and Where-the-Hell-Am-I."

Her eyes lit up. "Yeah, that's it. That's the most amazing part of it, isn't it? That something so beautiful is in the middle of nowhere. Could you imagine driving up to it and staying there? Like that was your house?"

"Are you doing a project on it or something?"

"Kind of—I'm writing an essay on Frank Lloyd Wright and organic architecture for art, but . . . I think that's what I'd like to study. Architecture. It's like math and design all rolled up into one. I'd love to— Sorry, you're here for this logo, not to be bored off your ass." She shut down the window and opened up another file.

"No, it's cool. It's just, wow, I feel like a jerk for asking you to do this, obviously you're into bigger and better things."

"Please, 'bigger and better'—this was fun. Well, it will be, if you like it," she said, clicking through a few pictures before coming up to it. "I worked up three—all pretty simple, straightforward. I mean, you want kids to doodle this on their notebooks when you become a household name."

"Ha."

"Here," she said, getting up. "Just click through these, see which one speaks to you. Want something to drink?"

"Uh . . ."

"Water? Soda? No fancy leaf patterns, though."

165

I grinned. "Okay, water's good."

She disappeared into the kitchen. The first logo was simple, just *Yellow #5* in old typewriter lettering. The second one was a little funkier-looking, like the letters were dripping. Definitely something that could be doodled on a notebook. The third one popped. The *Y* in *Yellow* had a long tail and became part of the hashtag, and the five was stylized. They all spoke to me, maybe this one a little more. All of them made me wonder how much work she'd put into this. They were amazing.

She came back in, two bottles of water in her hand.

I flipped my bangs out of my eyes, but they flopped back into place. "I think I like this one the best."

"That's my favorite too—I got inspired by looking at the back of labels. Tanner's right; you'll get loads of free advertising. Although I guess the whole unnatural food-dye thing is a little scary."

"What do I owe you for this?"

"You don't owe me anything. I can use this for my application." She took her index finger and moved my hair across my brow, more serious than flirty. She tilted her head to the side, studying my face, then ran her fingers through my bangs, pulling them straight before letting the hair flop across my forehead again.

"Application?" I said, trying to ignore what having her touch me, even in the most innocent way, was doing to my insides. *Just be cool.*

"Who does your hair?"

I laughed. "*Does* it? I don't get my hair done. I get it cut. Vito. I know, I'm due."

"Would you . . . I could do it," she said.

"Yeah, right."

"No, I can—it's sort of my thing."

She wasn't joking.

"When, like, right now?"

"Unless you have somewhere you have to be. Sorry, I just think you'd look really good with it a bit choppier, maybe even a darker shade. It would stand out onstage more. I did Wren's hair a while ago, blue highlights, but . . . Oh god, I'm being pushy. I just think, it might be fun."

If letting her dye my hair meant having her touch me again, she could give me a purple mohawk with hot-pink tips. "No, let's do it."

"Excellent," she said, tapping her fingers together like a mad scientist. "To the kitchen."

What had I just signed up for?

"Is that a good tee you're wearing? 'Cause these are some heavy-duty chemicals. We're going blue-black." She dragged a chair across the floor so it was situated next to a small café table where it looked like she'd set up a makeshift hair salon.

"We are?" Dark was one thing; blue-black was really dark. She waved her hand dismissively.

"My mother can fix any hair disaster, so if it looks awful,

you can change it before you play in Hoboken. Sit," she said, gently pushing on my shoulders until my butt hit the seat. She shook out a black plastic cape and it billowed around me, falling into place as she snapped it closed at the back of my neck. Then she tucked a small black towel around the collar.

"This probably isn't the best time to ask, but where'd you learn to do this?"

"My mom's a stylist. She has a few clients who only come to the house, so I sort of learned by assisting her. I do my own, otherwise I'd be this horrible shade of dishwater blond that would make me just disappear in the crowd."

"You? Disappear in the crowd? Right." It had come out without thinking—a friendly thing, but it sounded flirty. Was I flirting? Madison was anything but a disappear-in-the-crowd kind of girl. Even now, without makeup or anything fancy, she was pretty. But that night at the dance . . . damn. Maybe I *was* flirting.

She chuckled as she lined up three bottles in various sizes on the table. She placed a black bowl, a flat black brush with a long thin handle, and a little thing that looked like a whisk on the newspaper. Then she began hooking up the portable sink to the one in her kitchen.

"Do you need help or anything?" I felt lazy just watching.

"Nope, just let me have my way with your hair and we're good."

Was she flirting with me?

Once the sink was hooked up properly, Madison grabbed

a small jar of Vaseline and stood astride my legs. Her fingers were in my hair again, the tips grazing my scalp, smoothing the hair away from my face. She was so close—I could smell her lip gloss, something sweet and sugary like bubblegum. The way she was standing I could easily pull her down to my lap, run my hands along the smooth, soft curves outlined by her jeans, taste her mouth. My tongue felt on fire.

"What's, um, what's up with the Vaseline?" I asked, the words thick and hot, lava spilling from my mouth.

"It'll keep the dye off your face," she said, popping open the lid, oblivious to how this was affecting me. I was glad to be covered in a cape.

She dabbed the Vaseline along my hairline with her thumb, her hand anchored to the top of my head. My heart swelled, aware of the space between us, her fingertips gliding along my skin. I sat stock-still, afraid if I moved, I'd actually do the things I was imagining doing with her.

Cool it, Jess.

I tried to think of something to say to keep my mind from getting too twisted up in dirty thoughts. What about that guy she was with last week at Mugshot? Had that been her dance date? Was he her boyfriend? Bringing that up would be such an obvious fish for information but . . . I'd been that guy. The one who'd been oblivious to something going on right under his nose. Not that there was anything going on. Oh, hell. I just wanted to know.

"Who was that guy you were with last week at Mugshot?"

She put the lid back on the jar and wiped her hands on a paper towel.

"Zach? I introduced you, right?"

"Yeah, is he your, um, boyfriend?"

She bit her lip as she poured white liquid from one of the bottles and began whisking the mixture in the bowl. "He's a boy, and he's my friend, so . . . I dunno, that sounds so serious. *Boyfriend*. We hang out, how's that for a definition?"

"I guess it's good." Was it? I'd seen them together. They looked like a couple to me, but I was here now. Were we hanging out? Dyeing hair was probably number one on the Best Ways to Stay in the Friend-zone top ten list. Hard to have sexytimes when your hairline has a strip of petroleum jelly on it. I relaxed into the chair. Perviness subsiding. Talk of the other guy the equivalent of a cold shower.

Just then the front door groaned open. Madison's eyebrows rose in surprise. Heavy footsteps and the sound of paper rustling followed until a tall guy with sandy hair walked through the doorway, arms full of brown grocery bags. He stopped, looked at me, then Madison.

"What's up?"

ELEVEN

"WHAT'S UP?"

Paul smiled as he walked into the kitchen. He'd decided to stay with us until he found a place of his own, but his schedule with the corporate-jet gig had been pretty full. We hadn't had the chance to talk except to say, "We should really talk," since my mother had broken the news. Part of me was really okay with that. I wasn't sure how to act around him, which made me even more self-conscious because I'd never had to think about acting a certain way around him.

"Hey, I, um, didn't expect to see you," I said as he placed the bags on the counter.

"The flight I was scheduled for got canceled."

Paul looked over my shoulder at Jesse. "Hair? In the kitchen?"

"Mom doesn't really use the kitchen to cook when you're not here," I said, chuckling. "This is my friend Jesse. He's in a band, I'm giving him a new look."

I picked up the whisk and resumed mixing the dye.

Paul put out his hand in greeting. Jesse wrestled his from underneath the plastic cape and gave him a hearty shake.

"This is Paul," I said, "he's a . . ." I stumbled—the word *father* would not come out.

"A friend of the family," Paul finished. "I was going to make my vegetarian stir-fry, but I see you're busy."

"We should be done here in about half an hour. I can dry him upstairs, if that's okay with you."

Paul nodded. He didn't know the no-boys-on-the-second-floor rule, but since it was a special situation, I didn't feel like I was taking advantage. And it's not like I was going to be doing anything else but drying Jesse's hair.

"Uh, yeah, sure, that's great." He unpacked the groceries— mostly veggies—and put them on the top shelf of the fridge, then grabbed an apple. "I'll be out of your hair in a minute— ha, hair."

I shook my head.

"It's Dana's late night, right?"

"Yep," I said, pulling on purple latex gloves with a snap. I wiggled my fingers maniacally at Jesse. He had a wide, curvy mouth that stretched into an adorable smile. It transformed him from broody to hot in two seconds flat.

"I'm not going to regret this, am I?" he asked.

"Nope, especially not when the Hoboken girls swoon."

"Hey, you guys mind if I turn on some music?" Paul asked, flipping through the mail on the counter. He grabbed today's newspaper and put it under his arm. "I'll just hang in the dining room until you're done."

"Go ahead."

Moments later Paul's favorite was playing in the dining room, singing a song about Atlantic City. Paul hummed along in between loud, crunchy bites of his Granny Smith. It wasn't a particularly romantic song but it took on new meaning to me every time I heard the chorus. Did it mean anything to Paul when he heard it? Did he think about winning at craps, a night with my mother? *Ick.* My cheeks grew warm. With Jesse into grunge or punk, or "grunk," I was sure listening to this must have been like nails across a chalkboard to him.

"Sorry for the, um, oldies," I said, working the dye into his hair.

"It's fine, he's cool. My dad listens to Springsteen all the time."

He smiled again. It was a smile I could trust.

"Mine too," I whispered.

"Jess, my god, you have the patience of a two-year-old—sit still," I said.

We'd moved up to my bathroom to let Paul begin his

culinary genius while I dried Jesse's hair. I'd made him sit on my fuzzy pink toilet cover, facing the tank so he couldn't look in the mirror. He kept squirming, trying to sneak a peek. I wanted the look to be complete before the final reveal. It came out pretty hot, if I did say so myself. His blue eyes stood out in contrast to his dark hair. I'd shaped his long bangs with jagged edges, so he looked a little like a manga character. He would be irresistible onstage.

"You know I pretty much run a towel across my head, no muss, no fuss."

"Even when you play?"

"Yep."

"No mousse, gel?"

"No and no. Just falls flat in my face after two minutes of playing, anyway."

"Well, you might want to change that; I can recommend something," I said, turning off the hair dryer.

"I'm playing a bar in Hoboken, not the Garden."

"You gotta start somewhere. Okay, get up," I said, covering his eyes with my hands.

"Is this really necessary," he said, rising up. He was tall and lean and deceptively muscular, not in a Zach way, but still, in a way.

My head reached a good two inches below his shoulders, and I had to stand on tiptoe to keep my hands over his eyes, my body brushing his back. We shuffled so we both faced forward. For a split second, I regretted that I hadn't cleaned my vanity and felt a wave of embarrassment at the sheer amount of product that littered it—the blob of dried toothpaste on the edge of the sink, an open tube of liquid base makeup, an oversize can of hairspray, the Hello Kitty gel cling that had been stuck to my mirror since I was eight years old. Then I remembered his smile. Even if he thought it was messy, I didn't think he'd care.

"Okay, one, two, three." I slid my hands off his eyes.

He clamped his hands over his mouth as he stared at his reflection.

"Holy shit," he said.

"Is that good?"

He whistled and moved his head from side to side to check out each angle.

"Holeeecy shit," he said again, louder. "Tanner is going to be relentless."

"You don't like it?"

"No," he laughed, "I mean, yeah, I like it, just have to get used to it."

"I think it looks great."

We stood side by side, looking at each other in the mirror. I still couldn't believe he let me talk him into doing his hair. I'm not sure what had possessed me to ask, either. I only knew I'd wanted him to hang out with me longer than saying, "I like this logo, see ya." He bent down bit, putting his head next to mine.

"We're like opposites now."

"Now?"

We stayed cheek to cheek for a long moment, like we were sitting in a photo booth about to get our picture taken. That's when it came into focus—we looked really *good* together. My heart surged hot with the realization. Had he put two and two together at all—that I could have easily sent him the logo files in an email? That there was no real need for us to get together other than I simply wanted to see him outside of ordering a hot drink?

Ever since I'd cropped that photo, I'd built up some imagined personal history of Jesse. I kept working on the sketch, refining his features. What would he do if he knew I was drawing a picture of him? It made me wonder about him, how he spent his time other than making coffee and band practice. Did he have any siblings? Did he have a girlfriend?

"Anyone hungry?" Paul called up the stairs.

"Ah, be right down." I stepped away from Jesse, occupied myself with unplugging the hair dryer and rolling up the cord. He slid his hands into his back pockets.

"Um, let me put those logo files on a flash drive for you, that way you can do what you want." I stowed the dryer away, stood up to face him. There was another beat where he didn't move, looked like he wanted to say something, but then he shifted, and I walked past him to the door.

"Yeah, cool, I'll show them to the guys," he said, thumping down the stairs behind me. "I'll let you know which one we go with."

Paul was at the dining room table, plate of steaming veggies and the newspaper spread out in front of him. My laptop was opened to the logos. I grabbed my extra flash drive and plugged it into the computer.

Paul looked up. "Wow, interesting."

Jesse ran a hand over his hair and grinned. "Yeah, I like it."

"He's a rock star, Paul, has to look the part."

"Really?"

"No, just a guitar player."

"What sort of music?"

They spoke about their musical likes and dislikes as the files downloaded, strangely enough finding some common ground with the Stones and Pink Floyd. Jesse looked so animated when he told Paul about playing at Whiskey Business. I knew I'd said I'd think about going to see him, but hearing him talk about it again made me want to be there even more. The eighteen-and-over thing could be a problem, but I figured since Gray was in the band, Wren would definitely be going too, underage or not. We'd put our heads together and figure something out.

"You sure you don't want any stir-fry? There's plenty," Paul said.

"No thanks, I have to get going," Jesse said, grabbing his jacket.

I handed him the flash drive. "I'll walk you out."

Paul raised his eyebrows in approval at me. I shook my head and threw my jacket over my shoulders, ushering Jesse out the door and onto the porch.

"You don't have to walk me out, it's cold," he said.

"I'm fine. You sure you like your hair? Because if for any—"

"It's great. Only I think I miss getting a root beer lollipop from Vito."

"Well, no lollipops here, only stir-fry."

He laughed and juggled the flash drive in his palm.

"Madison, are you sure I don't owe you anything for this? This is a lot, the hair, the logo. I just—"

"No, really, I was happy to do it, and the hair was a bonus. It's what friends do, right?"

"Yeah, but maybe I'll have to throw a couple of free chais your way."

"Now you have me figured out."

We laughed, our breath disappearing in cold, white wisps. Jesse's eyes were on mine, intent. He chuckled, shrugged his shoulders to his ears, and all at once something shifted—I had the feeling he was thinking of kissing me because I was thinking of kissing him, how easy it would be just to reach up and brush my mouth across his. The moment passed, and he took a step back.

"Thank you," he said. "I guess I'll see you at Mugshot."

"See ya," I said, waiting until he got to the foot of the stairs to go inside.

I was about to head upstairs, but stopped short. Something in the way Paul was just sitting alone in the dining room nagged at me. This was the first time we were together without Mom in the house. I went out to the kitchen and grabbed a small bowl of stir-fry, then took a seat at the dining room table. A happier, more upbeat Springsteen song played in the background.

"Seems like a nice kid," he said, turning a page of his newspaper. "I like him better than the shirtless guy, that one seemed like, what do you say, a player?"

I nearly choked on my brown rice. "Zach? He's not a player. He plays soccer, but that's about it."

"Is Zach your boyfriend?"

"Um, maybe we can talk about something other than my love life?"

"Awkward?" he finished.

"Yeah," I said.

"What should we talk about?"

"Maybe how weird it is to think about things we *should talk about?*"

"Maddie, I'm trying here. I mean, I'm still me and you're still you, we've never had trouble talking before."

He was right.

"Okay, tell me something a father would tell his kid," I said.

"That seems deep. Like what?"

"Favorite color?"

"Blue."

"Robin's egg or periwinkle? There's lots of different shades."

"Sky blue."

"Okay, there's a start."

"What is it that you like about art?" he asked me.

"That's a complex one," I said.

"Not really."

"I love creating something where there was nothing before. A sketch, a design on my hand. Who knows, someday a building, maybe?"

"Is that why you want to go to design camp?"

"You know about that?"

"Your mother told me about your summer plans. Where are you applying again?"

They'd talked about me? I wondered if it had been before or after.

"New Jersey Design Institute—it's a two-week thing. You study all different areas but the focus is on architecture and building up your portfolio. They have dorms, and field trips. I'm applying for a scholarship."

"I'd like to help."

At first I didn't understand what he meant. Help how? Drive me there? Then I realized he was talking about money. The funny thing was, if Paul had told me two weeks ago that he wanted to help, I would have been thrilled. Now I wondered if there was more to it. Did he feel like he *had* to help me? Or did he *want* to help me?

"You don't have to do that."

He took his time folding the paper, then tucked it next to his empty plate and sat back in his chair, arms folded.

"I want to do it, Madison. You're talented. Your sketches—"

"You've seen my sketchpad?"

"It was on the dining room table. I may have peeked. I'm sorry if I wasn't supposed to."

"No, no, that's okay," I said.

"Look, I have the money, and even if you weren't my daughter, I'd want to do this. If you have a hard time thinking of me as your father, think of me as, let's say, a benefactor. Someone who wants to see you succeed."

Benefactor sounded stranger than *father.*

"Why didn't you say something sooner?"

Jazz had convinced Wren and me to go on a slow run with her. I'd thought it would be a great time to tell them about my father news and it mostly was, except for the small problem of not being able to form words. Jazz sounded like she could have belted out a power anthem while Wren and I were chugging air. We were also on recon to casually run (or pass out) by St. Gabriel's lacrosse practice to stalk Logan. Sweaty, gross, and looking like someone had slapped my face several times was not the way I usually wanted to look in the presence of St. Gabe's boys, but for Jazz I made an exception.

"Wow . . . that's . . . a . . . to . . . tal . . . mind . . . fuck," Wren said between gasps for air.

I wanted to say, *YES!* Mindfuck *is the perfect word!* But one word was all I could manage.

"Yup."

"How are you handling it?"

I shrugged.

"I just can't believe you didn't tell us this before." Jazz didn't miss a beat, her bright purple sneakers barely making a sound as she jogged gracefully along the tree-lined trail. I stopped short, put my hands on my knees and my head down, trying to get my breathing back to normal.

"If you want the story . . . ," I said, "then . . . how about . . . a slow walk?"

"YES," Wren said, stopping too.

Jazz kept going until she realized we weren't with her, then jogged back with a grin.

"Geez, guys, prom season is, like, two months away, I thought we were going to keep each other motivated."

"I'll eat fewer peanut butter cups," Wren said.

"Ditto," I said.

Jazz stood there, hands on her hips, and waited for us to catch our breath, then we continued to walk as I told them about Paul. How I found out the morning after the dance. That I'd wanted to tell them about him but couldn't find the right time. What my mother said about Atlantic City. How

Paul wanted to be my *benefactor.*

"Wow, Mads. I look at my sister, and how much support she has around her—Junior isn't even here and I'm lined up for babysitting this summer. I can't imagine Brooke doing it all on her own. That must have been tough."

"I know, but still—why keep it from me all this time? I don't know if that's something I can get past. One minute everything's okay and I think I have a handle on it, then I get pissed about it again. She kept saying that Paul was different, that he might not have wanted to support her. I can't imagine that—he seems pretty generous now."

"You need to think about it differently. I mean, he's your father, he should give you some financial support—especially if he wants to," Jazz said.

"The benefactor thing seems weird—but it might be nice to just sit back and enjoy the free ride. It'd be crazy not to, right?"

Even as the words came out of my mouth it felt like I was trying too hard to talk myself into it. My mom always stressed the importance of being independent. She lived it. Even if it seemed like it was to a fault at the moment.

When we got closer to the lacrosse fields, Jazz motioned for us to stop.

"Okay, here's what we're going to do," she said. "Once we hit the bottom of the hill, we'll start jogging—there's some bleachers next to the practice field and we can stop and stretch there. And then maybe I'll just kind of wave. How's that?"

"Not obvious at all," I said. Wren laughed.

We started jogging according to plan. Thankfully the bleachers were less than a quarter mile away; anything more than that and my face might have exploded. As it was, Wren and I were panting.

"Is it just me, or does this feel really scripted?" I asked, reaching my arm up over my head and doing a side-bend. "Kind of like a soft-core porn film about sweaty lax boys."

"Mads, please," Jazz said.

Wren switched legs. "Oh, sweaty lax boy, can you help me? I just need a little assist from behind."

"I'll hold your stick for you." I stretched my quad.

"What the hell? Would you two stop?"

"All the oxygen we're huffing must be getting to us."

"Heads up!" someone yelled from the field. Jazz ducked as something whizzed by her head and ricocheted off the top step of the bleachers. The ball fell to the ground below.

"And this is how it starts. Cue the sexy music."

"Bow-chicka-wow-wow," Wren sang as she put one leg up on the bleachers and grabbed hold of the tip of her sneaker.

I deepened my voice, giving it a southern lilt. "Would you be so kind as to pick up my ball, Jazzabelle?"

"Oh my god, just grow up," Jazz said, but there was laughter in her voice.

One of the players walked over, lifted his helmet, and smiled.

"Thought that was you," he said. Logan. "Did you see where the ball went?"

Wren and I burst into a fit of giggles. Logan looked at us, confused.

"Yeah, I'll get it," Jazz said, crouching to get under the bleachers. She was trying to keep a straight face and wouldn't look at either of us. Wren's face was purple from silent laughter. Jazz walked to Logan and tossed the ball over the fence to him.

"Feel like going for a run after this?" he asked her.

"Looks like you're getting a workout now."

"Yep, but I could use a run to unwind after this," he said.

"Yes, please, these two can't keep up with me."

"Cool," Logan said, backing away from the fence and then turning to trot out to the rest of the boys who were still playing. Jazz could have heated up a whole galaxy with the smile on her face.

"A guy who takes a run to relax? Guess you've met your Prince Charming, Jazzy."

"So can we stop pretending to stretch?"

"Ooh, but you're quite flexible, Wren," I said.

"Thanks to Leif and his assists," she said.

"Hey, so I was thinking—you know how Gray's band is going to play out at that place in Hoboken?" Jazz asked.

"I'd hardly call it *Gray's* band—I mean, he is the newest member. It's really Jesse's band," I said. Both Wren and Jazz puzzled at my quick defense. "What? It's the truth."

"Anyhow," Jazz continued, "I was thinking of asking Logan to go. That's a good idea, right? And this way if he says no, it's not like I'll be that crushed because I'll still go with you guys, but if he says yes, then it can be our first official sort-of date."

"That sounds perfect. Is Zach coming, Mads?"

I hadn't told them about the *L* word yet, mostly because I was trying to forget about it myself. Avoidance had become my new pastime.

"Maybe. Live music isn't really his thing. Hey, but how are we going to get in, anyway? Are you forgetting the whole we're-not-eighteen issue?" I asked.

Wren smiled. "No worries. Grayson's got that covered. He knows a guy."

TWELVE

"JESSE'S NOT EVEN A GIRL, AND HE GETS TO DYE his hair, not fair."

The debate had been going on since I came home on Wednesday night from Madison's. Daisy pouted, looking from my mother to me. Tax season was never a time to negotiate with my mother, her last nerve always on the verge of being fried. I tried to communicate this with narrowed *Cut the crap* eyes to Daisy, but she ignored me. Ty had finally gotten used to my new look, but still eyed me while nibbling on his pancake, as if he were waiting for something else to change. "Both boys and girls can dye their hair. If you want a streak, that's fine, but I'm done with this argument. You can't dye your hair purple like the girl on YouTube."

TKO, Mom.

Daisy grumbled. My dad changed the subject.

"You guys sounded pretty tight the other day. Are you ready for next week?"

Were we ready? We'd been practicing together six times a week, dividing our time between Lot 23 and the garage. We were sore, fingers bleeding, throats raspy, but the fifteen songs we had sounded good, all except the original—we were still fumbling through the sound, and the guys wanted to cut it. I swallowed a mouthful of maple-syrup-soaked pancake before answering.

"I think so, but you know, if you're gonna blow it, blow it big."

Dad laughed and looked at Mom. "I have not heard that in years."

"You know it?" I asked.

"Declan's motto? Yes," my mother said, cutting up another piece of pancake for Tyler. "He justified more than playing music with that saying."

"What does it mean?"

"He had this voice instructor, real dramatic, old-school guy, and he used to say that. Cracked us up. We started using it for everything. But you know, he had a point. If you crash, own it. People will respect you more," my father said.

"I don't plan on crashing. We're cool." At least I sounded confident.

"Remind me to call the sitter, Sam."

The pancake hung from my fork as I stopped mid-bite, staring at my mother.

"You guys are coming to see us?"

"Of course, why?"

"I'm not a baby, I don't need a sitter," Daisy said. "Why can't I go?"

"Hell no," I said.

My mother frowned. "What did I tell you about that word at my table?"

"Jess, we'll leave the foam fingers and pom-poms at home, but as chief financiers of Yellow Number Five, of course we're coming. We want to support you. So we can say we knew you when," Dad said.

I had certain expectations of Whiskey Business and what the crowd would be like, and it didn't include my parents. But what if they were the only people there?

"Sorry, I'm just nervous. What if no one shows up?"

"What if a ton of people show up and hate you?" Daisy said, sticking her tongue out so quick that my mother didn't notice. I hadn't thought of *that*.

"Jitters are part of it. If you weren't nervous, you wouldn't be normal. And that stuff you're talking about? It'll all happen if you're in a band long enough. Those'll be your road stories. See this?" My dad pointed to a scar that cut through his right eyebrow. "That's from a beer cap flung at me when we played this dump in Manville."

"That awful place with the sawdust on the floor?" my mother said.

"Yeah, the regulars were not into the Sex Pistols."

"Pissstul," Ty repeated.

"What a lovely word for him to learn."

The doorbell sounded.

"OPEN!" Ty yelled.

Daisy popped up.

"Sit," my mother said as she got up. All of our attention followed her as we waited to see who it was. She pushed away the curtains and peered through the side window.

"It's Duncan," she said, reaching for the doorknob. My dad and I shared a puzzled look. My family knew my version of what had happened, that Hannah and Duncan were together, and they had lived through my phase as the soulless hermit from hell, but as far as I knew they'd never come face-to-face with Duncan since then. I wondered what my mother would say to him, and braced myself.

"Duncan, hey, come in out of the cold," my mother said, opening the door wide.

So much for solidarity.

He stepped inside, running his boots across the doormat and pulling his hat off his head. He saw us at the table and hesitated a moment before coming over.

"Hey, Mr. McMann," he said, holding out his hand.

My father stood up and shook his hand. "Duncan, long time, no see—how's the new band?"

Thunk. My father always knew how to throw the awkward right into the conversation. He sat down, smiling up at Duncan, appearing to be truly interested in what he had to say.

"Can-can," Ty said, slapping the little tray on his high chair. Duncan laughed at Ty. He and Duncan had had this drumming thing when he'd stay after rehearsal sometimes. I hadn't realized it made an impression on Ty. Only Daisy ignored Duncan. She gave me a quick look and rolled her eyes. At least one of my family members saw him as a jerk.

"New band's a'right," Duncan said, twisting his hat in his hands.

"Do you want something hot to drink, cocoa or something?" my mother asked, poised to sit down.

"No, no thank you, just stopped by to see Jess."

"We can talk in the garage," I said, pushing away from the table. Duncan followed as I walked into the kitchen and put my plate in the sink. He had to be here for the song. Again. He said nothing as we walked through the laundry room into the garage.

I flipped the switch on, rubbed my hands together. Our equipment was set up for rehearsal later that afternoon. I crossed my arms and looked at Duncan. He walked over to Grayson's drum set, ran his finger across the cymbal.

"How's he working out?" he asked, shoving his hands into his pockets.

"Good."

"Better than me?"

"Different."

He nodded, sniffled. "Kenny's such an asshat. He lost his nut when he found out you guys were doing the battle."

I smiled in spite of myself. "Good. What about you? Lose a nut?"

"Nah. Bring it," he said.

"But you want the song."

"Did you finish it?"

I nodded. He didn't need to know it sucked at the moment.

"I was thinking, maybe we could both do it."

"At the battle?"

"No. Like, split it."

I wondered if I was in Duncan's shoes if I'd be so eager to grovel at my feet. The truth was it could have easily been the other way around. I just happened to have the notebook we used to write it down. The song was okay. Nothing great. I knew I could easily write a better one, but not in a week. Not before the Whiskey. But I wasn't about to make it easy for him.

"What, like, in half?" I asked, smirking.

"I think you know what I mean."

"Why would I agree to that?"

"Because you're a decent person, Jess. And you're gonna blow us away anyway."

"Unless Kenny has a neighbor on the judges' panel again."

He laughed. "That's the only way. Come on."

"So you're asking me to give you an advantage?"

"No. I'm asking you to give us a friggin' fighting chance. We started writing it with the Whiskey in mind, remember? Just, you know, you guys can use it there and we'll play it for the battle. Seems fair, don't you think, since we cowrote it?"

Since it was more like a 60/40 partnership in my favor, I didn't think it was fair, but I was sick of going on about it. And when I looked it over the last time, I realized something. We both were probably thinking about Hannah when we wrote it. That song had a ton of baggage with it. If I thought I could come up with something new before next weekend, something we could practice that would sound as good as the rest of our songs, I'd attempt it. But between work and school and life, it wasn't going to happen.

"Fine. Sounds good."

He startled. "Really?"

"Yeah, why not? Are you coming to the Whiskey?"

"Oh, um, hadn't thought about it."

"Bullshit."

"All right, I don't know. Kenny said something about going but . . . it would be hard, Jess. For me. You know?"

I hadn't thought about what it would mean for Duncan. He'd wanted to play out as much as I had. I should have felt bad for him, but I didn't. Too much had happened, but maybe we could be friends again. Maybe.

"It would be good to see you there, Duncan."

"Maybe."

"Cool."

"You might want to rethink the hair."

"Dude, I think we need to drop the pipe dream of the original for now," Tanner said, wiping the sweat from his forehead with his sleeve. We'd been practicing for two hours and still couldn't get it right. I looked at Grayson, who in the past week had become so lightning-fast and tight on the drums, he'd far surpassed Duncan. We'd found our groove. Except for the original.

"Tanner's right, Jess. Definite weak spot in the set."

Tanner stood up a little straighter with Grayson's agreement.

I knew they were right, the song wasn't coming together, but I wanted to *kill it* at Whiskey Business. And playing an original would definitely kill it. I didn't want to let Declan down, either. Not on our first time out. We still had a week before the show. Plenty of time to make it happen.

"I think we need to try," I said.

"Why not just save it for now, Elvis," Tanner said. He'd been as merciless as I thought about my hair, karma for all the hat guff I gave him. "We've got until the battle to perfect it."

"Actually we don't," I admitted, looking between them. Just rip off the fucking Band-Aid. "I gave it to Duncan."

"What?"

"We agreed, we could use it for our show and they could use it for the battle."

"And who's *we*? Did he talk to you?" Tanner looked at Grayson, who shook his head.

"So just keep at it. We got this," I said, playing the first chord in the song. Neither of them joined in.

"No, we don't," Tanner said.

"What did you want me to do? I'm sick of him asking for it."

"How 'bout grow a pair and tell him he can't have it. Didn't he write, like, three lines in it?"

"More than you did," I said.

Tanner flinched, his face turning red. I regretted it instantly. The words cut him where it hurt. I was so sick of being hassled about the song, though. I'd made the decision and was sticking to it.

"That's it, then." Tanner unplugged his bass.

"C'mon, Tanner, I didn't mean—"

"Sure you did, man. It's always been about you and Duncan. I'm just the idiot with the bass and the stupid hat." He opened his case and pulled the strap over his head.

"You're overreacting."

"No I'm not, Jess," he said. "I thought we were finally coming together and then you go and do something like this, without even running it by me or Gray. This is *your* band, isn't it? Who was the one who got the word out that we were looking for a new drummer when you were too busy crying over Hannah? Who signed us up for the battle? Who found a deal on T-shirts? But why should I have a say in something so big?" He closed his case, locking the clasps on the side violently, then grabbed his coat.

"Tanner, c'mon, dude, stay," Grayson said.

He stopped a moment, looked at me, then back to Grayson.

"I have to get out of here before I say something stupid."

He swung open the door and left, not even bothering to close it behind him.

Gray got up from the drums and shut the door, folding his arms across his chest before walking toward me.

"Guess that's it for today," he said.

In all our years of friendship, Tanner and I had never as much as raised our voices to each other. He was the easy one, the go-with-the-flow guy. Not that we didn't have disagreements now and then, and he certainly knew when to kick my ass about something, but I'd never seen him react this way.

"What do you think?"

"I'm the new guy—what do I know?"

"You must have something to say."

He sighed. "He has a point."

I unplugged my guitar. "Really."

"You could have run it by us first. Or at least Tanner. Honest, Jess, I can't stand the song. It doesn't fit in with the rest of the set, and you don't sing it with . . . It sounds like you're just going through the motions."

I was about to defend it, but then I realized Grayson was right. I'd been holding on to the song out of some sense of . . . what? Pride? Revenge? Hannah and Duncan together still hurt me, but it was really less about them and more about what a chump I felt like that it had happened right under my nose. The song had been the only leverage I had, the final *fuck you both for doing this to me*. But really? It was a card in a game I didn't even want to play anymore.

"So you don't think we need it?"

"No, but we need Tanner. Maybe we should go get him. We could grab a pizza or something. Chill. All work and no play . . ."

"Sounds good."

"Hey, sexy, get in the car!" Grayson yelled. Tanner kept walking, oblivious or out of spite, I wasn't sure. Then I realized he had headphones in. I beeped the horn. Grayson hung out the small VW window and waved his arms. T finally stopped and scowled as he pulled out his earbuds.

"Dude, get in, we're blocking traffic."

A horn beeped behind us. Tanner stood still on the sidewalk. I finally had to pull up into a bus stop at the corner. Grayson got out of the car and walked over to him. He grabbed T's case from his hand and they both walked back. Grayson slid into the backseat with the bass, and Tanner flopped up front. Still not looking at me, but at least he was in the car. A few cars went by until I was able to pull out into traffic.

"Feel like getting some grub?"

"No," he said.

"C'mon, you're always up for something."

He shook his head. We drove a few blocks in silence.

"Maybe pizza," T finally said.

"Leaning Tower?"

"Anywhere but there," Grayson chimed in from the back.

"Palermo's, then?"

We finally agreed on something. Palermo's was open 24/7 and it looked it. The place had a layer of grease over everything and the jukebox only had songs from the eighties, but it had the best damn pizza this side of the Hudson. We ordered at the counter and sat at a table near the back. Tanner ripped off the paper from the end of his straw, then blew the rest of it directly into my face for a bull's-eye hit.

"Okay, I deserve that. You're right, the song's not ready for the Whiskey. And I'm sorry I gave it to Duncan without asking—I should have run it by you."

"Why? I didn't do anything for it." Tanner pulled the hat off his head and shoved it in his coat pocket.

"T—"

"No, look, I'm not saying I didn't want to punch you for saying that, but you're right. Sometimes I wonder why I'm even playing anymore—it's not like it's gonna get me anywhere."

"Who says you need to go anywhere with it?" Grayson asked.

"Why do it at all?"

The order-up bell rang.

"I'll get it." Gray went up to the counter and came back

with the pizza. Tanner's question still unanswered on the table.

"What if we suck next Saturday?" Tanner pulled apart the paper plates and handed me one.

"Is that what this is about?" I asked.

"We're not gonna suck," Gray said.

"How do you know?"

"Because we just worked our asses off for the past three weeks and I think we sound pretty damn good. Are we the next Nirvana? No, but who is? And what's the big deal if we suck anyway? At least we're playing somewhere. You know why you'd never heard of me before? Sticky Wicket couldn't even get out of the basement. So this? For me? I may as well be playing the Beacon. It's gonna be fine." Gray wolfed half his slice, and looked from me to Tanner, waiting for a reaction.

"If we're gonna blow it, blow it big," I said.

Tanner laughed. "What?"

"Something I saw in Deck's office—you know, just go for it and if it sucks, so be it."

"Exactly—you know, when I auditioned for you guys I had no clue if I could handle this. Sometimes you just have to throw yourself into something. I didn't worry about why you would or wouldn't pick me."

"That goofy-ass Muppet shirt did not help," I said.

"My Animal shirt? Dude—it's old-school, what's not to like?"

"Just don't wear it Saturday." I bit into my pizza.

"If we're really confessing—he picked you because you know Madison."

"T."

Grayson cocked an eyebrow. "Really?"

"No," I said, taking a sip of soda. "Okay, maybe. Did you see the logo she designed?"

"You were my first choice," Tanner said.

"Who was my competition?"

"*No one*, we're just messing with you," I said.

"Some dude who played 'Tom Sawyer.'"

"Damn, Neil Peart? I wouldn't have picked me," Grayson said.

"He was a show-off," I said.

"And he didn't know Madison," Tanner added.

"Tanner, quit it."

"Any girl you let make you look like that you must have a boner for."

Grayson had to cover his mouth when he laughed.

"I like it," I said.

"I've seen more stylin' merkins, Jess, come on."

"Says the dude with the ancient toboggan hat."

"What's with that, anyway?" Grayson asked.

Tanner shrugged. "My lucky hat. That's all."

"So, Madison? She's cool. You should go for it," Gray said.

"We're just friends. I'm focusing on the Whiskey. After that we'll see."

THIRTEEN

MOM HAD LEFT ME A MESSAGE TO MEET HER AT the yoga studio. Wren bailed because she needed to study for a monster chem test. I planned on getting to class before everyone else so I could grab some prime space up front. The eight-block walk to yoga helped clear my head, got my blood pumping. I stole a quick peek through the Mugshot window to see if Jesse was working. He was behind the counter with Tanner. A smile stretched across my face. Chai or Mexican hot chocolate tonight?

I fully expected to be the first one in the studio for class but was surprised to see my mother in scorpion pose, being assisted by Leif. His hand supported the small of her back, lips moving with words that sounded like humming from where I stood. I waited in the doorway until she finally came out of the pose, one foot and then the other. They turned to see me, and my first instinct was to bolt—it felt like I'd walked in on something private, but both of them smiled.

"Mads, you're here early." Mom's face was flushed pink, her hair held back with a tribal-print headband. She looked radiant. Ten years younger. Leif smiled at me.

"Ready for some heart openers?"

"I, um, guess so."

Leif padded out to the front desk. My mother wiped down her face with a towel. I unfolded my sticky mat next to her. "When you said to meet you I just assumed you were stuck at work."

"Oh, no—there's an advanced class before this one; I wanted to see if I could handle it."

"Oh." For some reason, her taking a class without me bothered me. When she first started, she'd practically bribed me to come with her. It was cool she'd found something to throw herself into, but at the same time it felt like she was moving on from me. Why hadn't she asked me to come?

"You're taking our usual class too?"

"Leif told me this is going to be more of a slow stretch tonight. Will you catch me if I topple over?"

I remembered what Wren said—how my mother rocked mermaid pose. I hadn't really noticed, until now. Yoga wasn't a competition; you weren't supposed to compare yourself to anyone else, but Mom excelled at it.

"You made scorpion look easy."

"Did I? My arms were shaking, I thought I was going to flop on my head."

"Couldn't see that from where I was standing."

She tossed the towel onto her mat, grabbed her water bottle. "So if I was leading a class, I wouldn't look out of place?"

I shook my head. Friendly chatter filled the studio as people arrived for class. I walked over to the prop station and grabbed a strap and a block, then sat down cross-legged on my mat.

"Teacher training starts next week."

"Wow, already? I thought you were just thinking about it."

"Why don't we go next door after class, hang out instead of getting our drinks to go. Catch up, sound good?"

"Sure."

Seeing Jesse, his dark hair sticking out of his baseball cap, made a grin that started somewhere in my toes break out across my face. It could have been wishful thinking, but I swear his smile widened ever so slightly too when he saw me.

"Hey, I have something for you." Tanner pointed at me and disappeared into the back room. I furrowed my brow at Jesse while he rang us up. Tanner came back holding a light yellow T-shirt. He fanned it out over the counter.

"The logo, wow." I couldn't say anything else—my work right there on the shirt. It was such an odd feeling to have something that had existed in my brain on a T-shirt for the rest of the world to see. I knew Jess had said they were going to use it for promotional stuff, but I didn't think he meant this. It was pretty cool.

"That looks great." My mother ran a hand across the logo. "Are you selling these?"

"Not sure yet, we might just give them out—get our name out there," Jesse said. "You can take a few if you want."

"Really?"

"Consider it an early birthday present," Tanner said.

"Not too far off." My mother picked up the shirt and hummed with approval.

"It's your birthday?" Jesse asked.

I flinched at the question. "No—"

"Maddie's, in two weeks," my mother said. "Do you have an extra small? I'll buy one."

"No, really, you don't need to pay. T, give them a few before they go. We'll get those drinks to you in a minute." Jesse peered behind us at the growing line.

I grabbed my mother before she shouted out my bra size and Social Security number too. I had a thing about birthdays—I mean, they were fine and all, but for some reason they left me feeling a little down—like I was always anticipating something bigger to happen. We found a table for two over to the side, right under the neon Mugshot sign.

Five minutes later, Jesse placed two wide-mouthed cups in front of us. Chamomile for my mom and Mexican hot chocolate for me. There was a flower shape in the foam. I smiled as he went back behind the counter.

Mom took a cautious sip of her hot tea.

"So," she said, placing the cup back on the saucer and leaning toward me.

"You start training next week."

"Yes, it's a six-month program—the most intense parts are on the weekend, so there'll be at least a weekend a month that I'll be out more than I'm home. You're okay with that, right?"

"Yes. Did you have to hit up my summer program fund?"

She played with her bangs, running her fingers through and swiping them to the side. "No, I told you I'd never touch that. Paul sharing half the expenses has really helped. That's part of what I wanted to talk to you about. Are you still interested in the summer program at Pratt?"

"I'm, well . . ." Pratt was about three times the price of NJDI; I was interested, but Paul living with us couldn't have freed up that much cash. "I'm fine with the Design Institute. I think I have a really good shot at a scholarship."

"But you don't need it now, I spoke to Paul—"

"Mom, I wish you hadn't."

"He wants to help."

"I don't want his help, okay, not for this, it feels weird. Like—" I didn't want to say what I was thinking.

"Like what?"

"Like the only reason you decided to say something was because we were a little strapped for cash."

She cringed at the words.

"Is that really what you think?"

"No. It's just a lot to take in, like I'm magically supposed to think of Paul in a different way, and I'm forcing it. I keep expecting something to change, to make me think of him as . . ." I was suddenly aware of the crowd at Mugshot, the noise—this seemed like too heavy a conversation to have with hot chocolate.

My mother took my hand. "Mads, he feels the same way. Helping you pay for school feels like something concrete that he can do."

"I guess."

"Just think about it, I won't push it."

Pratt. Damn. I remember drooling over the program description. The challenging classes. Living in New York. A taste of what life would be like in college. Then I saw the price tag. Yee-ouch. Too steep. But the experience. Would it really be so awful to accept some personal funding?

"How is everything?" Jesse came over to the table, a small Mugshot shopping bag in his hand.

"Excellent as ever."

"Here's the shirts," he said.

He stood there between us, smiling—waiting, it seemed, for something to do so he could linger. I liked it. He finally spoke.

"Hey, are you coming to see us Saturday night?"

I took a sip of hot chocolate, my mother's eyes on me too. I felt a slight stab of guilt for not thinking of Zach in this equation. It's not like I'd never done things without him before but that word, those three freaking words, suddenly made me feel tied down. And I hated it. Of course I was going to Whiskey Business, already thought about what I'd wear, but with each second that passed I felt a little rush of power. Jesse wanted me to be there. I put my cup down.

"Can't wait."

"Jazzy, hold still." One more swipe of liquid liner, some mascara, and she was done. I'd picked an eye-shadow combo of golds and greens that made her dark eyes stand out. The effect was mysterious stranger. *Rawr.*

"Let's see," Wren said.

Jazz batted her lashes.

"Wow."

She walked over to my vanity mirror to take a closer look.

"You don't think this is too much? It's itchy. What if I forget I'm wearing it and rub my eye? I'll look like someone punched me."

"For a run? Yes, too much. For a dark club on a first date with a running partner you think is hot? No." I dabbed some sparkly gloss onto my lips. Done.

"It's not really a date—it's a let's-meet-there kind of thing. When he heard Gray was playing, he said he'd bring a few friends too. So, I don't know."

"What friends? Lax team guys?" Wren asked.

Jazz shrugged. "Hey, what about Zach, is he meeting us there?"

"Nope." Zach had texted me throughout the day. His indoor league game had been canceled and he was prowling for something to do. I was too pumped for a night out with my friends. It sounded mean and I knew it, but ignoring was not the same as lying, right? I couldn't handle the love question tonight.

"Gray texted. They're turning the corner now." Wren shoved her phone into the front pocket of the teeny-tiny skirt she'd purchased during our Sadie Hawkins spree. She wore over-the-knee boots, so only a sliver of skin showed. It was not her usual look, but all those months of yoga had given her the sort of curves guys drooled over, and she rocked it. I had cut the collar off the Yellow #5 T-shirt, so it hung open over a black cami, and I paired it with denim cutoffs and black studded boots. No one would question us about being over eighteen.

We grabbed our coats and thundered down the stairs. Mom and Paul were in the living room.

"Wow," Paul said as we met him at the landing. He pulled out his phone. "Let me get a picture."

"Paul, it's not prom." I laughed. My mom walked over and stood next to him, arms crossed. If I didn't know better, if I was just some stranger looking in on the scene, I would think they made a nice-looking couple. They looked like parents, about to see their kids off for the night. Which I guess they were, but not really.

"C'mon," Wren said, pulling us together. We mugged for the camera until we heard footsteps on the porch. Jesse peered through the window.

"All right, gotta run."

"Time, Mads."

"Before midnight?"

"Sounds fair. Have fun."

"Not so much fun that I have to bail you out," Paul said. My mother elbowed him as I closed the door.

Jesse smiled when he saw me.

"Hey, look, I'm representing." I gave him a quick peek of the shirt before closing my jacket.

"Cool."

"Nervous?"

"It's that obvious?" There were two cars in front of my house; well, one car—Gray's POS-mobile, and a monster Surburban. I knew which one I'd be traveling in.

Grayson stood near the Suburban, one arm casually slung around Wren's shoulder. Jazz waited next to them, peeking in the SUV and probably doing the math on which car she'd end up in herself. The side door was open, and Tanner sat on the edge, elbows on knees, chin propped up by both hands. Gray reached into his jacket pocket and pulled away from Wren for a moment.

"Here, lovelies," he said, holding out three cards to us. He took the first one and held it under the streetlight.

"You are Kenzie Renegar tonight, Mads," he said, handing me the ID. It looked like an authentic driver's license with my picture. There was a hologram and everything. I didn't want to know where he got it.

"Jazzy, you are Diara Jones. And last but not least, Wren is Olivia Green."

"So what CW cast were these names stolen from?" I asked.

Gray laughed. "I didn't request names. They should be fine—lie low with them, you know, don't call attention to yourself. You probably won't be carded—just think of them as insurance."

"Walk in with us, carry something, no one will stop you," Jesse added.

"Are we going or not?" Tanner stood up and climbed into the middle seat.

"Shotgun." I grabbed Jesse's arm. "If that's okay."

"Yeah, it's great."

Jazz looked at Wren and Gray. "Do you have room?"

"Half the backseat is yours if you want it," Grayson said.

"All right, so we'll meet there—you know where it is?" Jesse opened the front door and held out his hand to me.

"Yep, see ya in twenty." Grayson, Wren, and Jazz walked back to the car.

I took Jesse's hand for support and climbed into the front seat.

"I'm stoked you're here," he said, before closing the door.

"Me too."

We pulled into the cobblestone back alley behind Whiskey Business and the guys began to unload the equipment. Wren grabbed a cymbal. Jazz and I grabbed mic stands and we walked in following Jesse's lead. The guy holding the door open for us didn't say anything but copped an eyeful as we each walked by. We were in.

"Grab a table, we got the rest of this," Jess said after we deposited the equipment on the stage, ending our short stint as Yellow #5 roadies. The guy who'd been holding the door came over to us. On closer inspection, he was a bit of a fox. Midtwenties, blond hair, yellow shirt with a Yoo-hoo logo on the front. It stretched taut across a subtly buff chest. Strong arms. Uh-oh. Moment of truth, Kenzie. Think eighteen.

"Hold out your wrist," he said. Wren was the first to put her arm out, and the guy wrapped a purple band around her wrist. Followed by Jazz, then me.

"Eighteen, right?" He smiled as he secured the tab.

"Yep." I had the feeling he knew the truth and didn't care.

"What can I get ya? Once it starts filling up, table service stops, but anything for now?"

We ordered a round of Cokes. Whiskey Business was the sort of club I'd dreamed about hanging out in. It's like you could feel the ghosts of nights-out past still echoing through the space. A crackle of anticipation was in the air—the emptiness just waiting for another incredible night to happen.

"This is going to be awesome," I declared.

"What if we are the only three here?" Wren asked. We looked around at the empty space. I thought about what Foxy Yoo-hoo Dude said.

"Nah, it's early, it'll fill up," I said. At least I hoped it would, for Jesse's sake.

An hour later, Whiskey Business was packed so thick we couldn't see the bar from our table anymore. Jesse, Grayson, and Tanner were still in back, but a tall guy in a leather kilt came out every so often to announce when they'd be on. We still had fifteen minutes. Jazz's phone went off.

She swiped for her messages. "He's here."

Jazz waved her phone over the sea of heads. Logan broke through the crowd, followed by Luke Dobson and another guy with shaggy hair. They each had a beer in their hand. Guess they knew the same guy Grayson did.

Okay? Jazz mouthed to Wren. Gray's old friends weren't exactly friends. They were more like frenemies from a past life. Wren shrugged.

Grayson came out from the back and edged his way through the crowd on the dance floor. The moment he laid eyes on Logan, Luke, and the shaggy blond dude, he cracked a smile.

"Andy, what are you doing here?" He clapped him on the shoulder.

"Heard you were playing. Thought we'd check it out."

"Cool." Gray looked at me. "Mind if I steal Wren?"

"Haven't you already?"

He laughed. Wren got up and took his hand, ignoring the guys. "Be right back."

Andy and Luke drifted into the crowd. Logan grabbed Wren's chair and moved it toward Jazz. They leaned into each other. I took out my phone just so I had something to occupy myself while they chatted. Three texts from Zach. *Gah.* I shut down the screen without reading them. When it was obvious that Wren's *Be right back* was more like *Be back never*, I excused myself from Jazz and Logan's first date. No fucking way was I going to be third wheel.

"I'm going to find Wren," I said. Jazz nodded. I inched into the crowd, shouldering and shuffling and pushing my way through, until I spotted Wren, up front, stage left, arms crossed and waiting for the show to start. I bumped her.

"Be right back?"

"Sorry—Gray's nervous about tonight. Him, *nervous.* He needed a pep talk."

"Is that code word for something else?"

She smiled. "I knew you'd find your way over here. Is Jazz okay?"

"Yep. So far, first date is looking fine."

The guy with the leather kilt and black motorcycle boots strode onto the stage followed by Gray, Tanner, and Jesse— who looked more like they were on their way to detention than leading the crowd in a good time. Tanner appeared particularly freaked, his eyes blank, then Gray said something to him and he laughed. The room was electric, ready to party, but I had the feeling it was not easily impressed, or maybe not drunk enough.

Wren squeezed my arm. "Oh, god, they have to be good, right?"

"Of course, they're gonna kill it," I said.

Jess lost his queasy look once he pulled his guitar strap over his head. His features sharpened under the blue stage lighting as he strummed a little and stepped on a pedal by the mic stand. He stood a little taller, sussing out the crowd until he saw me. He smiled, but it wasn't that sweet, trustworthy smile. It was somewhere between a sneer and a smile that said *I'm about to throw it down, wanna come?* That smile torched my insides.

"Hey, hey, what's up, Whiskey Business?! Give it up for a band you'll be seeing more of if I have anything to do with it . . . Yellow Number Five." Leather kilt guy lifted his arms up and the crowd went insane.

Jesse turned around and stalked up to the mic.

"S'up, Ho . . . bo . . . ken . . ." he said, before launching the band into an Arctic Monkeys song. I kept bracing myself for some screw-up, a sour note, some weird misstep, but they were awesome.

Jesse commanded the stage, legs straight and slightly apart.

He held the guitar with a kind of lazy control that made him look like he might have had better places to be but was choosing to hang out with us for a while. Broody Barista was nowhere to be seen as he writhed to the music, eyes rolling up into his head when he sang, mouth barely caressing the mic with each word. His presence filled the room.

"Omigod, they're good!" Wren shrieked into my ear.

Grayson was sick behind the drums, precise and fast, his hair flipping around with his effort. Even Tanner made that stupid hat look cool.

Jesse picked me out again. His eyes on mine, I felt like he was sharing some part of himself that could only come out in the dark. That it was just the two of us. I moved with the music, *his* music. Anytime he looked away, I had the urge to throw myself into his line of vision again.

The crowd grew thicker, swelling, pushing us closer to the stage. People thrashed and pogoed and knocked into one another around us. I looked behind me, and between the bobbing silhouettes I caught a flash of Jazz and Logan, standing near the back and moving along with the crowd. And I caught a glimpse of . . . *Zach?* Shit. He stood by the wall, stock-still, a statue in the midst of pandemonium. I wasn't sure if he saw me.

Someone knocked into Wren and me, sending a spray of cold liquid across us. We both screamed from the chill and turned around. The burly guy held his hands up.

"Sorry, sorry." He gave us each a once-over and leered. "Hey."

A hand clamped on his shoulder and spun him around.

The guy in the leather kilt.

"Watch it," he said in Leering Guy's face. For someone in a skirt, he was pretty threatening. He shoved the guy back into the crowd. "Are you okay?"

Wren nodded. Zach worked his way through the crowd toward us. All I knew was that I couldn't stand up front with him. How long had he been here? God, did he see Jesse looking at me, because if he did, if he saw me . . . snagged.

"Zach's here," I whisper-yelled into Wren's ear. She raised her eyebrows. I wriggled over and met him in the crowd halfway.

"Did you get hurt?"

"No, I'm fine." I motioned toward the back of the room, covering my nose as I walked through a cloud of rank sweat and cologne. He grabbed my hand and snaked us through. Once we were past the mass of bodies, the air was cooler. I swear I could feel Jesse's eyes on me. The crowd went wild as he played the first chords of "Aneurysm." I had to force myself to look disinterested. We found an empty space near the edge of the bar.

"Nice shirt," Zach said.

I squirmed. Why hadn't I just answered his texts?

"Zach."

"That's the guy from the coffee place, isn't it?"

"We're friends, Zach, you know that."

"Friends like we're friends?"

"No." I crossed my arms. "What are you doing here?"

He tilted his chin toward the stage. "He told me about it, remember? My scrimmage was canceled and Kyle and I were looking for something to do, but you would have known that if you answered your phone. I don't get it, Madison, why didn't you just call me?"

My throat constricted, the air thick and hot around me.

"Why don't we get out of here?" he asked.

"No, they just went on. Let's stay."

"I don't want to. Kyle's having trouble finding a parking spot anyway; I think we're going to head back home, hit the diner."

"Okay, you do that."

He flinched.

"Fine." He brushed by me and wove through the bar crowd toward the front door. I squeezed my eyes shut. Counted to ten. He wanted me to follow him. Maybe it would all just go away, and we wouldn't have to have that conversation. The one I'd been putting off since Sadie Hawkins. I wanted to be in front of the stage again. When I opened my eyes, Zach had returned.

"Can we talk, out front? Please."

I relented and followed him through the bar. Foxy Yoo-hoo

217

Guy was sitting at the entrance and nodded as we walked out. We continued out onto the street, moving to the side of Whiskey Business so people could get in. The echo of the band still hummed in my ears. I crossed my arms against the cold. Zach paced in front of me.

"Does it make you feel good to ignore me or something?"

"No."

"Then why do you do it?"

"I don't—"

"Yes you fucking do, Madison. When we're alone, everything's perfect, but the minute we go out, or talk about doing something—other than each other, I guess—you get all weird about it. Have you even thought about what I said to you?"

Some passing girls who'd heard what he said burst out laughing. My mouth went dry. "Please don't talk about this here. Now."

"Why? Am I embarrassing you? Is that it? Am I such a fucking embarrassment that you can draw me in your little sketchbook but you can't really be with me?"

"Enough." I could feel the pressure building. Those words again, waiting to come out. Was I ready to say them? Why was I holding on to this? Whatever it was? Because sometimes it was better to be with him than to be alone? I'd never be able to say to him what he'd said to me.

"Why didn't you answer my texts today?"

"Because I don't want you here!" The words sprang out of

my mouth and right into his face. The anger he'd been direct-
ing at me dissolved. His face softened. His eyes. Hell, I had to
look away. "I'm sorry."

He stood next to me and leaned against the window of the
club. Shoulders drooped a bit, hands in pockets. "Don't be, at
least I know the truth."

"Zach—"

"Maddie, just shut up, okay? Shut up."

We stood like that for a few minutes, the streets alive with
Saturday-night bar crawlers. A bachelorette party, the bride
with a sash and a tiara, stumbled into Whiskey Business as a
couple of guys wandered out. Not just any guys.

"Logan?" I said.

He spun around while his friends kept walking, oblivious.
"Yeah?"

It was the first time I got a really good look at him. He was
cute—longish hair and an almost imperceptible chin cleft
that made his face interesting.

"Where's Jazz?"

"She's inside."

"Are you leaving?"

He looked toward Luke and Andy, who finally realized he
wasn't with them and stopped. "We got invited to this party in
a brownstone. She didn't feel like coming."

I wanted to tell him how nervous she'd been to ask him
out for tonight. How fucking lit up she'd been after fooling

around with him in the hallway at the dance. Why would he leave, if he knew how important it was to her? But who was I to give anyone advice? He waited for a moment, then turned and caught up with his friends.

"Hey, Zach." Kyle trotted toward us from the curb where his car was double-parked. "I can't find a fucking spot and I'm not paying twenty-five dollars for a parking garage so we can hang out for an hour. Hey, Madison." He acknowledged me with a nod—a nod that said he knew exactly what was going on.

"I'll be right there," Zach said. Kyle jogged back to his car. Zach turned to me.

"So, this is it, I guess."

"Zach, I'm sorry, I just wanted to hang with Wren and Jazz. I shouldn't have ignored you."

"It's more than that, Madison, and you know it."

"You don't have to go, really."

"Yeah, I do." He started walking away, then turned back. "I meant what I said that night. It's really sort of fucked up that you can't even . . ."

"You can't force me to say something I don't feel."

"The rush from this guy is going to wear off too."

"This is not about a guy."

"Sure it is. I see the way you look at each other."

"Zach." *How did I look at Jesse?*

"Just, good luck. Maybe you'll let him in, Madison." He

turned away then and got into the car without looking back. *Maybe you'll let him in?* What did he even mean? It was the most interesting thing he'd said to me in our five months together. I watched the car head down Washington Street until I couldn't see it anymore. He really wasn't coming back.

I felt like I should cry, or yell, or *something*. Why would he just say that and leave?

"Kenzie."

I kicked the sidewalk, took a few deep breaths. How much of the set had I missed?

"Kenzie," a voice said again.

I turned around. Foxy Yoo-hoo Guy smiled at me.

"Your friends are looking for you," he said.

"Oh, um, right." *Kenzie. I'm Kenzie.* Wait, how did he know?

I walked back into the bar and was surrounded by cries of, *Kenzie!*

Everyone. Was. Saying. My. Name.

Or my faux name. Clapping. *Chanting.*

"Ken-Zie, Ken-Zie."

"Give me a hand wishing my friend Kenzie a happy birthday."

It was Jesse. Leading the crowd in "Happy Birthday," to me.

EVEN AS THE LAST CHORDS OF THE SONG ECHOED through the bar, I knew I'd made a huge mistake. I could see Madison clearly, out near the front, looking like she'd rather be anywhere else. I thought she'd like it, kind of a thank-you for all she'd done in the past two weeks, but halfway through "Happy Birthday," when she wasn't even smiling, my gut told me, *Jess, you just blew it big.*

We left the stage as Deck went back on and announced the band for the next eighteen-and-over date. The dance floor had cleared out a bit, but was still thick enough that I had to push my way through. Gray and Tanner disappeared into the crowd. Someone tugged on the collar of my jacket; a girl waved me over to her and her friends.

"You guys were sooooo awesome!"

"Thanks." I nodded at the four of them, hoping they didn't expect me to say much more than that, because I could barely hear my own thoughts over the techno that was now blaring through the speakers.

"You guys want to hang out?" she asked.

"We're, um, kind of hanging out anyway, here with some friends."

"Will you guys be back here to play again?" another girl asked.

I shrugged. "Not sure, hope so."

They let out an enthusiastic "Woo-hoo!" and high-fived. I didn't know what to do. We'd never had fans who were strangers before.

"Is the guy in the hat seeing anyone?"

"Ha, Tanner?" I shook my head.

The girl who'd waved me over tugged on my collar again and brought her mouth to my ear.

"I think you're hot. Text me when you play here next," she said, shoving something into my hand. It was a napkin. With her number.

"Cool." I tucked it into my pocket. "See ya."

"See ya"? You've got this guitar-god thing down great, Jess.

I found Madison, Wren, and Grayson by the bar.

Madison had her arms crossed, a different person from the beginning of the night. She looked bummed, all the excitement drained out of her. Zach wasn't around. I shouldn't have felt happy about that, but I did.

"So did you hate it?"

"Oh, what, you? No, you guys were great. 'Happy Birthday'? I just hate being the center of attention for something so corny. I know I probably don't give off that vibe, but, yeah that's me."

"Ah, I'll file that away for future reference."

A hatless Tanner popped up behind Grayson and Wren.

"Have any of you seen Diara?"

"You mean Jazz?" Madison said.

"Oh, I kind of like the fake name thing."

"Isn't she with Logan?" Wren asked.

"No, I saw him leave about half an hour ago. I haven't seen her since then." Madison's brow pinched and she looked at Wren. "I thought she was with you."

"She was with me until five minutes ago and . . ." Tanner leaned in like he was going to say something but put out his pinkie and thumb and tipped them back toward his mouth to mime drinking.

"No," we all said together.

"Yeah, had to step outside for some air; we came back in, I told her I'd grab her a water and now I can't find her."

"Maybe she's in the bathroom." Wren grabbed Madison's hand and began to walk away. Then a siren sounded, a red light pulsed on the far wall, and people climbed up onto the bar to dance. Everyone was clapping and laughing, even the bartender, so it must have been a regular thing at Whiskey Business.

"Ho-leeey shit. Found her." We followed Tanner's gaze across the room to the end of the bar. There was Diara/Jazz, standing on top and wearing Tanner's ridonkulous hat. She held hands with a girl who wore a sparkly crown and a veil. They waved their arms up over their heads as they swung their hips side to side along to the music.

"Omigod, she's really into it," Wren said, laughing.

Tanner cupped his hand around his mouth and yelled, "Di-ar-a! Woo!"

We watched until the song was over and the red light dimmed. Everyone climbed down from the bar. Jazz bounded over to us, the pom-pom on the top of the hat wiggling as she made her way through the crowd. "Did you see me?"

"Jazzabelle is out to play," Madison said, tugging on the hat strings. Jazz's eyes widened.

"Hey, this girl wants to meet you." She grabbed Tanner's hand and pulled him along. His face twisted with confusion but he laughed as they sliced their way through the chaos.

"Guess that is his lucky hat," I said.

"Jess," someone said, putting a hand on my shoulder. My parents. I'd almost forgotten they were here.

"We're heading out. Need any help loading up?" Dad asked.

"Nah, we're cool."

Mom clung to his arm, a big grin on her face as she took in the atmosphere. Her eyes landed on Madison's shirt, then she looked between the two of us and smiled.

"Are you the Madison who designed the logo?"

Madison lowered her eyes and laughed. "Guilty."

"Love it, and Jesse's hair, too."

Did she *have* to mention the hair?

"Thanks."

"Make sure you settle things with Deck. He was looking for you. See you at home." They waved as they made their way to the front and out of the bar.

"Dude, maybe we should go break down, before Diara starts dancing on the bar again. I don't feel like having anyone question her about her ID. Know what I mean?" Grayson said.

Once the Suburban was loaded, we went back inside to Declan's office.

"There you are," Deck said, taking out bright orange earplugs as he pushed away from the desk on his rolling chair. "Once that techno shit starts playing I have to put these in. Gotta do what brings 'em in, though."

It was the first time he'd said anything that reminded me that he was my parents' age. "Yeah."

"Yellow Number Five." He stood up and handed me the cash. I flipped through the bills—tens and twenties—and counted two hundred.

"There's too much here," I said, handing him back two twenties. He held up his hand.

"We did great tonight, consider it a bonus. Are you guys up for a date in May?"

"Hell yeah," I said.

"Cool, I'll put you down—second week. Hey, did you ever see this?"

He waved us over to the wall of pictures. Gray and I stood before it, scanning the photos.

"Recognize anyone?"

"That's Dad," I said, pointing to their band picture. The five of them stood in various poses, leaning against a brick wall. My father was shirtless under a denim jacket and tight black pants. I'd seen pics from his band days, but not this one. He was so thin, and looked bored, but in a determined way—if I didn't know him I would have assumed he was pretty badass.

"Is that, wait—" Gray pointed at a picture of Declan with his arm around a girl. She had long hair and was leaning back, laughing.

"Whoa." I laughed and inspected the picture again. I knew my mother had hung out with Backtalk, she and my dad talked about it from time to time, but I'd never seen pics of her. Especially with Declan.

"You know she used to sing backup when she was bored."

"My mother. Sing?"

227

"Yeah, she had a sweet voice, too. Never wanted to do more than that. She was too practical." Declan stared at the picture in a way that made me wonder how close they actually had been. No. Fucking. Way.

"Well, um, we're heading out."

"See you in May."

In the hallway, I handed Gray his share of the take. He paused a moment and counted it.

"It's all there," I said.

"Oh, yeah dude, I know. Never been paid to play. Feels kind of sweet."

In all the excitement, the nerves, the desire to get it right, I'd forgotten about that feeling. He was right. It did feel pretty sweet to get paid for something that I loved to do.

"It does. Doesn't it?"

We unloaded at my house first, then hit the Starlite diner, which was so crowded they didn't have a spot for six. We had to split up into two booths across from each other. Me and T on one side, Jazz and Madison on the other in a booth for four, while Wren and Gray sat in the booth for two near the window. Even though they sat across from each other, they were one unit, legs entwined, hands clasped across the table, as they read through the menu. There was familiarity there. Closeness. Comfort. I felt my wrist, a phantom buzz from the missing infinity band.

Madison already had her menu closed. When our eyes met, she looked away. God, I would have given anything to relive that moment onstage at Whiskey Business. The way it felt to have her look at me like that, like she couldn't look away. Here in the diner with the bright lights and the clanking of dishes and laughter, I felt too exposed to just stare at her. How could it have felt like we shared a secret in a crowded room, but here we couldn't hold eye contact for longer than a few seconds? She fiddled with the paper ring around her silverware.

After we placed our order, Jazz put her arms on the table and her head down. She looked content in Tanner's hat.

"So how much did you have to drink, Diara?" Madison asked.

Jazz sat up. "Only two itty-bitty beaker . . . no, wait, test-tube thingies of some really sweet-tasting blue stuff. I'm still a little buzzed, but I'll be fine after I eat. The girl in the tiara—the one getting married—just handed them out from this little rack. I was talking to her about Logan, and she told me to lighten up and live a little."

"Wait, what about Logan?" Wren asked.

Jazz waved her hand. "I. Don't. Want. To. Talk. About. It."

"Diara has spoken," Tanner said. Jazz convulsed with laughter.

"Ugh, don't make me laugh."

The waitress came back with our order. Two plates of disco

fries and rye toast with jam. Madison had a hot chocolate with a mountain of whipped cream.

"Check out this shoddy barista work. Amateurs." She took a spoonful of whipped cream from the top. I laughed.

Tanner grabbed his plate of disco fries and dug in. Jazz wrinkled her nose.

"Those look like a stomachache waiting to happen."

"Nah, these are the best. What's with the rye toast and tea? Are we dropping you off at the nursing home after this?"

Jazz laughed. "Training, Tanner. That plate of grease would probably take me about twenty laps around the park to burn off."

"Food of the gods, Jasmine. Live a little." He held out a forkful of fries dripping with gravy and cheese to her.

"You know my real name."

"Yep, like the rice."

Jazz snorted, putting her hand up to her mouth. Tanner waved the fork at her again.

"Suits you better than Diara. Going once . . ."

She took the fork out of his hand and nibbled at the tip of a fry before scarfing the rest of it.

"Mmmm . . . this is . . . No way."

"See, told you."

Madison arched an eyebrow at their exchange, then looked at me.

"Stranger things," she said.

I touched my fingertips to hers, across the table. She didn't snatch them away. Her eyes met mine again. She had smudged dark eyeliner on that made her eyes look so damn blue it was like they were lit from within. I kept waiting for her to glance away, but she didn't.

"What happened with Zach?" I asked.

"You saw that?"

"Well, no. He was there and now he's not."

"We broke up," she said, sliding her fingertips over mine. We weren't exactly holding hands, but it was something. Her touch made every cell in my body buzz. *Don't smile. Don't smile.* My mouth betrayed me. She pursed her lips to the side, fighting a smile, and looked away.

"I'm going to make it up to you—the birthday thing," I said.

"You don't have to," she said.

"Yes. Yes I do."

She tapped her fingers on mine. "I'd like that."

"MADISON, THESE PHOTOS ARE PERFECT." PIPER stood over our proposed Sadie Hawkins layout, a rare grin across her face. "I love this one, it's such a standout."

She pointed at the photo of the balloons, the one with the word *choice*. I'd edited it so the word stood out, and the way the shot was angled, the balloons looked otherworldly in the background. I'd put in a mix of photos in the layout, some student candid shots, the band, and some more esoteric shots. I also snuck in the one of me, Wren, and Jazz, hoping Piper would be okay with it. She wasn't one of those "Let's make the yearbook photos about the yearbook staff" people.

"Thanks, I think so too."

"I thought these pages would be a throwaway, but it's one of my favorite layouts in the book so far. This picture might be a bit much," she said, pointing at the one I'd been worried about. "But maybe I'll let it slide."

She moved on down to the next group of staffers. Wren was busy on her laptop, working on some copy for the page on the fall fund-raising walk.

"Hey, I forgot to send you something." I attached the picture of her and Grayson from the dance to an email and hit send. I'd cropped Jesse out of her photo but kept the original intact. Every so often I pulled it up and studied it, imagining what he'd been witnessing when the photo was taken. I was dying to ask him about it, but the other night at the diner didn't really seem like the proper place. I'd noticed he wasn't wearing that infinity bracelet he used to wear—maybe that had something to do with it? My stomach still turned to jelly whenever I thought of our fingertips touching.

Wren gasped. "Mads, I love this picture. I didn't even realize you took it! I'm making it the wallpaper on my phone." Jazz peeked over at Wren's laptop and smiled.

"Yes, too bad I didn't have a camera the other night. You can see a lot through a camera, like things people don't want to tell you." Jazz glanced away when I said this, busying herself with more typing.

Wren and I had dished our versions of Saturday night via text all weekend and every day since, but Jazz had remained quiet throughout. And really, out of the three of us, she hands-down had to have the most different version of the night. The most she'd said was that she didn't want to talk about it. We were close to wearing her down, though.

"It can't be that bad," Wren whispered, leaning in.

Jazz chewed her bottom lip and moved closer to us, sliding her laptop along to create a barrier, under the guise of doing work. She ducked behind it and spoke.

"Nothing happened, okay? That's the embarrassing thing."

"Why did Logan just leave?" Wren asked.

"And were you really cool with it? That's what he told me outside," I said.

She pressed her lips together, maybe trying to keep the story in still, but finally relaxed. "Yes, I was cool with it. Everything was fine when he first got there. We held hands, talked— well, as much as you can talk over the music. He wasn't really into the band and then his friends wanted to leave. They were going to a party at a brownstone that these girls at the bar invited them to."

"He said he asked you to go. Did he?" I wished I could go back to that moment I'd watched Logan leaving and stick out my foot to trip him.

"Yes, he said I could get a ride home with them, but I wanted to stay with you guys. When he left it was like a whole different night. I tried to make it up front, but the crowd was too much, and those girls from the bachelorette party kind of took me in."

"You should have texted me, I would have found you," Wren said.

"I don't know, it was fun being someone different, like, maybe I could be Diara Jones for a night. Diara did blue shots and danced on the bar and completely forgot about Logan. You know, he's cute, we talk, and I really like him as a running bud, but there's no . . . magic." When she said *magic* she brought her hands together and then slowly apart, wiggling her fingers a bit, in what I imagined was supposed to represent sparkly, magical love glitter.

"You watched *Sleepless in Seattle* again, didn't you?"

She laughed. "No. Haven't been romcom-ing it lately. I'm sick of pining for some meet-cute that probably won't happen but I don't know, isn't that how it should be, at least a little bit? That *something* you can't quite put your finger on? I feel like we're both just kind of forcing it, because he's a boy and I'm a girl and that's what we're *supposed* to do. No one has written the script about good friends, have they?"

Wren and I both shrugged.

"Anyhow, after I did those blue shots, I started feeling dizzy, and ran into Tanner and he walked with me outside for some air. It was cold, so I took his hat. Do you know that's his grandfather's hat? He was the one who got him into the bass."

Wren grinned. "Holy crap, you are totally crushing on Tanner."

Jazz bit back a smile, her eyes darting between us. "No, not really."

"Jazzabelle, you're blushing."

"He makes me laugh. It was like, one question about his

hat and he kind of cracked open into this whole other person. I'm not saying it was magic or anything, but I wasn't analyzing every move wondering if it meant something. It felt nice. C'mon, you both know what I'm talking about. I saw you and Jesse holding hands, Mads, not sure why I'm under a microscope here."

"We weren't holding hands," I said. "Just . . . touching fingertips."

"Whatever it was, you guys looked into it," Wren said. "How cool would that be if we dated guys from the same band?"

"Decidedly not cool. What would happen if one of us broke up, then what? We couldn't hang out?" Jazz said.

"Ha! So you are thinking about it," I said.

"No, not really. I'm not saying I want to start anything with Tanner, but it was a bit of a jolt, to see him in a different way.

"And now I'm meeting my platonic but foxy run buddy to try to shave five seconds off my five-K," she said. "Wish me luck."

She packed up her laptop and gave us a small wave as she went out to her locker. I stared at Wren.

"Tanner and Jazzy? You think?"

"That would be . . . interesting, but I'm more curious about what Jesse wants to do on your birthday. Did you find out yet?"

"No, he said not to worry, he's doing all the planning. What could that even be? Free chai for a year?"

Wren smiled.

"Do you know something?" I asked.

"Only that you really want to do more than touch fingertips with him."

Since Paul was flying a client to Chicago for the weekend and my mother was starting her RYT 200 intensive teacher training, we skipped our Thursday yoga in order to celebrate my birthday early. I picked Arturo's, our go-to special-occasion-casual-but-elegant place. We ordered our usual cheese-smothered garlic bread and fried calamari with pepperoncini, which we dug into.

"Omigod, this is so good, but I bet I'll still be tasting this on Saturday. Hope I don't reek for Jesse."

"Are you sure that's really the way you want to spend a good portion of your birthday—in a car?"

"Mom, for the tenth time, yes. I'm so ridiculously stoked for this."

When Jesse told me he'd make it up to me for singling me out at Whiskey Business with "Happy Birthday," I expected at most a movie, cake, a free chai at Mugshot. Instead he'd asked me if I wanted to go to Fallingwater, the house designed by Frank Lloyd Wright.

Mind = blown.

The downside was that it was five hours away.

The upside was that we were spending the night at his aunt's house.

The downside was the number of phone calls it took to plan it all. My mother and his mother, my mother and his aunt, the three of them at one point talking so long I thought for sure we'd be in on a vacation share in LBI with them during the summer or spending national holidays together.

Of course, my mother had wanted to make sure that said aunt really existed and that Jesse and I wouldn't be spending the night in a motel. Then there were my calls to Wren and Jazz. What to wear? Was this too much? Should I really consider doing something so big with someone I'd only just started hanging out with? It was all slightly embarrassing, but completely worth it. For the first time in a long time, I was so flippin' excited for my birthday, but I wasn't sure what it had to do with more—seeing Frank Lloyd Wright's work up close and personal or spending all that time alone with Jesse. Both, I supposed.

After my pre-birthday dinner, we stopped by the bakery for a small vanilla buttercream cake and then went back to the house.

"So what first, presents or cake?" My mother set the cake down in the center of the dining room table.

"Presents? Today?"

"I guess we have an answer," Paul said. He disappeared into the living room and came back with a large, flat package tied with a blue ribbon. My mother's grin stretched across her face as Paul handed me the present. I had to shove away from the table to make room for it. My heart raced as I untied the ribbon and ripped away the tissue paper.

It was an art portfolio.

I ran my hand across the soft, smooth leather. My initials, *MP*, were stamped into the front. I'd been keeping my things in a binder with page protectors; this was probably more extravagant than I needed at the moment, but it was perfect.

"Your mother and I picked it out, but if you really don't like it—"

"I love it," I whispered, opening it up and imagining how I would fill it. Slipped into the second page were a few papers that were stapled together.

An application to Pratt's summer program.

My throat tightened; the initial unease I felt when I spoke about being handed this sort of money danced in my gut. I'd talked myself into accepting NJDI as my only option, that it was what I wanted, what I needed, that earning it was a noble thing. I still believed that, but this? The love I felt at that moment overwhelmed me, filled me up so much that my eyes itched with backed-up tears. They believed in me. They really wanted this for *me*.

My mother cleared her throat. "Mads, we know how you feel about this, but we really think, if this was your first choice, you should reconsider."

"Think of it as sixteen years' worth of birthday presents;

when you look at it that way, it's really not that mu—"

"I'll do it," I said. "I'll apply, I'll go. I . . . Thank you." I placed the portfolio to the side and sprung up to give Paul an awkward, seated hug. He laughed and patted my arm, then I went over to Mom.

"You won't regret it, sweetie, really, you'll see." I threw my arms around her, pressed my cheek against hers. We rocked for a minute until she stepped back.

"And wait, there's more."

"Really?"

"More" turned out to be a set of colored sketching pencils and a pair of boots I'd admired at the mall. I even allowed them to sing "Happy Birthday" to me, softly and without any additions like "a pinch to grow an inch" or a countdown to how many birthdays I was celebrating. It all felt right somehow. The three of us there. A family—maybe with the seams showing, but still . . . together.

"Make a wish, Mads."

The candlelight made the shadows dance around the room.

The other part about birthdays I hated was the wishing. It's like my mind would go on overload, ever since I was little— what did I want? What did I *really, really want?*

I could never think of anything specific and I was afraid of asking for the wrong thing—like a genie story gone bad, where if you hadn't worded your wish correctly it would come out in some different way and burn you.

Wax dripped onto the perfect white buttercream frosting, while different wishes vied for approval.

A perfect weekend with Jesse.

An exciting summer going to Pratt.

Me, Wren, and Jazz becoming yearbook editors.

There was one wish—a whisper, really—that I wanted more than anything. It came on suddenly and surprised me in the sheer fact that it was corny as hell, a made-for-TV movie of a wish.

For that reason, I was sure it was doomed to fail.

But when I closed my eyes to make my wish, it's all that came to mind.

I whispered those words in my thoughts as I blew out seventeen candles.

Let it always be like this night.

SIXTEEN

JESSE

THE LAST TIME I'D WOKEN UP WICKED EARLY ON A
Saturday was my first year in soccer. I can still remember my
parents stumbling across the field with their cups of coffee, cheering me on as I tried my hardest to stay *away* from
the ball. While there was more to my demise in sports than
getting up early, it never meant anything good. This was different, though.

It was the Saturday to end all Saturdays.

The Saturday I'd spend with Madison Pryce.

After a quick pit stop at Mugshot to get provisions for our
ride, I drove to Madison's. All a part of my grand non-birthday
plan that I'd come up with the night after we played at Whiskey Business. I had wanted to surprise her, like *really* surprise
her, but not in the I-hate-to-be-the-center-of-attention way

again. It had to be unexpected. Impressive enough to make her eyes light up the way they did when she spoke about art or going to design camp. That's when I thought of Fallingwater, how stoked she'd been about the Frank Lloyd Wright project she was working on the day she showed me the band logo.

Perfect except for the endless-drive thing that made it next to impossible for a day trip. Enter Aunt Julia, more persuading than I'd done in Debate 101, and finally a birthday overnighter that I knew (or at least hoped) would rock her world.

Madison was sitting on her front porch, duffel bag at her feet. The moment I saw her, my mind went into panic mode— what if this was an idiotic idea? What if we had nothing to talk about for the five-hour drive? There was no turning back, and I kind of dug it. We were in this together. I put the car in park, grabbed her drink, and climbed up the steps to meet her.

"I only get up this early for Frank Lloyd Wright." She stood and swatted the back of her pants.

"Am I allowed to say happy birthday?" I handed her a hot chocolate I'd picked up at Mugshot and hoisted her bag over my shoulder.

She brought the cup up to her face, peeking into the spout.

"Okay I lied, getting up early for your hot chocolate works too." She closed her eyes and took a sip. "Mmmm."

Ms. Pryce stepped out onto the porch, opening her arms wide to Madison. "Give me a hug, birthday girl."

Madison opened her arms awkwardly, holding up the cup and raising her chin over her mom's shoulder, laughing. When they parted, Ms. Pryce looked at me.

"You don't text and drive, do you?"

"No, ma'am."

"Speeding?"

"Mom, come on."

"Nope, the VW sort of sputters when it hits sixty-five, so no worries."

Madison laughed.

"You have cash on you? Your phone is charged?"

"Yes and yes, Mom. And we'll make pit stops and eat when we're hungry. No worries. Thanks for letting me go. I don't know any yoga slang, but, um, bliss out today at training." Madison hugged her again.

"At least text me at some point today, okay? Or leave a voice mail, let me know you got there in one piece."

"Will do." Madison gave her a kiss on the cheek, then grabbed my arm.

"Let's go before she changes her mind," she whispered.

I tossed her bag into the trunk, and opened the passenger-side door. I remembered what she had said about Gray having a shitty ride and braced myself for her assessment of the Bug. It wasn't much, I knew that, but it got me from point A to point B without any trouble. I slid into the driver's seat and made sure I had the right address in the GPS.

"Omigod, you have an eight-ball stick shift? Cool."

Whew.

"So I made us a playlist, easy listening's your jam, right?" I said.

She wrinkled her nose. "What?"

I started the car as Green Day exploded through the speakers.

"Just messing with you."

Her smile fueled me.

Two and a half hours into the ride we had exhausted every hokey car game. Twenty Questions. I Spy. And a version of the license-plate game that hadn't started out as raunchy but quickly debased into third-grade humor. Madison had declared me the winner for *Astonishing Ass Wombat-3675* for using an unexpected adjective with a mammal native to Australia. We were already into Pennsylvania but still had about three hours to go. We were both about to tear the roof off.

"I bet we aren't even going to Fallingwater. You're kidnapping me, aren't you?"

"You're right. We're heading to California."

"Northern or Southern?"

"Um, Northern."

"San Francisco," she said, as if it were a real decision we were making. "What would we do there?"

"Ride a cable car?"

"Oh god, no."

"Ohhkay . . . then, what?"

She put her feet up on the dash, hugging her knees into her chest. "Is this okay? That my feet are up here?"

"You really have to ask?"

"Okay, then this is what we'd do—we'd get roasted peanuts and watch the hang-gliders on the bluffs, then we'd Rollerblade in Golden Gate Park."

"Rollerblade?"

"Yes, 'cause it's perfect and hilly and gorgeous, then we'd window-shop in Haight-Ashbury and get a headache from the incense in the head shop."

I laughed and glanced over at her. "A headache from a head shop?"

"Yeah." She grinned and looked out the window. "And then we'd get lost and take in all the insane colors of the old Victorians, and listen to the street performers and walk and walk until our legs felt like they were going to fall off."

"Wait, when does this get fun?"

"Then we'd find this little Italian restaurant that serves the best linguine and clam sauce you've ever had in your life. And we'd drink red wine since the waiter doesn't care how old we are because even babies drink wine with dinner in Italy. And when we come out, it'll be nighttime and the full moon along the skyline will make you feel like you're in another world. And it will be the best day ever."

She spoke with such detail and conviction, it sounded more like a memory.

"You've done this, haven't you?"

"There are perks to having a family friend who is a pilot. Paul took us when I was thirteen. Around spring break. We went for a long weekend. It's one of those places that just stays with you."

"Cool. Have you gone anywhere else?"

"We went to St. Louis once. You know you can go up in that arch? Total nightmare. And Houston . . . but nowhere worldly like Europe or anything."

"Well, the worldliest place I've been to is, like, the France pavilion in Epcot Center. We had to wait thirty minutes so my sister could get her picture taken with Beast. Go me!" I said, fist pumping.

She took her feet down from the dash and shifted in her seat so she was partially facing me. A good ten minutes passed with the sputtering of the Bug the only noise between us. We'd even exhausted my road trip playlist at that point. I concentrated on the road, but all I wanted to do was look at her.

"Everything okay?"

"That guy Paul, the one you met when I dyed your hair— he's my father."

"You call him Paul?"

"Yes, I call him Paul because up until about a month ago I didn't even know he was my father. He didn't know either.

My mother told us because, well, she's 'living her truth' in yoga, but that's a different story. He's here kind of figuring out some stuff, and I guess she thought why not throw this into the mix too."

I should have been able to come up with something that would make it all better, or to show that I understood, but all I could come up with was, "Madison . . . whoa . . . shit."

She laughed. "Yeah, that was pretty much my reaction."

"I mean, he seems cool."

"He is cool, and I think he's having the same problem as I am—how are we supposed to think differently about each other? But we're trying. I didn't want to put a downer on the day, Jess. It's a good thing, really. I just, well, I wanted you to know. It felt like I was keeping a secret from you and I don't want to do that. Friends know about each other's lives."

"Are they together?"

She shook her head. "No. They've been friends, like, forever, but I always wondered why they never got together. I guess they sort of did, at least for one night. Which is kind of weird to think about."

"Wow."

"Now you have to tell me something about your family."

I changed lanes to let a pickup truck speed by us. "We're not that interesting."

"It's all new, everything's interesting." She reached around to the backseat and rustled through the Mugshot bag, pulling out a small container of fruit and cheese. "Want some?"

I shook my head.

"C'mon, just a grape," she said, holding one out to me.

"Toss it."

"You're driving."

"You look like you have good aim." I opened my mouth as she tossed the grape. It grazed my ear. We swerved a bit. "Okay, maybe not a good idea."

"Here." She leaned over and popped the grape into my mouth. "Now give me something."

"Information for a grape?"

"Something like that."

I thought a minute while I chewed. "Those were my parents you met the other night. My dad's an ex–bass player turned adjunct professor wannabe author. My mom's an accountant. I still walk in on them groping each other—it's gross."

"Or adorable."

"No—it's gross, period. I have a little brother, Ty, who doesn't speak much yet, so he's okay, and a ten-year-old sister whose main mission in life is to make mine miserable."

"I think you're being mean. No grapes if you're mean." She smiled.

"They're okay, even Daisy when she wants to be. Better?"

"Yes." She fed me another grape. "Why don't you wear your infinity bracelet anymore?"

I practically did a double-take. "You noticed that?"

She flustered slightly. "Oh, um—you used to wear it in Mugshot. I always thought—well, I thought it was cool, and now I see you don't have it on."

"That story might cost you a cheese cube."

"Ha, here," she said, honoring my request.

"It was from my ex, Hannah. We had matching wristbands. She's with the old drummer from Yellow Number Five."

"Wait—is that—Was he in the band that played at the Sadie Hawkins Dance?"

"Yeah, why?"

Her brow raised, she chewed her lip and nodded, as if she'd just figured something out.

"What?"

"Nothing, how much longer do we have?" She clasped the top of the takeout container and put it back into the Mugshot bag.

"Our ETA is about two and a half more hours."

She yawned. "Mind if I catch some Z's?"

"Wait, so that's it? I don't get to ask you anything else?"

She reclined the seat, curling her legs up beneath her. "I'm so tired."

"I think you're just avoiding it."

"See, you know me already." She snuggled into the seat, closing her eyes. "And I may snore, so don't like me any less."

"Impossible," I whispered.

"Hey." I nudged Madison.

I'd managed to make it through the gates, and even paid the parking fee without waking her up. Her face was scrunched against the seat, mouth slightly open. She *had* snored a bit, but I decided to keep that to myself. She snorted awake on the third nudge, rubbing her nose and squinting as she scanned the wooded area we were parked in.

"Omigosh, we're here!"

Madison was out of the car before I wrestled the key from the ignition. She reached for the sky, staring up at the canopy of trees, then shivered, crossing her arms.

I shrugged off my jacket to her protests.

"What are you doing?"

"You look like you need this. I've got a hoodie in the trunk, consider it a birth—"

"Lalalalalalala," she said, plugging her ears. "We're not using that *B* word, okay?"

"Take it." I held it out for her until she put her arms into the sleeves.

We walked through woods, to a gazebo, and picked up our tour tickets. Madison wandered around the pavilion, as if she'd been a captive on a desert island and hadn't seen anything quite like this. She ran her hands across the railings, looked up at the rafters, out to the forest. Her lips moving every so often, she laughed to herself.

I waved her over and she took my arm again as we walked

with the other tourists, down to a mossy path that followed along a stream. The sound of rushing water echoed through the dense, bare trees as we squished our way along the soft earth toward the house. It was overcast, and slightly misty, but suddenly the house was there, across a wide ravine, in our sight. Madison slowed down while the other people in our tour group flowed around us.

She pulled me over to the side, so we were directly across from the front of the house, or maybe it was the back— I wasn't sure. It looked exactly like the picture online—all lines, windows, and rushing water, with a staircase that led to the water below—but smaller somehow. To be honest, I didn't understand what was so impressive about it. The colors were sort of oatmeal and that burnt umber crayon that's always broken and no one uses. Madison was captivated as she took in everything.

"You know, I really don't get—" She put her fingers over my mouth, still staring straight ahead, eyes darting over the lines and angles, until a small smile crossed her lips.

"It's real," she whispered, finally looking at me. She laughed. "It's real."

"One-thirty tour," a voice called.

"That's us!" She tugged on my hoodie, leading us over to the group. Madison dragged us front-and-center while the tour guide, a woman about my mom's age wearing plaid rain boots, gave her a head-to-toe once-over.

"You've got the coolest job," Madison said, instantly winning the woman over. By the end of the tour, she knew Madison's name. In fact, by then, everyone knew Madison's name. From the moment she set foot in the house, she was like me at thirteen on Christmas morning, the year I opened up the cherry-red Fender I'd begged for for three months. She flitted through the house, taking in the furniture, the artwork, stopping and staring and holding herself back from touching the flat stones that made up the walls.

"Look at this, isn't this just genius?"

It was the staircase to the water.

"Convenient for swimming," I said.

She laughed. "Weren't you listening? The water regulates the temperature when it's warm out: a built-in cooling system. And it's so pretty, isn't it? Bringing the outdoors in, and the indoors out? I love that. Can you imagine chilling here, reading a book or watching the world go by, probably drinking something like a Rob Roy?"

"I see trees," I said. "And what's a Rob Roy?"

She pinched me.

Madison's favorite words on the tour were *Can you imagine?*

Can you imagine waking up to this view?

Can you imagine Albert Einstein stayed here? We're walking where he walked.

Can you imagine . . . it's a freaking Pablo Picasso, right there in front of us, as art on your wall?

And all the while I looked at her. Experienced her. On the master terrace—sort of the nerve center of the house that went out over the water—she took my hand.

"Close your eyes, Jess, listen. Hear that?"

"Yep," I said, listening but not sure if the rushing sound was the water below or the blood through my brain as I felt her hand in mine. It was small and cold, but strong and soft at the same time.

"It wasn't enough for Frank Lloyd Wright that his client had a view of the waterfall, he *made* them the waterfall. They were in it."

She turned us around to face the house. "Open your eyes. See? See the lines now? How it just—"

"Makes sense. Feels like a part of the forest."

She squeezed my hand, then let go. "Yes!"

"You still can't walk naked through the rooms."

"Because that's what I look for in a house." She walked back into the house to join the tour again.

Her enthusiasm was contagious. She tossed out words like *cantilever* and *organic architecture* and when we reached a small room one of the occupants had used as an office, where a half circle had been cut out of a desk to accommodate the opening of a window so the room would have no corners, she whispered, *"Brilliant."* The tour ended up by the guesthouse, a place we reached by climbing a wide, winding stairway covered by a curved cement canopy that connected it to the main house. Whoever stayed here must have been in decent shape.

"Can you imagine this being your room? Your own swimming pool and everything? Damn. And look, see how it all starts here," she said, her finger following the line of the canopy that went to the house. "The cascading lines follow all the way down to that staircase to the water, to make it look like the waterfall."

"Hence the name Fallingwater."

That earned me another pinch. It was worth it. The ninety bucks. The five-hour car ride. The absolute undiluted joy on her face was worth it all.

"C'mon, I want to see it from the front again." She skipped off ahead of me.

I caught up to her and we walked toward a vantage point where a group of people were taking a picture.

"Your turn," I said, pulling out my phone.

Madison posed with the house behind her. First serious, then funny, then serious again.

"I can take a picture of the two of you if you like," said an older gentleman who'd been waiting his turn to get a picture.

"Yes, c'mon, Jesse."

I handed him the phone, already set to take a picture, and walked over to her.

"Don't push me in," I said.

She put an arm around my waist and pulled herself closer to me. I was sure the autofocus would zero in on my smile, clearly the biggest focal point. We thanked the guy for taking the picture.

"Okay, let's leave, if I stay any longer we'll be here until the sun goes down. I'm so starving I could eat a handful of that moss."

"Now on to phase two."

"Phase two?"

"Aunt Julia's."

SEVENTEEN

MADISON

MEXICAN HOT CHOCOLATE AND FRANK LLOYD
Wright.

Jesse McMann was wooing me.

There was no other word for it. Probably the kind of word
used when Rob Roys were *the* drink. And men wore smoking
jackets. And there were weekend visitors who actually stayed
at Fallingwater. He was *wooing* me.

And I was eating it up.

The day had been better than I ever could have imagined.
The fact that Jesse planned this for me was almost too much
to take in. This was a day I'd never forget, no matter what
happened, *if anything happened*, between us. And now I had
a clue as to what he might have been thinking about in that
picture from the dance—it must have been something to do

with his ex-girlfriend if she had been there. I wanted to know more about his family, about his breakup, about *him*.

We drove for a while through narrow winding roads with thick, dense forest on either side. The VW labored, puttering loudly uphill and chirping down. Finally there was a small clearing with a mailbox. Jess turned right, down an even narrower unpaved lane, which eventually widened into a large expanse of land. A few horses grazed in a fenced-in field. There were two corrals, and several large barns and a house that looked like a yuppie's version of a log cabin. Three dogs of various sizes and breeds came rushing up to the car, tails wagging furiously. Jesse slowed down. My jaw may have actually dropped.

"This is where your aunt lives?"

"Yep, cool, huh?"

"Cool? How about magnificent? Incredible?"

He smiled, cutting the engine. "How about—wait till you see the inside."

I looked out the window at our canine welcoming committee. Jess got out of the car first. The dogs ambushed him, hopping around and jumping up on hind legs as he made his way over to my side of the car. He knelt down and gave them each hearty scratches on the neck, going forehead to snout with the husky. A woman waved from the porch as two kids galloped down the stairs to greet Jesse. The dogs encircled all of them in a flurry of wagging tails and paws and lolling tongues as I stepped out of the car.

The small dog, a furball of a thing that looked like a cross between a fox and a miniature lion, came tearing toward me, yipping wildly.

"That's Pepper. She won't bite," a young girl with a long ponytail said.

"Hey, Pepper," I said, reaching out and running my fingers across the dog's soft fur. Her coat reminded me of a pair of earmuffs I owned. She sniffed my hand and ran her little pink tongue across my fingers. I laughed and pulled my hand away.

"This is my cousin Sara. Sara, this is Madison," Jesse said.

"Do you guys need help with your things?" she asked, scratching the dog behind the ear.

"Sure." Jess pulled the bags out of the trunk. Sara grabbed mine.

"You don't really have to do that," I said.

"No one should carry their bags on their birthday." She smiled and tromped off. I looked at Jesse.

"Does *everyone* know it's my birthday?"

"Kind of," he said.

We walked toward the house. Jesse's aunt was still on the porch, smiling as we approached.

"Hey, about time you got here," she said. "Charlie's been asking for you since he woke up this morning."

"Have not," said the young blond boy.

"Hi," I said, suddenly shy. I had the overwhelming desire for them to like me.

"Madison, this is my aunt Julia," Jesse said. "And that guy over there is Charlie, the little Jack Russell is Max, and last but not least is Duke, the Alaskan husky."

"And your uncle Vaughn, but he's away at a trade show in Louisiana," Aunt Julia said. "Happy birthday, Madison, we're so happy to meet you."

I widened my eyes at Jesse. Not the birthday thing again.

"How did you like Fallingwater?" she asked, leading us into the house.

"Oh it was amazing." I stopped immediately after crossing the threshold. Jesse was right. If I'd thought the log cabin was impressive from the outside, it was nothing compared to the inside. My jaw dropped again as I took in the high ceiling of the great room. The first floor was one big open space from the sitting area near the fireplace to the kitchen. The kitchen was separated from the great room by a long counter, with stools for seating. One wall was completely floor-to-ceiling windows. The view of the hills and the sky was breathtaking.

"Why don't you show Madison to her room, Sara," Aunt Julia said.

Sara still had my bag slung over her shoulder. She waved for me to follow her down a long hall. If I had to guess I would have pegged her for eleven or twelve, but she was already a good two inches taller than me.

"Here it is," she said, opening the door to a room that was twice the size of mine at home. Even though it was big, the dark wooden walls made it feel cozy. There was a large window that opened up to the same view as the great room. A wardrobe was on the far wall, and the bed frame was made from tree branches, the headboard a tangle of branches and vines, with a white gauzy dust ruffle. Sara tossed my bag on the bed, then sat beside it and proceeded to stare at me.

"How long have you and Jesse been together?" she asked.

"Oh, we're not together, like that anyway—just friends."

"Too bad, you seem really cool."

I ran my fingers through my hair, pulling on a tuft behind my ear out of nervous habit. A flurry of clicking and panting rushed behind me as Pepper raced across the wooden floor and leapt up onto the bed next to Sara.

"Thanks."

A knock on the door made us both turn.

"Sara, your mom wants you," Jesse said.

"Later," she said. With Pepper still in her arms, Sara skated in her socks across the floor and out of the room.

"Sorry if she was bothering you," Jesse said. He stood there, hands in hoodie pockets, his hair sticking up in a charming way.

"No, not at all, I'm fine—just, you know, tired I guess," I

said. "I just want to maybe change or something, or check in with my mom."

"Cool. I'm bunking with Charlie if you need me for anything. Hey, you know how to play Spoons?"

"Um, what?" I asked.

"The card game? Like Crazy Eights?"

I shook my head.

"I'll teach you." He smiled as he shut the door. I collapsed onto the bed, half expecting woodland creatures to appear and tuck me in. Could the place be any more enchanting? Before the road trip was over, I had the feeling I would know what it felt like to kiss Jesse McMann. *Breathe, Maddie.*

Dinner was a continuation of the complete and utter amazingness that had been my birth—um, special day. We made our own pizzas from scratch—well, the dough had been prepped beforehand, but Aunt Julia had put out all different ingredients in small bowls around the countertop. Charlie had so much pepperoni on his pizza it looked like shingles on a roof; both Aunt Julia and Sara made regular cheese and tomato sauce pies; I tried my hand at a margherita with fresh mozzarella and basil; and Jess surprised the heck out of me by making a Hawaiian, with pineapples and ham and cheese.

After dinner we sat near the fireplace and played Spoons, which involved matching cards and grabbing spoons, and I completely and utterly sucked at it and was the first one to spell out S-P-O-O-N. Charlie kicked everyone's butt. Jesse disappeared and came back with an acoustic guitar.

"Well, that was fun. Time for some not-birthday cake?" Aunt Julia looked at me.

"What's that for?" I motioned to Jesse and the guitar, anticipating another rousing version of the song I cringed over. He grinned and strummed.

"Mood music. I promise to get it right this time." He laughed.

I collected the cards, making room for the not-birthday cake, which we were going to chow down on near the fireplace. Aunt Julia carried the cake into the great room, the dogs following at her heels.

"Can we sing?" Sara pleaded.

I was about to say sure—I mean, really, how could I refuse?—when Jesse cut in.

"We'll do the version we sing to my dad—how's that?"

They all looked so excited.

"Okay."

Jesse strummed a few chords of the Beatles' "Birthday" song, and they all started singing and clapping to it. I blew out the one candle I'd allowed them to put on the cake, and grinned.

The cake was some sort of triple-chocolate blackout cake, which made me weak in the knees after three forkfuls and a half glass of milk. Full and lazy, I never wanted to get up from the couch.

"Jess, play that song you played at your mom's birthday party that time," Sara said.

He shook his head, swallowing a mouthful of cake. "Nah."

"Oh, come on, it's so pretty," Aunt Julia said.

"I'm eating," he said, looking down.

"Madison, you should hear it, it's . . . What was it?"

"'Claire de Lune,'" Aunt Julia said. "He learned it as a gift to his mom."

"Guys," Jesse said. "No."

"You play classical? Oh, you have to do it. It's my birthday, I demand it."

"You hate birthdays."

"Doesn't matter. Play," I said, pointing at the guitar and waving my hand to order him around. Being the birthday girl *did* have privileges, after all. He narrowed his eyes at me as he wiped his mouth with a napkin. He picked up the guitar and sat down on the edge of the couch, strumming softly and fiddling with the tuning knobs at the end a few times.

"I have not played this since last summer," he said. "So, you know, you've been warned."

He plucked the strings slowly, stopped, then started again. At first he looked down at the neck of his guitar. Each note precise and sweet. The song was familiar, like something I would have heard in school, but the way Jess played, it felt more like a dream. Quickening at some parts, slowing down and lingering over other notes. He hit a sour note and winced, laughed a little, and looked at me while he continued.

I blinked, looked away.

There was something so intimate and raw about the way he played. He couldn't help but be an open book when the guitar was in his hand. It had been the same way at Whiskey Business. It wasn't the dark, or the crowd, it had been his music that revealed a part of him to me. When I looked back, his chin was up, eyes closed, mouth trembling like he was whispering to someone. His hair fell across his forehead and he flipped it back, not missing a note. The longer he played, the more it seemed like he was playing with his whole body, not just his hands.

His playing slowed. I savored each second, not wanting it to end. He sighed, plucking the final sound, a high note. We all sat still, letting the tone reverberate, mixing in with the crackling fire and the soft hush of our own breathing. Sara broke the spell by clapping.

"You didn't hear those off-notes?" he asked.

"No, it was beautiful," Aunt Julia said.

Charlie yawned, loud and long. Jesse looked at me.

"It was great." *Great* seemed too brash and understated a word. *Magnificent* felt like overkill, but wow . . . I'd *felt* the song.

"Okay you two, time to get ready for bed."

"But Mom, we haven't played Clue yet," Sara protested.

"It's too late for Clue."

Then it occurred to me this mass exodus was for my benefit. For mine and Jesse's. To be alone.

So I did what any girl who'd been feted and pampered
would do.

I freaked the hell out.

"I, um, wow, I'm beat, Jess."

"Oh, yeah, me too." He said it, but I didn't believe him.
"What time do you want to leave in the morning?"

I stretched. "I don't know. Whenever. Not in a rush."

"Ten-ish sound good?"

"Sure."

We gathered up the dirty cake dishes and dumped them in
the sink. I helped clean up the empty cups and brought the
leftover cake to the counter.

"Thank you so much, for everything. This has been
incredible."

Jesse smiled, his eyes zeroed in on mine—asking me to
linger.

With him.

"Good night," I whispered, then bolted to my room.

Sleep would not indulge me.

I'd washed, changed into my fleece PJ bottoms, and even
put on the fuzzy slipper socks I needed to have on so my feet
wouldn't get cold. My mind raced. I jammed my eyes shut
again. Willing myself to Go. To. Sleep.

Nothing.

The comforter was down-filled, and hugged my body in a way that was heavy and light at the same time. The sheets were so soft and warm now, with a slight scent of lavender. The bed was a perfect, blissful sleep cocoon. There was no reason why I shouldn't be able to fall asleep. Except . . .

The haunting melody of "Claire de Lune" kept dancing through my brain. Any time I closed my eyes, it was there, as was Jesse and that look on his face, the way his fingers moved up and down the neck of his guitar.

Breathe, Maddie.

I was falling for Jesse McMann.

How could I not?

Wasn't that what this whole trip was about?

I felt mean thinking that way. None of it was calculated. It wasn't like this trip was easy. A five-hour drive. A weekend off from work and band rehearsal, when the Battle of the Bands was two weeks away. He'd done it for me.

That was scary, uncertain ground. I thought about what Zach had said when we broke up—*Maybe you'll let him in*. I didn't know what he meant until now. I could always box Zach up—as *fun guy, great kisser*. And whenever things seemed like they were getting deeper—I'd shut off, or down, because it was easier to feel in control that way. I wasn't in control now.

I tossed and turned a few more times before finally throwing off the cover and getting up with plans on raiding the kitchen for a glass of milk or something. Maybe another slice of blackout cake would put me into a blissful sugar coma and help me sleep. My door creaked, no matter how gently I tried to open it. I paused, waiting to hear any telltale clicking of little paws or feet. Nothing. I tiptoed quietly down the hall. The fire illuminated the great room, shadows expanding and flickering across the walls.

I froze mid-step, heart jumping into my throat. Jess was there, on the couch, staring into the fireplace. He nodded out for a moment, dozing.

Stop pretending, chica. *You didn't come out here for cake.*

I moved toward him, cleared my throat so I wouldn't completely freak him out. He jolted awake, sitting up when he saw me.

"Hey." He ran a hand through his hair.

"Hi," I said. His eyes moved across me, taking in my black fleece PJ bottoms with the fluorescent hearts, my thin white tee. I crossed my arms.

"You're still up." *Um, duh, Mads.*

"Barely."

I flopped in the corner opposite him, curling my legs up underneath me. The fire made my skin feel tight, warm, and dry. The flames were hypnotic.

"I can't stop thinking about the way you played that song," I finally said.

He laughed. "You missed the clunker notes."

"No, clunkers and all, it was . . . You were . . ."

He waited for me to say more, but I couldn't find the words. Nothing could describe it.

"Where do you go?" I asked.

"Hmm?"

"When you play, when you close your eyes it looks like you're whispering or something . . . you're gone." After I voiced it, the question sounded ridiculous. He stared into the fire, a small smile crossing his lips.

"C'mon," he said, standing up.

"What?"

"Let me show you what it feels like." For a moment I was disoriented. This was Stage Jesse, confident, holding out his hand to me, letting me in on his secret. What was he going to do? "Go get your boots on."

Not what I'd expected.

I went back to my room, pulled on my boots, and met him by the front door, heart racing. Where were we headed? He had on his hoodie, a patchwork quilt slung over his shoulder.

"Here," he said, handing me his leather jacket. I put it on, zipping it up to my chin this time, and followed him out into the frigid night.

My eyes finally adjusted to the dark, as we walked down a dirt path that cut between the barns. Soft whinnies echoed through the slats in the stalls; the sweet smell of hay and sting of manure made my nose itch. Aside from that, everything was still, peaceful, except for our feet scuffing against the hard road. Questions raced through my mind, but it felt like talking would interrupt something.

Jesse veered off the road, walking into a vast, grassy field bordered by a forest and looking over his shoulder to make sure I was following him.

"Be careful where you step," he said.

"How can I even see anything?"

"Oh, you'll feel it when you step in a pile of something," he said, chuckling. He looked up toward the sky and spun around, fanning out the blanket and letting it fall onto the field. "This will do."

"For what?"

He knelt down, patted the space next to him. "Madison, have you been disappointed at all today?"

I sighed, easing my way onto the blanket. It was cold. Correction: effing cold. But I was curious. I squatted till my butt hit the ground, ignoring the feeling of frostbite seeping through my PJ bottoms.

"Now what?"

He smiled, leaning back so he was flat on the blanket, hands folded on his chest. I did the same, sliding onto my back.

"So you go out to a horse pasture when you play the guitar?" I asked.

"Duh."

"Well?"

"What are you feeling, right now?"

"Freezing."

"Aside from that."

"I don't know . . . that the sky is so pretty. We see more out here than where we live because of all the pollution and lights, but then that sort of bums me out because the pollution makes me feel so helpless."

"Okay, right. Nothing more?"

I sighed. "It's all so big and beautiful and blah, blah, blah."

He laughed. "The *blah, blah, blah* is what everyone is afraid to let in."

There it was, that letting-in phrase again. What was I afraid to let in? This?

"I feel so small—like when I'm sitting here and looking up, I realize that nothing is ever still, those stars are constantly imploding and dying and new ones are born, and we're on some spinning hunk of rock in the middle of a galaxy and when you look at it that way, hell, you realize how insignificant we really are, and it's scary, but then you wonder, how can we be alone? It's pure arrogance to think we're all alone in the universe, and it's a nice thought—the not being alone.

"But then someone hurts you, or pushes you into a locker, or breaks your heart, and you realize how alone you are, and it blows. And it's that uncertainty that makes us all batshit crazy, right? What does life mean? What if it means nothing? Well, when I'm playing, when I close my eyes, it's like for a split second, just a sip of time, I understand stuff and I'm part of everything. And I know there's something more—can physically feel connected to it, can feel it going through me. So that's it, that's where I go when it looks like I'm whispering. I know it sounds weird but I think everyone has something like that, you know? I think you have it when you draw. I saw it today in your eyes, when you showed me your version of that house. It was fucking brilliant."

Time stood still in *that* moment. Listening to Jesse talk, the intensity behind his words, the mystery of the night sky, even the cold—it all filled me. Jazz popped into my head, her sparkly, magical love glitter . . . a person cracking open. Jesse had always been open, with his smile, his foam art at Mugshot, when he played the guitar—I was the one cracking open into a whole other person.

"Please, say something."

"I think the whispering thing is sexy," I said.

He was silent, but I felt the movement of his head on the blanket as he shifted in my direction.

A star imploding, another one being born. I was cracking open, letting him in, I couldn't stop it.

"Jesse, I lied about the birthday thing, about not liking to celebrate. I think because it never lived up to what I thought it should be. That people tried too hard to have a good time or make sure I was happy. This is the birthday I never knew I wanted."

I turned toward Jesse, knowing when our eyes met that I would be a goner. My lips tingled at the thought of touching his, but a large shadow loomed over him. I sat bolt-upright, my hand covering my mouth in a silent scream.

He shot up too. "What . . . oh, shit."

Jesse blocked my body with his, laying his hands down on either side of me. I peered over his shoulder, grabbing on to the hood of his sweatshirt.

A massive buck stood about five feet away. Towering over us with long, spindly antlers sprouting treelike from its head. He pawed at the grass and grunted, white tendrils of breath coming from its snout. We sat frozen on the ground, waiting for something to happen.

"Is he going to charge at us or something?" I had visions of being gored with those antlers, right through both of us. *And I never kissed Jesse.*

"I don't know," he whispered.

"Should we run for it?"

"No, just stay still." He sounded confident, but his heart was pounding as fast as mine. I could feel it through his sweatshirt.

The buck grunted again and lifted its head, frozen a moment except for its ears, which pricked up, twitching. Glassy, dark eyes stared unblinking. I wasn't sure how long we sat like that, but it felt like forever, until more shadows emerged. There were five to ten more deer, walking slowly across the field. Jesse laughed, low. I didn't feel threatened anymore, just fascinated. They were beautiful, graceful without even trying. The buck stamped its foot once again before galloping off to join the others.

"Well, that was interesting," he said, letting out a ragged breath. He leaned back on his hands, legs out in front of him, feet moving back and forth releasing pent-up energy.

My heart still throbbed from the rush. "You sat in front of me."

"I did," he said, looking up at the sky. A smile crept across his face.

"Very chivalrous."

He leaned toward me and nudged me with his shoulder.

"You said I was sexy," he said, straightening up, still looking at the sky.

I wrapped my arms around my knees, hid my face, and laughed. "The whispering thing. I said that whispering thing was sexy."

He swept his fingers into my hair, raking past my ear to the nape of my neck. I shivered, resting my cheek against my knees so I could look at him.

"You know where else I was when I played that song?"

I shook my head.

He kept his eyes on mine, moving closer. I straightened up,

tilted my face toward his. The tip of his nose grazed mine. I closed my eyes, anticipating the kiss, but Jesse only nuzzled my face, his lips brushing my cheek. He kissed my neck, the hollow below my ear, and sent a flood of warmth through me, my skin electric.

"Jess," I whispered, lips trembling.

He nipped my earlobe. "I was here."

Kissed my temple. "And here."

I grabbed a fistful of his sweatshirt, turning toward him. The leather jacket was suddenly awkward and bulky, squeaking as I moved. He hesitated, hands on either side of my face, our foreheads touching. Our eyes were open as our lips touched, lightly at first. Jesse closed his eyes, kissing me full on the mouth, his tongue coaxing my lips open, as we fell back side by side, onto the blanket, our legs tangling up together.

Broody Barista could *kiss*.

I unzipped the jacket, grabbed his hand, and brought it toward my waist.

"Mmmmmm," he moaned, moving his hand up my back and pulling me against him. We kissed that way for a while, shifting positions, dissolving into each other. The air nipped at the sliver of bare skin between my tee and PJ bottoms. Reality.

"Jess," I said between kisses, "I can't feel my fingers."

He laughed and grabbed my icy hand, enfolded it in his. "Same here."

"Do you think . . . maybe," I said, hesitating. What did

I want? I wanted more of this, of him, but where? Could I really ask him back to my room? It felt odd.

He looked toward the house. "No one's awake, we could . . ."

"Sneak into my room," I said.

He touched his forehead to mine.

I continued. "Not to, you know . . . just . . . There's a door that can shut."

"Exactly," he finished, kissing the now-frozen tip of my nose, my lips again.

Jesse stood up first, held out a hand and pulled me to standing. He gathered the blanket and threw it around both our shoulders as we headed toward the house. It looked so far away. He stopped and pulled me in for another kiss, before we decided to run for it. Tromping up the stairs, I was dizzy at the thought of picking up where we'd left off. He opened the door. We were greeted by three little fur faces, panting and wagging their hello. Aunt Julia was in the kitchen, stirring a pot on the stove.

"I couldn't sleep. Anyone want cocoa? You guys look frozen."

Jess and I looked at each other and laughed.

"That sounds great, Aunt Julia," he said.

THE SMELL OF COFFEE AND BACON NUDGED ME awake. And then a flash of last night—kissing Madison. Had it really happened? That five minutes—or five seconds—seemed like an eternity. Then, our night cut short.

I could just hear Tanner. . . .

Dude, cock-blocked by cocoa? Epic.

Not that there would have been enough of anything going on to block, but the thought of being alone with Madison made a beat pump through my brain. When would that happen again? Last night had been perfect, like stars and planets aligned perfectly. Was it Fallingwater? The chocolate cake? My guitar playing? A magical combination of everything? God—the way she looked at me—being around her was a total rush.

Charlie burst through his door.

"C'mon, everyone's awake. Breakfast!" He raced out of his room with more enthusiasm than anyone should be allowed to have in the morning. I grabbed a shirt and made a pit stop in the bathroom to gargle with a swig of mouthwash before heading out to the kitchen. Madison was up already, talking to Sara as they sat side by side at the table.

Dead puppies, great whites, genital warts. Be cool, Jess.

My smile was a force that could not be stopped.

I grabbed a plate and sat across from Madison.

Don't stare.

Her presence was a magnet pull. It took all my effort not to look at her because once I did, I knew I'd just start laughing or dropping silverware or losing control of my senses because all I wanted to do was swipe the breakfast dishes away and continue where we left off last night.

"I taught my friend how to do a fishtail braid, so yes, your hair is perfect for that," Madison said to Sara. "Hey, Jess, we have time before we go, right? I can fix Sara's hair?"

Her eyes planted on mine. Gone was that hungry look. Her face was so neutral, she could have been ordering a chai from me. As if we hadn't swapped spit out in the pasture, or I hadn't saved her from a mutant buck, or dazzled her with my guitar prowess. Nada.

"Ah, yeah," I said.

"Great." She dug into her plate of eggs. Something tickled my foot. I flinched and looked under the table, expecting to see one of the dogs. Madison's socked foot slipped under the cuff of my jeans. Proof last night wasn't a dream. I bit back a grin and reached for some bacon.

After breakfast and showers and hair braiding, we said good-bye and started the long trek home. The farther away we got from my aunt's house, the more unreal it all seemed, at least to me. Madison stared out the window, taking in the scenery as we drove. It was a good day for a drive—perfect, cloudless blue sky and open roads.

When we hit the first two-lane road, I pulled into a gas station and shifted the car into park.

"Jess, I think it's closed."

I unhooked my seat belt and leaned toward her, my hand in her hair. She paused, before bringing her face toward mine. Our lips touched, soft, sweet. I squeezed my eyes shut, imagining last night's starry sky, the perfection of that moment, of this one, of her. Her tongue teased mine as we kissed deeper. I could not get enough of her. I kissed the tip of her nose, her forehead, finally breaking away.

"I wanted to do that all morning," I said.

She put her fingers to her lips and smiled. "Me too. Does it have to end? Can't we just go back? Screw school."

"We could squat at Fallingwater. You could sketch." I pulled the car back onto the road.

"And you could entertain everyone with your guitar. Could you imagine? How freakin' awesome would that be?" She hunkered down, propped her feet on the dash, and put her hand over mine, nudging her index finger underneath my pinkie on the eight-ball stick shift. I smiled.

"Although, we couldn't walk around naked or anything," she said.

I laughed. "Are you trying to make me drive off the road?"

"Never." She squeezed my hand.

"We could just live in that guesthouse, have our own private pool."

"You *were* paying attention."

"Of course," I said.

I could have driven like that forever, just one long winding road, with Madison holding my hand. My mind kept interrupting, though—making me *think*. Questions I was afraid to ask because I knew they would wreck the mood, but I wanted to know the answers anyway. What were we doing? Could I kiss her again? *Were we . . . together?*

Why ruin the moment with reality?

Madison spoke first.

"So why did you and Hannah break up?"

Ah, so she had questions too.

"Where's my grape?"

She smiled. "No grapes today. You don't have to talk about it if you don't want."

I peeked over at her. She chewed her thumbnail and studied my face. Talking about Hannah didn't bother me, but the dose of reality made it seem like Hannah was in the backseat, leaning forward, waiting to hear what I would say about her.

"It's cool. Ask away."

"How long were you together?"

"Forever."

She shifted in the seat, taking her feet off the dash. "Hmm, that sounds like a long time."

"We live on the same block, so I don't know, it has always sort of felt that way, but we weren't *together*, together until the end of her freshman year."

I spilled more than I planned, but something about being behind the wheel, driving through the mountains, not looking her in the eyes, made it easier to talk.

"What made you break up?"

"You'd have to ask her."

"So *you* didn't want to break up?"

There was something in the tone of her voice that made me want to change the subject. The whispering, sexy, chivalrous guitar god was turning back into average-Joe barista in the noonday sun.

"I, um . . . at the time, I guess no. I didn't really expect it, I was sort of blindsided. They're happy together—it hurt to see them like that at first, but now, it's okay I guess. I mean, I don't want to hang out with them or anything, but, you know, if I bump into them, I think I'll be all right."

"Did you break up because of the drummer?"

"At first I thought so, but it was more than that. We didn't spend any time together. And then I was late for her birthday party. Sweet sixteen. Shitty thing to do, but at the time—"

"Her birthday?"

"Yeah."

Her brow furrowed. "Ironic, no?"

"Huh?"

"Think about it. We just had this awesome time for my birthday. Maybe you're trying to make up for that. Subconsciously or something?"

"No. That's ridiculous." *Wasn't it?*

She laughed. "Chill, Jess, I'm just fooling around. Wielding my AP Psychology knowledge. I didn't mean to hit a nerve. Sorry."

"You didn't hit a nerve."

She curled her feet underneath her and fiddled with the radio.

"Man, do you think we can find a station without static?" She fiddled around until she hit upon what sounded like a pop station. Closed her eyes. End of conversation.

Was it true? Had I just orchestrated this whole thing for Madison's birthday because I was still somehow trying to make up for my mistake? No. *No.* The truth was, it never would have occurred to me to do something like that for Hannah, and that made me feel worse. My relationship with Hannah had been easy, I never had to work for any of it. She was pretty and easy to talk to and we had this history, but Madison challenged me. I'd wanted to surprise her, to do something that would really matter. I was over Hannah. Over us. And our breakup had nothing to do with Duncan and everything to do with me.

We finally reached Madison's house at dusk. I pulled into the spot in front of her house and killed the ignition. I'd been so confident after last night, and in the morning when I'd pulled over at the gas station, but in our everyday reality, the spell was broken. She made a move to get out.

"Wait," I said.

"What's up?"

"What you said before—the whole subconscious thing—"

She slumped back down into the seat. "Jess, I'm sorry. I didn't mean anything by it. I was being a smartass. That's sort of what I do, when things get too real."

"Real?"

"The past twenty-four hours have been maybe some of the best of my life. It flew by, and the thing is—I never even thought about wanting to be anywhere else. Or with anyone else. It was nice."

She played with the string on my hoodie, pulled me close.

"I like you, Madison. I didn't do this to make up for anything. I did it for you. And I really hope we can do this again. Not this exactly, but do stuff. Together."

Maybe I *was* being too real, but I couldn't help it.

"Me too, Jesse," she whispered, and put her lips to mine. "Walk me up?"

"Yes."

NINETEEN

JESSE SLUNG MY BAG OVER HIS SHOULDER AND WE walked up the stairs to my porch. Normally I climbed them two at a time, but I took it slow, feeling the railing under my fingertips, clinging to the last moments of our road trip, because once we said good-bye, Fallingwater would be in the past. A memory. I wasn't ready for that. I hadn't even given Jesse back his jacket. Maybe if I didn't say anything, I could keep it overnight, wear it to school, keep the weekend alive even in a small way.

The porch light was on, but the house was dark. *Odd*. My mother was supposed to have been finished with her RYT class by early afternoon. Her car was in the driveway. She should have been home. Not that I expected a welcoming committee but I thought at least she'd want to hear how my unofficial birthday road trip went. Whatever.

"I need my bag," I said. Jesse handed it to me and I knelt down to rummage through the side compartment for my keys. I tucked them into my pocket, rezipped the bag, and stood up. A few weeks ago when I'd dyed his hair, Jesse and I'd been in the same face-to-face position to say good-bye. I'd thought about kissing him then, but now I wanted to act on it. I tugged his hoodie strings.

"Come here."

"What do you want?"

"You."

He smiled under my kiss, then finally surrendered to my persuasive tongue. I'd spent the better part of last night tossing and turning, imagining what might have been if his aunt Julia hadn't greeted us with cocoa. This was worth the wait. I pulled back. Why not take advantage of my mother's absence?

"Wanna come in for a bit?"

He scratched the back of his head. "Uhhh—"

"Or not, I just thought—"

"Yeah, sure. Kind of not ready to go home yet."

My fingers were noodles, useless after the kiss. *Key in lock, Mads.*

I finally turned the knob, and pushed open the door. The house was still.

"Hello?" I called, shutting the door behind us.

Silence.

I walked through the kitchen and flicked on the light. Everything was in place. Not even a note on the table. Living room the same. Then I took a breath and creaked up the stairs.

"Hello?"

I turned on the lamp at the top landing. All the doors on the second floor were open.

We were alone. For how long I wasn't sure, but I didn't care. My mother obviously didn't either or else she would have been home.

Jesse stood at the foot of the stairs. Waiting. I slipped off the jacket and hung it over the banister. I raked my fingers through his hair.

"Close your eyes."

"Madison."

"Trust me."

He relented.

"So we're walking back from the meadow and no one is awake—what would we have done?"

I brought my forehead to his, tracing his lips with the tip of my tongue. His hands found my waist, caressed the curve of my hips as he kissed me full, taking my tongue in his mouth. I threw my arms around him, closing the space between us. He staggered back and my feet left the ground. I wrapped my legs around him, but the momentum made us fall back onto the stairs. My butt at least softened the blow. His hands were on either side of me.

"Are you okay?" he asked.

"Just kiss me." For the moment his mouth was the perfect sedative, and who cared if we were in this awkward position on the stairs—they always did this sort of thing in the movies, fade to black. The reality was different, though, and about a minute in, the pain in my back went from dull to sharp. My spine wasn't meant to follow the angles of stairs while Jesse did the equivalent of a push-up—breaking the laws of our own organic architecture.

"Maybe we should take this somewhere else," I said between kisses.

"Mmmm . . ."

"Come on, Jess."

As we got to my bedroom door, my mother's face popped into my head. What if she came home now, would it piss her off? I turned on my bedside lamp, and Jesse's eyes wandered the room.

"Hey, you did this?" He pointed at my dresser to a model of Hearst Tower, which I'd built out of Popsicle sticks for a sophomore art project.

"Guilty. I love that design."

"Cool," he said, moving over to my desk. I resisted the urge to dart in front of him and body-block it. It was a disaster zone. Koh-I-Noor pens with missing caps, crumpled paper with failed drafting attempts, rubber-band bracelets that I still wore sometimes. I noticed something else, something he was about to pick up.

"Oh, um."

I froze, fingers on my lips. My cheeks burned. I normally didn't blush but it felt like I could light the whole room. This was too personal. For both of us. He looked at the sketch—the one I drew from the picture of him from that night at the Sadie Hawkins Dance—without saying a word. I wouldn't have blamed him if he wanted to leave—I wanted to leave. Why had I asked him in? Where the heck was my mother when I needed her to intrude?

"Is this—?"

"You? Yes." I stepped from one foot to the other. "From that night at the dance. You were in the background of this picture I took and when I saw it I thought—it made me wonder what you were looking at, and I just started doodling and, I know, it's awful."

"No it's not." He tilted his head as he studied the sketch.

The question that inspired me to draw the picture prodded my brain.

"Were you really just there to see the band that night?"

He nodded, placed the paper back on the desk, and turned to me. His eyes were different, or maybe I was—he had the upper hand, he knew somehow he had caught a glimpse of me in that picture. He knew that I thought about him. I stepped back as he came toward me.

"I saw Hannah that night—with Duncan. That's the night I realized they weren't together to screw me over. They were just together. I took off that infinity bracelet after that."

"Oh."

His fingers traced my jawline, snaked up into my hair.

"So you don't think I'm a total creeper for drawing you?"

He answered me with a kiss so soft and sweet it was like taking a sip of a warm drink; heat crept down to my toes, to my fingertips as I put my arms around him. His heart thumped against mine. We fell back onto my bed, tangled up in each other—my knee between his, his hand on my hip.

His lips explored my cheek, my forehead. I kissed his neck, the space below his ear. He sighed and pulled me closer.

"Stay," I whispered, laying my cheek against his chest, feeling the rise and fall of his breath underneath me. His laugh vibrated in his rib cage.

"Sure."

I snuggled against him, my head fitting perfectly in the crook of his neck. I closed my eyes.

So perfectly.

So perfect.

So perf . . .

"Madison."

I opened my eyes, my cheek still on Jesse's chest. It took a moment to orient myself. How much time had passed? I propped myself up on my hands.

My mother stood at the foot of the bed. A crease formed on the bridge of her nose as she looked at Jesse, then me. I nudged Jess. He kind of gasped awake, running a hand across his face, eyes soft with sleep. He looked so damn cute as he sat up, all I wanted to do was push him back down and kiss him. Well, maybe if my mother hadn't been boring holes into my brain.

"What time is it?" I prayed she wouldn't start in on me about him being in my room. She had to see it was innocent.

"It's a little after eight." Her voice was clipped.

"Wow." Jesse blinked a few times before standing up. I followed, ignoring the weight of my mother's glare.

"Where were you? I thought you'd be home when we got here," I said. Her features softened slightly.

"A few of us went out after class. Why are you up here? How long have you been home?"

I looked at Jess; his face was blank but he'd caught my mother's miffed vibe. He shoved his hands so deep into his hoodie pockets, the front stretched taut.

"Around six maybe," I answered.

She nodded and looked between us.

"Jesse, Madison's not allowed to have guests on the second floor. I guess she didn't mention that."

She hadn't yelled, but somehow that made it worse. My gut wrenched with shame. "Mom."

The room became a vortex of awkward. Jesse eyed the door and then looked at me, his eyes pleading to make a run for it. I nodded.

"I, um, didn't realize it was so late, I better get home," he said.

"I'll walk you out."

"How was the trip, guys?" My mother followed us down the stairs.

She really expected a lighthearted convo after she'd just humiliated me?

"Oh, it was great," Jesse answered. "We had a good time."

"And the drive?" she asked as we hit the landing.

"Long," we said together. I bit my tongue to stop myself from saying *jinx*. It seemed like too much of a fun, casual thing to say after getting caught upstairs. Even though we hadn't actually been doing anything. I reached for the door. My mother opened her mouth to say something.

"He has to leave," I snapped. It came out a little more forceful than I meant it to sound. She recoiled slightly.

"Well, have a safe ride home, Jesse. I'm making tea, Mads, want some?"

"Nope." I closed the door behind us and stepped onto the porch. "I'm so sorry about that."

"Don't sweat it." He leaned down so his mouth was by my ear. "It was worth it."

I growled, tugged on the front of his hoodie. "I don't want this weekend to end."

"Maybe," he said, "we can think of it as a beginning."

"Jess."

We kissed.

"I'll call you." He backed off the porch, keeping his eyes on me until he finally realized going down the steps in reverse in the dark might not be the smartest move. He turned and jumped over the last two stairs to the sidewalk. I waited until the VW was down the street before heading back into the house.

My mother was in the kitchen, standing over the kettle. Her cup and saucer already on the counter, chamomile tag hanging out.

"Why did you have to do that?"

She looked at me, the same face as she had on when I saw her at the foot of my bed.

"I could ask you the same thing. You know how I feel—"

"We didn't do anything except fall asleep."

"It's one rule, Madison."

One ridiculous rule.

"I'm seventeen, Mom. Maybe it's time to change."

She seemed to consider it. "I'll think about it, but for now, you broke a trust—I'm not happy about that."

Her words sunk in.

Trust.

Not happy about that.

I stomped out of the kitchen.

What the frig? I stomped right back in.

"You said I broke a trust? What about you? You've done nothing but lie to me my entire life."

"That's not fair."

"Another word that you should stop using."

"Madison, enough—I'm not talking about my choices, I'm talking about yours. My rule about not going upstairs is about boundaries. Don't blow this up into something it's not."

"You're the one throwing around the 'trust' word. It makes you a hypocrite."

"What do you want from me? I can't go back and change anything. I can only deal with what's in front of me. I screwed up. I know that. I'm sorry."

"Sorry doesn't make anything better!" I left the room in a huff. She followed.

"Don't you think I know that? Paul's angry with me. You're angry with me—and for that I'm actually grateful—we both thought you were taking this too well. You have every right to be outraged."

"You're grateful that I'm angry? So now even being angry isn't my choice either, you're *allowing* me to feel this way because it's the right thing? Thanks, Mom."

"You know that's not what I meant. All I'm saying is getting angry is part of it—yell at me, don't talk to me, whatever it takes for you to get through this, so you can find your way to forgive me."

"Omigod, just cut it with the earthy-crunchy pop-yoga speak already." I opened my arms wide as I walked through her meditation space. "I could probably meditate for twenty years and still not find my way to forgive you."

I tripped over the edge of the bolster, flailing to keep upright. My fingertips grazed the statue on the mantel and I watched in horror as it slipped over the edge. I reached out to save it, but Laughing Buddha smashed to the floor into several little plaster chunks. It sobered me up from the fight. The kettle whistled from the kitchen. My mother stood still, hand over her mouth. Her eyes grew glassy. Why did I go off like that?

"I'm . . . I'm sorry," I whispered, bending down to clean up.

"Don't touch it."

"Mom."

"Just go. I'll deal with it."

She walked back into the kitchen. The kettle sputtered and went silent. I flew upstairs to my room, slamming the door behind me. I waited for my mother to storm up the stairs and yell at me for making the house rattle, but there were only the sounds of her puttering through the rooms downstairs. I guess I could have insisted on cleaning up the mess I made. Was she really that broken up over the statue?

No. Of course not, it was everything before that.

It felt good to get that off my chest, but maybe I'd been a little too dramatic about the trust thing. I knew she felt bad about everything, that if she could change things she would, but—she couldn't. The only thing we could change was right now. Put together some new version of us with Paul included—like *form ever follows function* in architecture, we'd shape a new family to suit us. And it was about time the second-floor rule was retired.

I wasn't a latchkey kid. I could handle myself. I'd be on my own in the summer program—and in a little over a year, if all went well, I'd be on my own in school.

Once she finished her tea she'd probably knock on my door—I could apologize, really tell her about the weekend—but when she came up the stairs her footsteps went past my room. The lock on her door clicked shut.

Screw it, then.

I took a scalding-hot shower and changed into a tee and PJ bottoms. While I brushed my teeth I heard a drumming noise. My phone. *Jesse.* I ran out of the bathroom and into my room, doing a quick scan to figure out where the ring was coming from, then realized it was from downstairs. I clomped down the stairs, nearly tripping again, before I realized I'd left my phone in the pocket of Jesse's leather jacket, which still hung over the railing. I grabbed the jacket, rifling through the pockets for the phone. The ping of change echoed through the hall as the contents of one of his pockets spilled onto the stairs.

"Shit."

The phone stopped ringing. I tapped in my unlock code and swiped the flashlight feature so I could pick up what had fallen out of the pocket. There was a small rectangle of gum, a few coins, a green guitar pick, and a napkin from Whiskey Business with some sort of writing on it. I gathered it up in my palm and went back to my room to sort it out and check my messages.

I sat on the bed and slid the change back into Jesse's pocket.

I unwrapped the gum and put it in my mouth—cinnamon. Ha, I'd pegged him as more of a spearmint guy, not sure why. I held the green guitar pick between my fingers. It was smooth—the word *Fender* worn off slightly in the center of it. I tucked it back into his pocket.

The Whiskey Business napkin had writing on it. There was a name—Becca—written in swirly blue lettering and a phone number underneath. I smoothed it out on my bed, just to make sure I wasn't seeing things—maybe it was just the number for the bar, maybe this was some special marketing gimmick to make it look like pen—but as I looked closer it was indeed a girl's name and number, in blue ink that had smeared. The surge of jealousy that flared in my stomach surprised me.

I scrolled through my messages. There were four from Jesse. The last one read:

Asleep?

And a voice mail to call him at any time. He'd be up for a while.

And then there was a text from . . . Zach?

Miss u babe. HB!

The date stamp was from the previous night and must have been delayed due to me being in the Middle of Nowhere,

Pennsylvania. Maybe it was a drunk text. He hadn't looked like he was going to miss me when he hopped into the car that night in Hoboken. The phone rang. *Jesse.* I let it roll over to voice mail.

You're overreacting. A number in a pocket doesn't mean anything. And look, Zach texted you. Are you going to tell Jesse that?

I said these things to myself, even understood them, but the ragged feeling ate away at me anyway. Without thinking I flattened out the napkin and called the number. After two rings, a girl's perky voice sang, "Hello?" on the other end.

What was I doing?

"Um, hello?"

I deepened my voice. "Can I speak to Jesse?"

"Who?"

"Jesse McMann?"

"Wrong number." *Click.*

I stood up and threw the phone on my bed. I didn't do jealousy. The voice on the other end took on the phantom form of some leggy, hot girl named Becca, ready to leave lipstick stains on Jesse's skin without a thought if he had anyone else.

Why did this bother me so much?

All of the things I'd done with Jesse over the past twenty-four hours came back in a rush. What I told him about Paul being my father and the way I felt about birthdays. How right it felt to kiss him in the meadow, to wake up in his arms in my room, no matter how much trouble it got me into. How could a napkin with a number just pull it out from under me?

297

I'd cracked open, let him in, and I hated how vulnerable it made me feel, that this feeling had some sort of power over me, made me do ridiculous things like call a stranger.

Maybe we can think of it as a beginning.

How could I begin anything, when I couldn't even trust—

Trust. That fucking word again.

I flopped back down on my bed, picked up my phone, and dialed.

He picked up almost immediately.

"Madison? Hey."

I needed a dose of the familiar.

"Zach . . . thanks for the birthday wishes."

I COULDN'T REMEMBER THE DRIVE HOME. ALL I
could think of was her face, the way she looked up at me,
the gentle curve of her jawline. All I could hear was that beat
from the morning when I first woke up—the one that went
through my brain when I thought about being alone with
her in the meadow. I thought about the stars, the heat of her
mouth when we kissed. Fragments coming together. And
then words . . .

You come in like a storm.

I was writing a song, without even realizing it. My fingers
burned to bring the sound to life.

When I got home, the house was quiet. My parents were
parked in front of the TV watching a movie where dragons
battled an army in the desert. I leaned over the top of the

couch to say hello, but they were both sound asleep with Ty's baby monitor on the end table next to them. I backed away quietly and went upstairs. There was a sliver of light coming from Daisy's room. I poked my head in.

"Hey, I'm home," I said.

She looked up from her book. "Yeah, so."

I laughed; her enthusiasm killed me. "Night, Daze."

I flicked on the light in my room and closed the door behind me. My acoustic sat in its stand, abandoned since Hannah-Dunk. I took off my hoodie, grabbed the guitar, and sat on the edge of my bed. All went silent in my brain. I put down the guitar. Grabbed my phone. Sent a few texts to Madison, hoping some interaction would inspire me. Nothing.

I called and left a voice mail.

She'd probably changed her mind about having tea with her mother. Her phone could be dead.

Or possibly you should calm the fuck down and stop acting like a drooling love zombie.

I picked up the Yamaha again, wishing I were one of those divinely inspired musicians who could come up with a song in an hour. The guitar had fallen out of tune. It took a few seconds to hit that sweet sound, but when it got there, I started strumming, trying to pin down the melody in my head.

Eyes alight with fire.

Another line.

I grabbed my song notebook from my desk, opened to a fresh page.

There was a knock on the door.

"Yeah."

Mom stood in the doorway, her eyes darting across the bas-relief my dirty clothes formed across the floor. "Jess—this room."

"Oh, sorry, I'll clean it. Did I wake you?"

She came in and sat on the foot of the bed. "Nah. I thought I heard Ty stirring. How did I miss you come in?"

"You guys were sleeping, I didn't want to bother you. Must have been some movie," I said.

"Your father picked that out. Anytime I get a moment to sit still, I end up falling asleep these days. Tax season, ugh. I wanted to make sure you got in okay."

"Yep, I'm in."

She nodded, looked around the room again. "So . . . are you going to tell me how the weekend went? Or am I just going to have to get the skinny from Aunt Julia?"

I laughed and strummed.

"Like you haven't already."

"You know me, yes, we talked, but it's only because you're so tight-lipped."

"Madison liked it, a lot."

"And I heard you guys took a little moonlight stroll."

Aunt Julia. *Nothing was sacred.*

"See, I don't need to tell you anything. Did Aunt Julia say anything else?"

"Only that it was nice to see you happy. She thought you

and Madison made a very cute couple."

"We're not a couple, yet," I said, not even sure what I meant. I knew that I needed to take things at a glacial pace, but my heart had other ideas.

She saw my notebook and smiled. "Writing again too, I see."

"Trying to."

"It'll come. Don't try so hard, sometimes the best stuff pops up when you're unfocused." She stood up.

Musical wisdom was usually Dad's forte—hearing this from her made me think of what Declan said that night at Whiskey Business.

"Mom."

"Yeah." She paused at the door. I tried to picture her as that long-haired girl from the photo in Deck's office. My mother, so straight-laced and organized, who could spend hours poring over tax returns and find it a challenge, didn't exactly strike me as a singer, backup or otherwise.

"Why didn't you ever tell me you sang with Dad's band?"

She laughed, leaned against the doorjamb. "Who told you that?"

"Declan. The picture in his office."

"That's another life, Jesse. Wow. God, Deck used to play some real awful places, and whenever my friends weren't around, I'd sing backup to avoid getting hit on."

"And you never thought to do it more?"

"I could carry a tune, but it really wasn't my thing. Declan's the one who wanted me to take it more seriously, there were some clubs he wanted to play where it was a plus to have a girl in the band. I went to one of his voice lessons with him—the one we were talking about with the voice coach who said, 'If you're gonna blow it, blow it big'—and I couldn't stop laughing. Kind of pissed him off—so that was my short-lived singing career."

"Was Dad there too?"

Mom looked up, chewed the side of her lip before speaking. "I knew Declan before your father, Jess. Backtalk was together for a year before your father joined."

I'd only assumed in the band stories that my father told that Mom was always—well, I knew that's how they met but . . . the picture from Declan's office came to my mind.

Holy effing shit.

"Mom, what are you saying?"

She actually giggled and waved her hand at me.

"I can be tight-lipped too, Jess. Good night. Keep it down. And make sure you pick up this room at some point this week."

"Good night, Mom."

I strummed the guitar again, playing around, letting the words collide in my brain. I picked up the pen and scribbled a few more lines.

Then it hit me.

Dad was freakin' Duncan.

"Must have been one helluva weekend if you were inspired to write a song, but I don't see how we can make it sound good by Saturday, especially if you're still working on the lyrics." Tanner plucked at his bass. We'd been practicing for just about an hour at Lot 23 and still couldn't get the song to gel the way I wanted it to.

"John Lennon wrote 'Across the Universe' in a night," Grayson said.

"Dude, thanks, but I'm not John Lennon."

"Just saying, it's not impossible."

"And I'm saying it is impossible, if we want to win the battle. And I don't want to just win, I want to crush Kenny," Tanner said, playing the bass line to Pink Floyd's "Money" and grinning.

I wanted to win the battle and crush Kenny too, and an original song would give us an edge. There was more to it, of course. Whether I'd admit it to the guys or not, the song was for Madison. The few words I had seemed so ordinary and disconnected that I was close to scrapping the whole thing. *You come in like a storm. . . .* What did that even mean?

"We know Plasma is going to do an original, so—"

"Don't bring that up. You're the one who gave our song to Duncan, Jess," Tanner said.

"And I'm trying to make up for it with something better. Just take it from the bridge." We started again, but it sounded pretty much like three dudes making noise. Gray went off a bit on the drums and stopped. What had sounded amazing in my head and on my acoustic was not translating. It was so damn frustrating.

"Sorry, start again," he said.

"No, you guys are right. Let's just run through the set we did at Whiskey, and I'll work on the song later. Maybe if it comes down to it, I can just do it solo on the acoustic for the battle and we can have it finished for when we play out again in May."

"We can't win if you do the song on your own," Tanner said.

I thought for a minute he might be screwing around, but his face was serious.

"What?" I asked.

"It's in the rules. Every person in the band needs to play or you're disqualified. Unless you're a solo act, of course, and you're not, so, we all need to play if we want to win."

"That's a stupid rule."

"Yeah, well, Kenny's neighbor probably made it up."

I didn't like giving in so easily, but I let it go for the moment. We concentrated on playing the set we'd done at Whiskey Business once through. We'd really gotten it down—so comfortable we were able to riff off one another. It felt good to get lost in the music, to not think about life outside the rehearsal space for a little while, because no matter how incredible the weekend had been something didn't feel right.

Madison had not returned my calls—even though I told her she could call at any time. I'd texted again before school—to make sure things were cool with her mom—and she just texted:

yes.

That's it.

Not: Yes, stud.

Or: Yes, amazing rock god who inspires me to draw pictures.

There weren't even any silly emojis.

She didn't owe me any sort of explanation, but she'd said she didn't want the weekend to end, didn't she? That seemed pretty straightforward. Enthusiastic. My mind flipped through the entire weekend, the tour of the house, sitting by the fire, the ride home, everything had been perfect. A glimpse of what we could be. Or at least it felt that way to me. What if things had been too perfect, like we'd created some small space in time that was ours only, and now, back in reality, it couldn't stand up? Maybe I wanted too much at once. Maybe I was freaking her the fuck out with overtexting.

"Again?" Tanner asked when we finished the set.

"Nah, have to meet up with Wren, practice tomorrow, right?" Gray said.

"Tomorrow."

We loaded up the equipment in our cars and headed out. Tanner and I grabbed a quick bite at Burger King before I drove him home. I knew better than to allow T in my car with food. He spread out in the front seat, reclining it a bit, leaning back with his hands clasped behind his head.

"So, are you and Madison, like, a thing now?"

I shrugged.

"Because I know the *real* real reason you want to do that song."

"Tanner, don't start." I turned onto Avenue C.

"Jess, we're finally at a place where we're decent again, probably better than that, I don't want to see you get all wrapped up and moody over a girl. Been there, done that, running out of vodka. She's great and all— so are her friends—but I dunno, you don't have to let it get to you."

"What are you talking about?"

"When you do something, you do it a hundred and ten percent, and I think maybe it's the band's turn to get that. Be with her, have fun, but dude, don't, like, cut her name into your arm or anything. I'm not up for the fallout."

"There won't be any fallout, T. I know how to keep it light."

"Yeah, right. 'Cause writing a song for someone is light."

I couldn't argue with him about that.

"Hey, so what do you think about Jasmine?" T asked.

"What about her?"

"We hit it off that night at the bar. She's cute. Funny. Obviously has a hidden wild side. Wren mentioned she was into movies, so I thought, maybe we could, you know, all go out or something. After we crush the competition; we need to keep focus, of course."

I laughed. "But wait, Tanner, what about giving a hundred and ten percent to the band?"

"Dude, please. I can always spare at least forty percent for the chicks. I know how to multitask."

"Wow, you're a true ladies' man," I said as we pulled up to his house. He got out and shifted the seat to grab his bass from the back.

"Welp, you're the songwriter, Romeo."

That remained to be seen.

TWENTY-ONE

RED BULL AND CHIPS AHOY! WERE NOT CUTTING
it in yearbook today. My mood was a complete flatline. I sat,
head down, waiting for Piper to hand over our next assignments while random thoughts scrambled around my brain.

It was Wednesday and my mother and I were still not on
pleasant speaking terms. I wasn't sure if she was just giving
me space, letting me find my own path to forgiveness, or if
that Buddha statue had secretly been something she'd wanted
to bring on *Antiques Roadshow* and she was heartbroken it was
now in smithereens in our garbage can. We spoke, but it was
day-to-day details. We hadn't even dished about my weekend.

And then, Jesse.

My feelings for him were too raw, new. I hated the way I'd
acted about that stupid napkin. Yellow #5 had been on fire
at Whiskey Business—why wouldn't he get some attention?

Getting so close to him, in such a short time, was scary. Pushing him away was much easier. Now I was in control. Only it didn't make me feel any better.

"Sadie Hawkins girls, can I talk to you for a minute?" Piper had her serious editor in chief face on. I glanced at Wren and Jazz, who both threw me perplexed looks. We got up and walked to Piper's desk. She motioned for us to come around to her side to look at something on her computer screen.

The Sadie Hawkins layout was pulled up on her laptop. I managed a smile. Out of everything I'd done for the yearbook so far, this made me most proud.

"So no final tweaks or changes? We can put this to bed?"

The three of us looked at each other and nodded at Piper. "Excellent. There's something else I'd like to tell you. It's not completely official—well, not until the end of the term—but I wanted to let you know I'm recc'ing you three for editorial positions next year. This doesn't mean you can slack or anything. I'm telling you as incentive to keep up the good work."

"Well where's the fun in that?" I asked. "Aren't there any perks?"

"You'll find there are a lot of people who suddenly want to be your friend—not that I take advantage or anything." Piper grinned. "I'll have more assignments next meeting. You're finished today if you'd like to leave early."

That was perk enough for me at the moment. We collected our things and walked out to the locker bay.

"I'm already thinking about all the ways I can make Ava

Taylor suck up to me," Wren said, grin so wide it made my cheeks hurt just looking at her.

"We don't have the job yet," Jazz said.

"Don't be a buzzkill. We should celebrate—how about an after-meeting chai or something."

"Can't today—I'm meeting Logan for a run."

"Really? So this friend thing with Logan is really working out," I said.

"Yeah, weird, huh? It's like, after we hooked up, we realized we're better as friends."

"Can't kiss to save his life?" I closed my locker and put on my jacket.

"Mads."

Jasmine laughed. "Nah, he knows what he's doing."

"You can really just be friends even after you swapped spit?" Wren asked.

"It's weird, I guess, but I'm trying to take a play out of the Madison Pryce handbook."

"I have a handbook? News to me. You should loan it to me sometime."

"You know what I mean—I've always liked the way you can be cool, not let the physical stuff mess with your head. Logan's been a great running partner. Keeps me on pace, challenges me on the trail. Kind of better than a boyfriend right now. Beats always running with my dad, too."

"I'm impressed." I was flattered she looked at me as a sort of relationship guru, but that was far from the truth at the moment. Everything about Jesse messed with my head. I envied her blind enthusiasm.

"I'm just, you know, experimenting. We'll see. Hey, I switched my schedule this week at my mother's office, so I can go to yoga—why don't we just have our celebratory chais after class then?"

"Do you mind?" I asked Wren.

"No, sounds perfect."

"Great, see you later," Jazz said, trotting up the stairs, gym bag in tow.

Wren stuffed the rest of her books into her messenger bag and twisted the combination dial on her locker.

"Ready to slum it on the bus?" she asked. Now that Yellow #5 was practicing every day, she was back to being rideless after school, at least until after the Battle of the Bands was over.

"Lead the way."

We climbed the stairs from the locker dungeon and went out through the side doors. Spring was on its way to being sprung—new buds forming on the trees that lined the drive-way of Sacred Heart—but there was still a bite in the air. I pulled up my collar, wishing I'd worn Jesse's jacket instead. After finding that number in the pocket, I couldn't bring myself to touch it, let alone put it on. It was still in a heap on my bedroom floor. No handbook page for that one.

"So does Jesse think they have a chance on Friday?" Wren asked.

"Haven't talked to him since the weekend."

"Why? I thought you said you had a great time."

"I did, it was, like, best-time-of-my-life good, but . . . there's something I didn't tell you. Something I feel supremely stupid about."

We walked a few feet in silence. I'd told both Wren and Jazz about how great the weekend had been, and about the weirdness with my mother, but I left out the napkin, and what I did when I found it. I'd been burning to spill my idiocy to someone, but I still felt, well, idiotic about it.

"And?"

"I called Zach."

Wren stopped in the middle of the sidewalk. "What?"

"He texted me happy birthday, and I called him."

"Why would you do that?"

"Self-sabotage?"

"I don't get it, you said you had such a great time."

I looped my arm through hers and leaned closer to her as we walked toward the bus stop. "I found a girl's phone number in his jacket pocket. On a napkin from Whiskey Business. And . . . I called it."

"Madison Pryce. You're jealous?"

"Shh," I hissed, looking around as if someone really cared about what we were saying. "I think I am, was, anyway—wouldn't you be?"

Her face scrunched in thought. "If the number was still in his pocket, what are the odds he even used it?"

I hadn't thought of that.

"What happened when you dialed the number?"

"Nothing, the girl on the other end didn't sound like she even knew his name."

"So, that's why you called Zach?"

"I'm not sure why I called Zach. It wasn't like one of our, you know, sexytimes calls. We talked. It was friendly. Normal. He's already with that sophomore from the Sadie Hawkins Dance that was drooling all over him. And the thing is—that didn't even bother me. Why would a napkin with a phone number drive me to such batshittery but I was all, like, 'Hey, that's great, you make a nice couple,' when Zach told me about that girl?"

Wren smirked.

"What?"

"You really don't see it?"

Of course I saw it, but I didn't get it. At all. We crossed the street with arms still looped.

"Zach's hot and fun, but you guys never had that *thing*."

"What thing?"

"That thing where you hang on to the other person's every word because everything they say is one more piece of their puzzle. Zach's puzzle wasn't that complicated. I think that's why it was easy for you to keep your distance. Deep down you craved a bit more than that—even though you pretend you don't."

"How do you know that?"

"Because you're a pretty complicated puzzle yourself. Like attracts like. The secret of attraction."

"I'm not sure I can handle all this angst. What would you do if you found a girl's number in Grayson's pocket?"

"I trust him, maybe it seems naive, but I do. He loves being in this band—and I know he'll probably get his share of numbers, but at the end of the night, he's with me. And when he's with me, he's completely with me. So I don't think of all the other stuff. That may be a direct quote from the Madison Pryce handbook. You should take your own advice. The guy is smitten, Mads, so what if a girl gave him her number? Fuck jealousy. It's a waste of time."

"So is 'fuck jealousy' from the Wren Caswell handbook?"

She laughed. "Sure. Let's make T-shirts."

When I got home, I took out my leather portfolio and laid out all the pieces that I wanted to include in it. The sketch of my floor plans for an extension on our house. The logo for Yellow #5. My prize photo of the Ferris wheel from the fall. The *choice* photo from the Sadie Hawkins Dance. There was a pastel landscape from art class, and I'd taken a photo of my Popsicle stick version of the Hearst building to showcase my model-making skills.

Then there was the sketch of Jesse—I wasn't sure if I wanted to include it. Was it too personal? I guess that was what art was all about. Getting your heart and soul on the page for all to see. I'd always had such trouble drawing Zach's face right—was it because I really hadn't seen him? Wasn't interested in his puzzle enough, like Wren had said? I let my eyes go unfocused as I stared at my work, dreaming up the order that I'd put them in for the most impact, wondering what pieces were strong enough to include. The process made me so unsure, but it thrilled me too.

When I thought I knew where to start, I opened the portfolio. The Pratt application fell out. I picked it up and read over the first page, which was just a form for basic information: name, address, emergency contact. I let my focus blur, the lines becoming swirls on a white background, and dreamed of what it would be like to go there over the summer.

Was I ready for Pratt? Is that what I really wanted?

I knew that's where I wanted to go after high school.

Wouldn't it be better to do something different before then?

I did have a choice. I could delay going to Pratt—go somewhere and gain some experience and build up my portfolio. Sure, NJDI was smaller, but so were the classes. And if I was being upfront with myself—earning my own way would mean more to me than someone swooping in to pay all my bills. Maybe it would be a mistake to turn down the money, but it would be my mistake.

There was a knock on the front door, then the click of a turning lock.

"Hello?" Paul.

"Hey, I'm in here. Why are you knocking?"

He stepped inside, closing the door behind him.

"Didn't want to barge in."

"It's not barging if you live here," I said, continuing with my project. He lingered in the entryway, silent for a moment.

"Well, uh . . . I actually found another place to stay."

I looked up. He still had his jacket on.

"Oh. When?" I asked, chewing on my thumbnail.

"Today. I just thought it might make things less confusing."

Less confusing for who? I wanted to ask, but held back, forcing myself to look at my work again. My concentration was blown. Paul walked over and surveyed the table.

"Feel like going for a ride?"

"I'm sort of in the middle of this."

"It won't take long. There's something I want to show you."

"Um . . . yeah, sure." I grabbed my jacket, turned off the lights, and followed him out to his car.

Our first stop was the bakery—the one with the good doughnuts. Five minutes later he returned with the telltale grease-stained white bag and drove to the park, down to the bottom by the bay. I got out of the car, bracing myself against the wind coming off the water. It felt good to be outside. Like everything that had been bothering me would expand to fill the space. What could he possibly want to show me here? I'd thought we would probably end up walking on the path by the water, but instead Paul sat on the hood of the car, fished out a doughnut, and took a bite. I leaned next to him. He held out the bag to me.

"Can I call this dinner?"

"Wouldn't be the first time I did that." He laughed.

We sat and ate as a tugboat sliced through the bay. He put the bag on the hood of the car and swiped his hands clean.

"When I was a kid, and everyone was over there playing soccer or flag football," he said, motioning to the sports fields behind us, "I'd be over here watching those planes take off and land from Newark airport. Watch, that one is going to turn, that's heading to Florida." He pointed to the sky, my eyes followed.

"Lucky."

"And that one?" he said, pointing to a plane that was headed out over the Manhattan skyline. "That one's going to France."

"How do you know?"

"Can see the Air France logo."

I laughed, took another bite. "Is this what you wanted to show me?"

"Seems like the kind of thing a father would tell his kid."

I got the sense that Paul was trying to have a moment with me, something significant, parental. Had he been coerced?

"Did my mother put you up to this?"

He turned sharply to me. "No. I know it's her late night; I was coming over to make dinner anyway, thought you might want some company."

"I've survived her late nights on my own for a long time."

"Sorry about that." He rustled open the bag and reached in for another doughnut. Multicolored sprinkles. He offered me the bag. I shook my head.

"You don't need to apologize. I don't need you to rescue me. I'm fine on my own."

"Rescue? The last thing you or your mother needs is rescuing. I just thought it would be nice to spend some time together."

I shifted away from him, kicked a phantom rock with my foot.

"If you wanted to spend time with me, why did you find another place to stay?"

He picked at the sprinkles on the doughnut before tossing it in a nearby trash bin. It hit the rim before falling in. He looked at me.

"Mads, I've changed my mind about the summer. I've got a job offer in San Francisco. I'm going to take it."

I repeated his words in my head before asking the obvious.

"Does Mom know?"

"Yes."

"So again, I'm the last to hear about something."

"It's not like that—"

"Then what's it like?"

He sighed, jamming his hands in his pockets and stepping away from the car. "I don't know how to do this. The father thing."

"You haven't even tried." My voice caught in my throat. The anger behind the words startled me. I think it startled him, too.

"Before . . . when you asked me why I knocked?"

"Yeah?"

"I know how to be that casual guy, the one who shows up and surprises my friend and her daughter with great meals, and gets to hang out and tell stories and come and go as he pleases. And for a little while I can pretend that there are actually people who look forward to being with me, people who matter."

"We do look forward to being with you. You do matter. Why leave now that you know you're part of the family?"

"That's just it. Now that I'm supposed to belong there, I don't feel like I do. You and your mother are this unit. You're a family already and I'm—"

"My father."

"But what is that, anyway? I haven't earned it."

I didn't know what to say to that, maybe because it was the truth.

"I'm not sure I can ever forgive her for something this huge," I said. "I don't get why she didn't tell us sooner."

I zipped my jacket up to my chin, crossed my arms. It was getting a bit much having a heart-to-heart outside. I wanted to be home, putting my portfolio together. This father thing wasn't something that could be sorted out in a night over a couple of doughnuts.

"I was really angry at your mother, Madison. You're right, it's a huge thing to keep from us, but after a while, when I stopped being so pissed off about it, I realized something. She's not vindictive. I have to believe it was hard for her, too.

She didn't tell us because she genuinely thought it was the right thing. And the more I thought about it, remembered what I was like back then, I think she was right."

"How can you say that?"

"Hard to admit, but . . . I didn't want a family. I wanted to live overseas, fly jets in Europe, be unattached. I'd like to think if I'd known, I would have done right by the both of you, but I can't be sure of that answer."

"But don't you . . . You love her, right? That's what she said to me, that you loved each other." I felt my birthday wish slipping through my fingers.

He looked straight up to the sky. A beat passed before he answered. "I'd always sort of hoped if I ended up with anyone, it would be her. And you. Maybe somehow, I knew all along. Remember that time in San Francisco? When we had dinner at the Italian place that served you wine and your mother took it away and I let you sneak a sip?"

He remembered that too?

"Yes."

"When I paid the check the owner told me I had a beautiful wife and daughter. You both had already gone outside. I was about to correct him, but I couldn't. I just thanked him and we left, and it felt nice. I'm thinking maybe that's why I want to go back, to be in the place where I felt the best about it."

"That was a great trip."

"I'm going to treat this job as a trial—maybe I'll hate flying tourists around and pointing out the sights. Maybe I'll love it. It's a huge change, but I'm ready for something on my own terms. I can keep my feet on the ground, stay in one place for a while."

"But, if you want to stay in one place, why can't it be here?"

He shifted, leaning back against the hood. "I think this is a lot to take in—becoming an instant family, something maybe we need a little time and space to get used to. I'm not saying it's going to be perfect, or that you won't get angry about it all over again, but we know the truth now. And that's all that really matters, isn't it?"

"I guess."

"C'mon, I promised your mother I'd make her penne and vodka sauce tonight. We can keep our dinner a secret."

I laughed. "Sure."

Back at the house, while Paul whipped up a meal for my mother, I pored over my work again, thinking about what he said—that we needed a little time and space to get used to the idea of us, as a family. I wasn't sure if I believed it—that space was the answer—but what choice did I have? I guessed it was a start.

There was a quote I remembered from my essay on Frank Lloyd Wright: *Space is the breath of art.* I thought I understood it—the space thing—that it could be light or dark, positive or negative. It was part of a work, though. Essential. Maybe space would help us shed a little light on what was important to us, too.

Paul poked his head into the dining room. "You sure you don't want any of this?"

"No, I'm good. Are you guys eating in here? Give me a minute to put this away."

"We can eat in the kitchen when your mom gets home. Hey, how's the application for Pratt coming along? Did you send it in yet?"

"I'm rethinking Pratt for the summer."

He leaned against the doorway, and folded his arms. "Rethinking?"

"Yeah, I'm not sure I want to be there yet, I think I'd like a little more experience first. I'm going to try for that scholarship to the Design Institute, like I planned. I mean, that's okay, right? I appreciate your offer—the money—but could I put that toward—"

"It's there for when you need it, Mads."

"Thanks."

I continued packing up my work. The sketch of Jesse was on the end of the table. I picked it up to put it away, taking a moment to look it over. My heart warmed. Had I let enough space come between us? Why was I so afraid of opening up to him? Was it really easier to push him away? All at once I wanted to see him, to apologize for being so weird. I slipped the sketch into my portfolio and ran upstairs to grab Jesse's jacket.

"Paul, I'm headed out for a while, I've got my phone," I said, thundering down the stairs. I didn't wait to hear his reply.

TWENTY-TWO

JESSE

MUGSHOT WAS SLOW ON WEDNESDAY NIGHTS. There was a study group in the one corner commandeering the crushed-velvet chairs, and a couple sitting close to the window, holding hands, in their own world. I was alone and kept looking at the clock. There was less than an hour to go and I could shut down. I'd already cleaned a few of the pitchers, and restocked the paper products. I didn't mind not being busy because it gave me more time to focus on my song.

I stood at the counter, bent over my notebook, frustrated at the scribbles on the pad. I'd been trying to figure out a way to describe her eyes in the song, but yeah, that wasn't happening. And it was too cheesy. Madison would not like cheesy and this was for her, even though I couldn't tell her that. Learned my lesson at the Whiskey. But she'd know. Although at this point

I wasn't sure if she was going to the battle. I wasn't sure where we stood at all.

A shadow passed across the counter and I looked up. I'd been so involved in the song that I hadn't noticed someone come in.

"Hannah." I glanced behind her, at the door, waiting for Duncan to appear, but there was no one. She smiled.

"Hey, Jess," she said. Her hair was in a braid to the side, her volleyball warm-up jacket zipped to her chin.

"What's up?"

She leaned on the counter, looking into the bakery case. There was next to nothing left—mostly crumbs. Her eyes found my notebook and she glanced across the page. I closed it fast, then tucked it on the shelf below the register.

"Hmm, new song?"

"What are you, a spy for the enemy?" I kidded.

"Pfft, as if," she said. "Are you working on something new, though?"

"Maybe," I offered. "Where's Duncan?"

"Where do you think? Where he's been for the past three months—rehearsing."

"Decided to sit this one out?"

"I can only take so much," she said, "and Lot Twenty-Three smells like feet."

I laughed. "Are you sure that's not just Kenny's band you're smelling—*oh!*"

"That was bad."

"Yes, but it had to be said. What can I get you?"

"I'm in the mood for one of your peppermint mochas."

"Sure." I grabbed a to-go cup and attempted to do the Tanner flip-thing that he'd perfected.

"That's to stay," she said.

The cup fell just out of my grasp and bounced onto the floor.

"Oh, really?"

"Yeah, thought I could sit with you till closing. Do you think . . . maybe you could give me a ride home?"

"Er, sure, why not?"

"Great," she said, smiling. "Hey, I like your hair. What made you do that?"

"A friend suggested it," I said as she took a seat at the table I used to consider her "usual." I got to work on her mocha.

When we were together, Hannah closed with me a lot. She'd sit with a book or work behind the counter with me, pouring coffee or filling baked-goods orders. The last time she'd helped me we stayed a half hour after closing and messed around in Grace's office. It was a memory I'd put out of my mind until this moment. She kept looking at me. I concentrated on the drink. Maybe she just wanted to be friends. Could I do that?

I didn't get that jangled-nerve feeling—the one that felt like every moment I looked at her, it physically hurt. It helped that Duncan wasn't with her, but even thinking of him, or the two of them together, didn't jab me the same way it used to. I brought her drink to her table.

"Aren't you going to sit down?"

"Working."

She looked around. "Oh, yeah, you're swamped. C'mon. Sit a minute."

She pushed out the chair across from her with her foot.

"Now I know you must be doing some recon for the enemy," I said, sitting down.

"No, but if you want to ask me anything I can tell you." She wiggled her eyebrows and took a sip of her mocha. "Perfect, as always."

"Are they doing the original song?"

"Yes, but it's not as good as they want it to be. Kenny's sort of a . . ."

". . . tyrant," I finished.

"Yeah, that. They've been practicing every day. If I tell you something, you have to swear to keep your mouth shut," she said.

"Who would I say anything to?"

"I mean it, Jess. Just swear on the VW, or your Fender or something."

"I swear on the Beetle, what gives?"

"They were there at Whiskey Business and got totally psyched out by Yellow Number Five. Duncan couldn't believe

327

how great the guy you replaced him with played."

"Really," I said, trying not to show her how good that made me feel. "I didn't see them."

"They didn't stay long, but they stayed long enough. Guess it's going really well with the new guy. Duncan misses you and Tanner; he doesn't get along so great with Kenny."

Considering the past few times Hannah and I spoke she was trying to subtly wheedle the song from me, I suddenly had the feeling that she wasn't there for a friendly visit—she wanted something. Or wanted something for Duncan.

"Look, the band broke up, and Grayson is a good fit, so if you're here to see if Duncan can get back in—"

"I'm not here for Duncan, Jesse."

"Then what are you here for?" I asked, getting up.

"I'm here for you."

The words made me pause; a jolt crackled through me when she looked my way, her eyes friendly, warm . . . familiar.

"Don't say that," I said. One of the guys from the study group came up for a refill. I walked to the counter to help him, letting her words and her eyes do their number on me.

"We'll only be about another twenty minutes," the guy said.

"No worries," I said, filling his cup with the last of our house blend.

When I turned back, Hannah was sipping her drink, as

if she hadn't just dropped a bomb of epic proportions. Maybe her being with Duncan didn't bother me, but I still felt *something* for her. I'd be lying if I said it didn't feel good to hear she was there for me.

We had a history. A mostly nice one. One that I'd counted on until HannahDunk screwed me, or I screwed them, or however it all went down. I was done analyzing. I was done, period. I was still in that zone, though: the no-longer-boyfriend, but-not-ready-to-be-friends zone. I wasn't sure we could ever be friends—maybe friend*ly*, like bumping into each other on the street or in the Stop N' Shop one random night years from now, like in a country song or something.

The couple at the window left, and Hannah shot up to clean off their table. I grabbed the counter mop and followed her.

"Hannah, you don't—"

"I want to, Jesse, come on, you can get out of here quicker," she said, handing me the dollar the couple had left as a tip and grabbing their mugs. I wiped down the table as she took the cups into the back. When I turned around she had the box of raw sugar packets and began restocking the self-service stand.

"This is what you're really here for, restocking," I said. She always said it cleared her mind to refill the self-service stand, like putting each thing in its place gave her a sense of order and calm. It was one of the jobs I hated the most, so I never minded. She tossed a raw sugar packet my way and grinned.

I reached below and handed her the box of stirrers.

"I guess, while you're at it," I said, handing them to her.

"You're right, I like doing this," she said. She looked at my wrist. "You're not wearing your infinity bracelet—band—anymore."

"Why would I be?"

She lifted up her forearm and pulled back her sleeve. The infinity symbol glinted in the light. My stomach dropped.

"I noticed you were wearing yours the last time I came in."

"Does Duncan know you're here?"

"I'm not sure Duncan even knows when I'm in the room," she said, patting down the sugar packets into their compartment.

I turned away, heading into the back room to set up the dishwasher. Whether she was doing this to mess with my head or not, I wasn't sure. It wasn't like her to flirt *just because*. Maybe she wasn't doing it purposely but I refused to let it get to me.

I thought about Madison. How different it felt to be with her. Everything was up in the air, and unexpected, and I wasn't ready to let that go. Even if I had no idea where I stood with her.

By the time I returned out front, the study group in the corner was finally calling it quits. The guy who'd come over for the coffee brought some of the cups to the counter for me, and shoved a five into the tip jar.

"Thanks, man." I followed them to the door. It was five

minutes to nine, but I locked the door as they walked out and turned the slate that hung on the door to CLOSED.

Hannah was busy collecting the rest of the dishes from the study table.

"Duncan's not ignoring you. This battle thing, getting ready for it is pretty intense," I said, grabbing a bin to put the dishes in. "I'm sure he knows you're in the room."

"Did you?"

"What are you doing?"

"I'm just," she said, putting the cups into the bin. "I don't know. I miss you, Jesse. Our talks. Duncan doesn't—"

"I don't want to hear it. Please. I can't talk about him, about you together, what don't you get? You broke up with *me*."

"I'm thinking that might have been a mistake."

A knocking sound got both of our attention.

"We're closed," I said, keeping my eyes on Hannah. They knocked again.

Grace would have flipped out if she heard me talk to a potential customer like that, so I took a deep breath and walked toward the door. I saw her hair first, the light blond tufts falling every which way. I quickened my pace, undid the lock, and pushed open the door.

Madison scampered in, chilly air following her. No dark-lined eyes, hair swept back with a headband. She was wearing my jacket, her fingertips hanging out the bottom of the sleeves, making her look so tiny.

"What's wrong?" I asked.

She shook her head, stamped her feet for warmth.

"I, uh," she began, then looked past me.

"Hi," Hannah said over my shoulder. I stepped aside.

"Madison, this is Hannah," I said. Madison's eyes widened slightly when she recognized the name.

"Hannah, Madison. She's the one who, um, made my hair this color," I said, pointing to my head. *Fucking brilliant, Jesse.*

She smiled at Madison, then looked at me as if she expected me to say something more. I'd seen the recognition in her eyes when she noticed my jacket. *Did it bother her?* The three of us stood there as the world turned s-l-o-w-l-y. There was no reason for me to feel awkward, but I did.

"What, um, what brings you in?" The words were out of my mouth before I realized how idiotic they sounded. I didn't care what brought her in—she was there, in front of me. All I wanted was for her to stay.

"I wanted to see you, that's all. You seem like you're in the middle of something." She shuffled back and forth, looking between Hannah and me.

"No, just cleaning up," I said. "Do you want something? You look freezing. Here, please, sit down." I pulled out a chair, and reached out a hand to her. She hesitated a moment, but then relented.

"I can make you something if you want. Hot chocolate? Chai?"

"No, everything's clean, you're closing," she said.

"It's not a problem."

"Maybe a hot tea," she said.

"I'll get it," Hannah said.

"I'm going to clean that table, and close down, and then we can do whatever you want, okay?" I was talking to her like she was a three-year-old, but I couldn't help it. She'd come there to see me. I didn't want her to leave, or change her mind. She nodded.

I raced over to the table and tossed the rest of the dishes into the bin and then ran back to fill the dishwasher. On the way I collected Hannah's half-finished mocha cup and glanced over my shoulder. Hannah had brought Madison a cup of tea and sat down with her. The sight of the two of them together was surreal.

I finished up with the dishes quickly, turned on the washer for a ten-minute power-wash, and went out to turn off the neon MUGSHOT sign with a *click*. The girls sat in silence.

"So, um, do you want to hang out?" I asked. Madison shrugged.

"I was going to give Hannah a ride home, we can do whatever after."

Hannah stood up. "You know, I can walk, it's fine."

"No, it's pretty cold out. You should take the ride," Madison answered, sipping her tea.

"Let me get my jacket."

I walked to the back, grabbed my stuff, and made sure everything was set for closing. The last thing I needed to do was set the alarm code for the door. I punched in the numbers and the three of us walked toward the VW. As we reached the car, Madison stepped forward so she could hop into the backseat. I wanted to say something, but what? *Get up front?* Hannah didn't do anything to change the situation, either.

By the time we reached Hannah's, we'd managed to make some small talk about the Battle of the Bands. I put the car in park and waited.

Hannah turned in her seat toward the back. "Nice to meet you, Madison."

"Yes, nice meeting you too."

Hannah leaned closer to me. "Bye, Jess, see you at the battle."

She kissed me on the cheek, paused a minute, and whispered, "Bye" again before getting out of the car. We waited until she was on the porch and in the house. Madison remained in her seat.

"Why don't you sit up here?"

"Do you want me to?" she asked.

"Do you have to ask?"

"So, that was Hannah. *Hannah*-Hannah."

"Yes."

She climbed over the console.

"Hold this." She handed me the tea so she could flop down

properly into the seat. Once she was buckled in, she took the cup.

"She just, I don't know, stopped by to say hello." I shifted gears and puttered off down the street. It felt weird to drive by my house without stopping.

"I don't think she was there to say hello," she said.

"Where do you want to go?" I asked.

"Home," she said.

"Sure?"

"It felt like I was interrupting something."

"You interrupted me cleaning up."

"She's pretty, Jesse."

We stopped at a light. The car stalled as I tried to shift into first when the signal turned green. Complete brain fart. It rolled a bit until I gained control, and sputtered to life. I cracked my neck, trying to shake off the direction Madison was leading the conversation toward. Neither of us said another word until we reached her house. I parked in front of her driveway and turned off the engine.

"Tha—"

"You came to see me tonight. Why?" I asked.

She blinked, then pointed to her tea.

I grumbled. "You're lying."

"Jesse."

"Why are you acting like everything's okay? If something's bothering you, just talk to me. I called you twice, texted you, what, maybe a hundred times—"

"Don't exaggerate," she said.

"*You* came looking for *me*."

She pressed her lips together and turned her face away. Were we fighting? Why? I didn't want to argue with her. I wanted to make her laugh, kiss her; what could have happened to make her change in three days?

"It made my night," I added.

The side of her mouth rose slightly, but then she was all business. "I don't know, I just—I know I haven't—well, you called, and I didn't call you back. I'm sorry about that. I'm in a weird place right now, Jess. I had a huge blowout with my mom after you left last Sunday. And Paul is leaving, taking a job out in California, and I wanted something to be normal, for us to be okay, but I really don't know if I can do this."

"What do you mean?"

"I mean, get attached to someone who's obviously confused."

"I'm—me? You think I'm confused?"

"I know you said you were over Hannah, but—"

"I had no idea she was coming to the shop tonight. I don't know what she was doing there."

"It was pretty obvious." She took a sip of tea, then put the cup in her lap, tracing the rim with her thumb. "She kissed you before she got out of the car—you don't do that if you don't care."

"Madison." I reached over, took the cup out of her hand,

and placed it in the holder. She looked at me. I traced the outline of her face, the way I had in her room, and touched my mouth to hers. She was rigid at first, but then she softened, lips parting so her tongue could meet mine. I wanted the kiss to say all the things I couldn't put into words. To erase anything that she thought she saw at Mugshot. Her kisses got stronger, more insistent, her fingers in my hair, on my shoulders. She pushed me back.

"Hey." I laughed.

She kept her eyes on me and slipped out of her jacket—my jacket—and tossed it over the seat, then climbed over the console and straddled me.

"Doesn't this go back?" She reached along the seat to the handle and gave it a pull. With our weight, the seat reclined almost horizontally in one swift motion. She unzipped my hoodie, then put her elbows on either side of me, pressing against me while she did that thing with her tongue—tracing my mouth—which was so brain-frying-hot I could barely move.

It felt so amazing, having her there on top of me, that rational thought disappeared. Mugshot, Hannah, Battle of the Bands, all evaporated with the heat of her mouth as we kissed. My hands found her hips, the fabric of her yoga pants so thin, her body so warm. She rocked back and forth, gently pushing against me. A million different nerve endings exploded inside of me, but something was off.

I turned my face to the side.

"Hey," I whispered.

"What?" She kissed my cheek, my jaw, her tongue trailed along my neck, stopping below my ear. I opened my mouth to speak, but forgot what I was going to say, closing my eyes as she nipped my earlobe. She unbuttoned my jeans, her fingers slipping under the band of my boxers. She nuzzled my nose with hers, kissing me again.

"Madison," I said between kisses. I caught her wrist before she could take it any further.

"Don't you want this?"

"Yes, I do, but not in my car, in front of your house."

"C'mon, the thrill of getting caught is hot," she said, kissing me again.

I gently shifted her away. "You seem pissed off."

"Why would you say that?"

"Are you?"

"Now I am," she growled, pushing herself off me and sliding clumsily back into the passenger seat. I adjusted the seat upright. My heart thrummed in my ears. I ran a hand through my hair, forcing my breathing to return to normal.

"Maybe you can't do this because you still have feelings for Hannah."

"Are you trying to pick a fight with me?"

"No, but . . . What if I hadn't stopped by and you ended up driving her home, alone? Would you be doing this in front of her house?"

I banged my head back on the seat cushion, then turned my face to her. "Christ, Madison, I don't have feelings for her. Not the way you think. I'm here. Next to you. I don't know what more I can do. If you don't feel the same way, or whatever it is you're trying to say, fine, but don't tell me how I feel."

"Fine, whatever." She got out of the car and slammed the door.

"Madison."

She was halfway up the stairs, but turned around and stomped back down, opening the door.

"I'm—"

"I forgot my keys." She grabbed my jacket and fished her hand inside the pocket. As she pulled out her keys a cascade of change and other crap came tumbling out. She looked at the seat littered with stuff, then at me. Her brow furrowed and she dropped the jacket, leaving again. I got out of the car and stood up, realized that my pants were still unbuttoned.

"Madison, wait, come on."

"Go home, Jesse." She disappeared into her house.

What.

The.

Hell.

Just happened?

My blood still raced as I slid back into the driver's seat. I tossed my jacket in the back, picking up the random change and shoving it in my hoodie pocket. There was a guitar pick, and a napkin with numbers on it. Huh? I laid it flat on the dash and turned on the interior light. *Becca*. Those girls from Whiskey Business. Had Madison seen this too?

Fuhhhhhhhhhhhhck.

How could she even think this meant anything? The song I'd been writing, her song, buzzed through my head again. Bits of words again right there for the taking. I reached into the backseat, dug around my backpack for my song notebook. No pen. I sighed, looked up at her house, debating whether to ring her doorbell and insist we talk.

No.

There was no clearing this up right now, she had to cool off. Whatever it was she was going through, she didn't need me in her face. I started up the Bug and drove home, playing the song over and over in my head, eager once again to pick up my guitar. This song meant so much to me, now more than ever.

I needed to get it out of my head.

For her.

TWENTY-THREE

"CONSIDER THIS A YOGA-VENTION, YOU NEED TO go." Wren tugged on my foot.

"You can't miss my first class," Jazz said.

They both flopped down on the foot of my bed while I put a pillow over my head and screamed into it. It was forty-five minutes before class started and I had no interest in finding inner peace, no matter how bad I needed it. I'd broken the cold-shoulder routine with my mother and begged her to let me take a mental-health day from school—from life, really. Playing the I-just-found-out-who-my-father-is-and-he's-leaving card might have been a bit dirty, but she'd agreed on the condition that I put my portfolio together and attended yoga class that night, since it would be her first time assisting and she needed the moral support.

I'd finished my portfolio, but I was waffling on the class, which had more to do with being in the vicinity of Mugshot than anything else. I sat up and pleaded my case again.

"I don't know myself anymore. Why would I angry-kiss Jesse and pick a fight? I can't be trusted to be within ten miles of the boy."

"C'mon, Mads, you're going through an insane amount of stuff, you're allowed to act a little crazy. And angry-kissing is kind of hot. I'm sure he got over it," Jazz said.

"Is that Jazz or Diara speaking?" I asked.

She blushed. "I'll never tell."

I flopped back down onto my pillow and stared at the ceiling. They were breaking me down about yoga, but there was something else I hadn't told them—something that had me even more unsettled than my father leaving or the whole Jesse situation. After I'd put together my portfolio, I researched summer programs in the Bay Area. I'd been doing it for fun, on the off chance that there was something interesting.

The tuition was ridiculous and it involved transcripts and letters of recommendation and it was totally, totally insane, and I hadn't even bookmarked it or anything.

And yet I couldn't stop thinking about it.

That would be an experience. It wasn't much more than Pratt. And Paul had offered to pay for Pratt. I could do the father thing with him and my mother could *live her yoga* without me underfoot for a while. It could be a win-win sitch all around. Maybe she could even come out and visit and we could fly home together. Could he handle living with me under the same roof for a month? Could my mother?

"So you got jealous, and had a pissed-off make-out sesh. You're human. And you both promised me celebratory chais, so I'm holding you to that. Besides, you have to wish Jesse good luck, or break a leg, or whatever it is you say to someone before a battle," Wren said.

She stood up and rummaged through my dresser, pulling out my favorite pair of yoga pants—the ones with the daisies up the side that made me smile every time I was in downward dog. She tossed them over to me and they landed on my head, one leg draped over my face. I grabbed them and playfully narrowed my eyes at her.

"If that's not enough to convince you, I saw on the calendar that Leif is focusing on inversions tonight. Which means his shirt will be flipping up a lot. Which means a one-way ticket to abtopia."

"Does Grayson know you lust after Leif?" Jazz asked.

"I don't lust after him. I'm just admiring the view."

"Yes, every time Wren catches a glimpse of Leif half-naked she thanks the universe for creating such perfection," I said. Maybe going to class to drool over Leif's abs would be a good start on the road back to normal. It wouldn't be the worst way to spend an hour.

"Right. As long as he doesn't assist me, I'm fine."

"Then she turns into a melting lust puppy."

"Wait—assist? He might touch me?" Jazz asked.

"Melting lust puppy is exaggerating," Wren said. "And Mad's mom is there tonight so you only have a fifty-fifty shot of being assisted by Leif. No worries."

"The lust-puppy thing sounds fun, though," Jazz said, grinning.

My mouth dropped open. "I'm liking this side of you, Jazzabelle."

"Okay, then are you in or not? We've got, like, fifteen minutes to get there for decent mat space," Wren said.

Showing up for my mother was the right thing to do—she wanted me there, and it would be an olive branch, a small step in the right direction, especially if I was going to run the study-in-Cali idea by her. We couldn't turn back time to change her decision not to tell us, but Paul was right—my mother wasn't a vindictive person. I had to keep telling myself that; her choice not to tell us was not out of spite, even if I didn't fully understand it. I sat up and grabbed my yoga pants.

"All this talk of lust and abs, fine, you win, I'll be ready in ten."

Leif introduced my mother, and another student who would be assisting, at the beginning of class.

Mom looked almost shy, hair back in her tribal-print headband, standing to the side and giving us a modest wave before snapping into serious yogini mode. We started the class with a meditation. Leif's voice was practically an opiate.

"Take everything that's bothering you, all the dreck that makes you crazy, roll it together like a big ball of clay and put it to the side of your mat. I promise it will be there at the end of class and you can pick it up again, but for now, feel how much lighter you are without it."

The ball of dreck I collected was the size of Jupiter. My mother, Paul, my new idea of a summer program in Cali, Jesse . . . I put them all away for a moment and focused on me. Hearing Leif's calm, even voice made it all seem possible, to step away for a moment and just exist on my mat.

My hamstrings were so tight that I could barely touch the floor in forward fold. After a few rounds of sun salutation, my hands were wrapped around my toes. My breathing propelled me. I imagined I was slicing through the air during swan dive, focused on putting my forehead to my shins, enjoying how each move made my body more open and relaxed.

"We're going to open up with trikonasana—if you need a block, raise your hand." My mother distributed blocks to those who wanted them as Leif talked us through setting up our alignment.

I prepped for the pose—after five months, I didn't need to listen, could just feel what was right with my body. I reached out, tipping at my waist, placing my hand on my shin.

I felt warmth on my lower back. A hand.

"Your hip is tilting slightly forward, here." My mother placed a firm hand on the point of my hip bone and gently nudged it back, causing a muscle I hadn't even known existed in my lower back to smart. I snapped to standing so fast, I nearly knocked us both over.

"What are you doing?"

She shook her head slightly, blinked. I hadn't meant it to sound so snotty. I'd been doing the pose for months without anyone adjusting me, why all of a sudden did she think I was doing something wrong?

"Your hips were out of alignment." She demonstrated the first part of the pose herself, showing me how to square my hips. Why was she calling me out? If she could so easily point out what was wrong with my pose, why couldn't she use that same focus to figure out where she went wrong in her own life?

Olive branch . . . olive branch . . .

"Sometimes when you reach too far, you compensate by rolling your hip forward, and your hips go out of whack." She demonstrated by overreaching and turning her body in such a way that her butt stuck out. The woman on the mat in front of mine stopped mid-pose and watched my mom. Jazz was suddenly behind me, observing too. The tips of my ears were on fire.

"I don't do that."

My mother stood up, and held out her arms as if she were gathering me up.

"Try the pose again."

"Mom, stop."

The woman in front of us resumed stretching. My mother took a deep breath, eyes on me, looking like she wanted to say more. She nodded, though, and backed off. Jazz, ever the peacemaker, asked her a question about foot placement and the unpleasant moment passed.

Leif moved on to inversions.

"Inversions are challenging because most of us are afraid of going out of our comfort zone—and being upside down is about as out of your comfort zone as you can get when you're a biped. But reversing gravity's pull helps the body eliminate waste, improves circulation, and," Leif said, putting his hands on the floor and bringing his legs in the air in one nimble move that made the room go silent, "it's just kind of fun to see things from a different perspective."

His gray shirt flipped up, displaying his washboard perfection as he walked on his hands a few feet across the studio floor before landing on his feet again. I could practically hear the collective cougar-roar from the class, but I didn't peek over at Wren or back at Jazz to see their reactions. When it was time to partner off to practice headstand, I feigned a coughing fit and left the room.

"Madison."

I turned to see Leif right behind me, pulling the door to the studio gently shut.

"Oh, hey."

"Are you okay?"

I coughed into my fist to continue the charade. "I have a

tickle in my throat, wanted to get some water."

"I noticed you seem to be a little overwhelmed today."

"Nope."

"Because it's understandable to feel that way."

The last thing I wanted or needed was some catchall yogic wisdom, but I was curious. Did he know my situation? My mother couldn't have possibly blabbed about our personal stuff to him, right? That would have been weird.

"What way?"

"It's hard to adjust, to see a person in a different light, but change is the only constant in life."

I wasn't sure if I was relieved to hear someone acknowledge my feelings or ticked off that my mother had shared what was going on with Paul. All I knew was that I was sick of hiding behind my angry face. Being pissed off at the world had become a real energy-suck. I didn't feel totally comfortable talking about it with a stranger, but if my mother had trusted Leif enough to tell him, maybe he could offer some objective insight.

"I am a little overwhelmed, actually."

"Yoga training can really shuffle a person's beliefs, kind of rock them to their core—so it's natural to maybe feel threatened by the changes your mom is going through. When I started—"

He hadn't been talking about Paul at all.

"Wait, you think I'm threatened by my mother?"

His dark eyes went blank, lips pursed to the side. I'd never seen him look puzzled. It made him less mystical yogi, more human. "'Threatened' might be a strong word. I saw things got a little tense when she adjusted you."

I hadn't realized it was that obvious. "Oh, um, yeah."

"I know you started practicing together, so it's probably hard to see her as a teacher, and that's fine—I just wanted to make sure you know it's okay to feel that way. Your being here at all is great support for her." He stepped back toward the studio door. "I have to get back to class, see you in a few."

I nodded and watched him reenter the classroom, feeling slightly off balance again after I'd assumed he'd been talking about something different. My face felt hot, I needed a cool splash of water—something, *anything*, to reboot.

The bathroom was the same peaceful shade of sage green as the studio with a soundtrack of bubbling water and nature sounds playing softly in the background. I sat on a small bench along the wall, pushing down the sudden inexplicable urge to cry. What the hell was wrong with me? Was I really so infantile that I couldn't handle a simple correction in a yoga class? Had Leif been right? Did I really feel threatened by my mother?

I'd started taking the class as a fluke and I liked it, looked forward to it, even, but it was different for my mother. She was beyond that—it was more than a class for her. It was becoming a way of life for her—a way of life without me.

The realization hit me so sharply.

Was that why I was thinking of studying in California? Was it less about living with Paul and more about leaving her because I could feel her leaving me? No, not totally—I did want to make my own way, separate from her, but I also wanted to know Paul better than just sporadic visits. Even though they weren't together, I could never separate Mom and Paul. They were their own unique pair, connected by their shared history and now, me. I'd have to find a way for both of them to be in my life.

By the time I got back to the studio, the class was in final meditation. I didn't want to interrupt, so I waited in the reception area. There on the counter was the same kind of Buddha statue I'd accidentally knocked off our mantelpiece. The girl behind the desk was busy working on what looked like next month's class schedule. I cleared my throat.

"Excuse me, do you know where I can get a Buddha like this one?"

"This guy?" She picked up the statue. I anticipated some exotic locale, or Zen.com or something, but she looked on the bottom and smiled. "That home-accessories place on the back highway."

Sure enough, the sticker on the bottom was from the home store, and it was $10.99 to boot.

"Thanks."

When the final meditation was through, I went back into

350

the studio to collect my mat. Mom came over to me. I spoke first.

"That was a great class. Nice adjusting."

She smiled. "Are you okay—you left, I thought—"

"Nope, just had a tickle in my throat," I said.

"Ready?" Wren and Jazz sidled up to us.

"How did you enjoy your first class?" my mother asked Jazz.

"Very relaxing. I'll be back."

"Great. Maddie, I'm assisting with the next class, too—you do have a ride home, right?" she asked.

"Grayson's picking us up," Wren said.

"Yep, guess I do," I said, rolling up my sticky mat. "See you later."

"Let's go, chais on me tonight," Wren said.

"Why don't we get them from Quick Chek?" I asked, semi-dreading the apology I owed Jesse.

"You can't be serious, Mads."

"Only a little," I said.

The three of us left the studio and went next door to Mug-shot. Jesse was behind the counter with Tanner. At the sight of him my heart quickened—what did he think of me, after I'd practically attacked him in his VW and just stomped off? I knew I had to face him sometime, and maybe a well-lit, noisy café would be a good buffer against my angst. I'd been emotionally fragile with him, there was no going back from that, and I had to deal with all the weird, jangled feelings that came from sharing so much of myself with someone.

I kept my eyes down as we inched up to the counter. How would he react to seeing me? Could I blame him if he didn't want to deal with me? I imagined the worst, but when I looked into his eyes, they were soft, inviting. He smiled at me from under the well-worn rim of his Mugshot hat.

"Hey," he said.

"Hey."

Wren spoke up. "Three chai lattes, for here. Oh, and a black coffee for Gray. He's stopping by to pick us up."

"Ah, *here*—you're throwing me off my game." Tanner put down the cups he'd been about to juggle and cast a side-long glance at Jazz. She smiled back at him. Their flirtation momentarily lightened my mood.

"You don't mind. We can hang out awhile, right?" she asked him.

"You can hang out as long as you want, Jasmine," he said. "I don't know about those other two, though." Tanner winked at us. Winked. The boy had grown a pair and developed some flirting skills. There was some hope for him after all.

Wren nudged me and grinned. "They'd kind of be cute together."

She handed Jesse a twenty and we found a table near the window. Five minutes later he brought our drinks to us. He lingered a moment, looked at me. My stomach hollowed out.

I should have been the one to make the first move.

"Can we talk a minute?" he asked.

I slipped out of my seat and followed him to a narrow hallway behind the counter. We leaned on opposite walls.

"About last night—"

"Jess—I was totally out of line, I'm sorry. I believe what you said about Hannah. I do. I don't get like this normally. I like you. A lot. And . . . this—" I was spluttering. Uncomfortable. Jesse waited, a small smile crossing his face.

"Me too." He leaned down and gave me a kiss on the cheek.

"So you're not mad I attacked you, then basically ran off?" I asked.

"Um, no —I hope we can do it again sometime, well, in a more private place, without the running off."

I laughed, feeling the heat rise in my cheeks. "That would be awesome."

"I was worried you were upset about that number in my pocket, you know, the napkin. . . . I thought . . . you do know about that, right? The way you looked at it."

I briefly entertained the thought of lying. Not a good way to start, though.

"Yeah, I did, but I figured if it was still in your pocket, you probably didn't use it," I said, using Wren's wisdom to cover my jealous ass.

"Cool."

"Hey, Jess, I hate to break this up but—" Tanner motioned with his head to the growing line.

"Be right there." He stood up straight, adjusted his hat.

"So, um, are you coming to the battle tomorrow night?"

"I wouldn't miss it," I said.

"Great," he said. "See you tomorrow."

We left the hallway and parted ways. I turned back.

"Hey, Jess."

"Yeah?"

"Good luck."

"Thanks."

Grayson was sitting with Wren and Jazz when I returned. The three of them had goofy-ass grins on their faces as I sat down. I sipped my chai and ignored them.

"Hey, do you have to go right home after this?" I asked them.

"I don't."

"Me either."

"Guess not," Grayson answered. "What's up?"

"Think we could make a slight detour before heading home? There's something I need to get."

The following night, I took my time getting ready. I wanted to look special for Jesse . . . for me . . . because it felt good to be going somewhere with my friends and that my main concern was perfecting my smoky eyes and picking out my skirt and boots for the evening. The finishing touch was the Yellow #5 shirt. Wren's dad was dropping us off at the high school and I had fifteen minutes left to get ready. There was a knock on my bedroom door.

"Hey, Mads." My mother walked in holding the Laughing Buddha statue I'd stopped by the store to get last night after class. She sat on the foot of my bed and smiled. "Noticed this on the mantel this morning. Thank you for replacing it, you didn't have to."

"Yes, I did. I'm sorry about that. I know I haven't been that supportive of you getting into yoga. What you're doing is incredible, Mom. You're going to be an awesome instructor."

"You really think so? Sometimes, I wonder."

"It's a good fit for you. And you look cute in the yoga pants."

She laughed. "Where are you off to tonight?"

"Jesse's in the Battle of the Bands over at Bergen Point tonight. Going to cheer them on."

"Sounds fun, what time does that start?"

"Eight-ish. Not sure what time he goes on. Wren and Jazz will be here in less than fifteen."

"Oh . . . Paul is coming by tonight. He's leaving tomorrow, you know that, right?"

I stopped mid–swirl of blush application and looked at her.

"Wait, what? He said he found a new place."

"Yes, at a hotel near the airport."

Anger I thought had subsided bubbled up again.

"He didn't mention he was leaving, like, now."

My mother shook her head. "It doesn't surprise me. I had

to bribe him with Palermo's pizza and a bottle of his favorite cab to even stop by tonight; he's not one for good-byes. He doesn't really consider this good-bye, though."

"But it is, isn't it?"

I thought about my tentative plan to apply to summer architecture programs in California. What was the use now? If he hadn't even wanted to say good-bye, why would he want me to live with him for a few weeks?

"Mom, I'll try to get back, but I need to see Jesse. It's important to me."

"Well, maybe he'll still be here when you get home."

"I doubt it."

My mother stood up and put a hand on my shoulder. "Madison, it's a lot to take in. We won't figure this out all at once. I told you before—this *is* happy news to Paul. Very. Don't forget."

"So happy he's pretty much running away."

"Well—you know, sometimes it's hard to change."

"Maybe he should start taking yoga, so he can live his truth."

"I'll have to tell him you said that."

TWENTY-FOUR

"DUDE, YOU HAVE TO CALM DOWN, WE'VE GOT this thing," Grayson said.

"I'm trying," I said.

Being stuck in a vestibule along with the other bands and various equipment was about as fun as being naked in a cage with a rabid honey badger. Although, truth be told, a honey badger would have probably smelled better. Not everyone, it seemed, cared about hygiene, and the small space made that painfully evident. My nerves were live wires; I could barely stand still in the two feet of space we had surrounding us. At least the door had windows so I could see into the gym.

There were two stages, so as one band played, the other could set up their equipment. Thankfully, Plasma didn't share our staging area; they waited in the hallway on the other side of the gym. Sharing a cramped space with Kenny or Duncan would have made me even edgier. I'd seen them, nodded in a sort of "Good luck, may the best band win" kind of way, but they had just sort of stared, trying to psych us out. Out of six bands, we were set to go on third. Smack-dab in the middle. Not the most enviable spot, but it was the luck of the draw. Plasma was the closing band. Tanner thought it was fixed.

I paced back and forth, occasionally peeking out into the gym, which did nothing to calm my nerves. The Battle of the Bands always drew a decent crowd, and the space was already starting to fill in. I kept looking for one face, though, and ten minutes until the battle was supposed to start, Madison was nowhere to be seen. Her absence wasn't the reason I was nervous. She said she'd be there and I believed her.

The real reason it felt like my blood was replaced with pure adrenaline was that I was about to throw the competition and I had no idea how I was going to break it to Tanner and Grayson.

After the weirdness with Madison in my car, I'd gone home and finished the song. Her song. I couldn't handle playing it for her one on one, I'd be too self-conscious—but being on a stage where I could get lost in the energy of the crowd would somehow make it easier. I didn't plan on singling her out, I knew how she felt about grand gestures, but she would know it was for her.

Grayson would be easier to persuade. This was all new to

him, and while I knew he wanted to win, he wouldn't think twice about me doing the song. He'd said as much at practice.

Tanner was a different story. It was now or never. I grabbed his arm.

"Dude, I have to talk to you," I said.

"Shoot," he said.

"Not here."

His upper lip curled. "Where we gonna go?"

I looked around. He had a point. I turned my back to the small area, forming our own corner, and motioned for them to come closer.

"Okay, I'm starting to feel like a douche, Jess, are we going to join hands and do a power chant or something?"

"This from the guy wearing the hat," Grayson said.

"*Lucky* hat."

"The song is done. It's good. I want to play it for Madison."

That was as plain as I could make it.

Tanner breathed out hard, staring up at the ceiling before answering. "I thought we talked about this. Just save it for May."

"I just . . ."

"Want to impress a girl. Did you know about this?" He turned to Gray. Gray shook his head.

"No, this is sort of a game-time call. Look, I can't explain it, I just think she needs to hear this. We're already better than Plasma—we know that, does it really—"

"How could you spring this on us now? Why is it more important than us trying our best to win this thing?"

"Because it just is."

Tanner's face fell. He shook his head. "It's still all about you."

He spun away, knocking into the girl singer from the band who was set to go on first. "Sorry," he mumbled as she scowled.

"T, wait," I said as he shouldered his way over to a set of double doors. Through the glass window I saw him storm off into the locker room, out to the area where we unloaded our equipment earlier.

"I shouldn't have asked."

"Jess, you wouldn't have asked if it wasn't important. I'll go talk to him," Gray said.

I nodded as he walked off in search of Tanner. Was Tanner right? Was it all about me? I hadn't meant for it to come out like that. I wanted to win, I did, but wasn't music more about reaching people, making them feel something instead of this stupid competition?

I peered out into the gym and finally spotted Madison, standing between Wren and Jazz. She wore the Yellow #5 shirt. Her smile a small, still vote of confidence in the crowd. My heart wigged out at the sight of her. What the hell had I been thinking? The song was too personal to share, it needed work—I sounded clumsy. What if I totally screwed it up and blew it?

Mr. Katz, our gym/driver's-ed teacher/emcee for the night, tapped a mic on the far stage, welcoming everyone and announcing that the first band would be on in five. My stomach coiled tight. I needed to find T and Grayson. I wove my way around the other bands, pushed through the doors, and found the darkened locker room. There was a door open to the outside on the far end. I raced toward the sliver of streetlamp and out into the parking lot behind the school. Tanner sat on the curb. Gray stood next to him.

"Hey, you know, just forget it," I said. "We'll do our five best songs, that's it."

"No, do the song, Jess," Gray said.

"I can't."

Tanner sprang up.

"Now you need me to tell you how great you are, right? Because that's how it always works with us."

"No, you were right. We wouldn't be here if it weren't for you putting up the money, filling out the application. I'm just, it was stupid of me. Arrogant."

He breathed out, crossed his arms.

"Chickenshit."

"What?"

"Just play the song you wrote for Madison. Okay? You're wimping out, that's worse than losing on purpose."

"What if it sucks?"

"It won't. It never does," Tanner said.

"Okay, gather in," Gray said, motioning for us to huddle.

"Dude, I was serious about the chanting feeling. Not right."

"I was lacrosse captain, just huddle, it brings a team together, and we are about as not together as you can be at the moment."

"Fine, but if you start telling me to breathe deep—"

I jabbed Tanner to stop it. The three of us put our hands out and brought them together.

"Now what?"

"Someone say something inspiring. As front man, Jess, I think that falls to you."

My mind was blank. What to say? Two months earlier I'd wanted to give up, and here I was with a viable band, both Tanner and Gray were better than they thought they were. We could be great. Blow them all away. That was it.

"If we're gonna blow it, blow it big."

"From the Whiskey. Cool, I like it," Tanner said.

"Me too. So on the count of three, um, 'Blow it big.'"

"Do we—"

"Just say it." Gray shot Tanner a look.

"One . . . two . . . three. . . . Blow it big!"

We pulled our hands away, and Grayson howled. Tanner punched the air a few times.

"Let's do this."

I could never be sure at what point it happened, when Stage Jesse took over, but it was something I could always count on.

The fear of failure, the nervous anticipation, and the energy of the crowd all converged and fueled me. The last piece of the puzzle was my Fender. I put the strap over my head and ran my fingers across the strings. Gray slid into his seat, giving me a stick up that he was ready. Tanner nodded. I stomped my foot, holding the guitar close to my body, and walked up to the mic.

"S'up, Bergen Point. Are you ready for some Yellow Number Five?"

There was a cheer, but not a loud one.

I screamed into the mic, "Are you readeeeeeeeee?"

I didn't wait to hear a louder response, just launched into "Welcome to Paradise" and the crowd was infused with the music, a wave of people under our control, at least for the duration of our set. I looked over at Tanner; he grinned, tassels on his hat whipping around with his movement. We owned the stage and it felt fucking amazing.

We went into the next song, a Say Anything cover, without breaking. I scanned the faces in the crowd, now more visible, looking for her. She was there, her face flashing green, then blue, in the stage lights. A smile when our eyes met that fired up my confidence. I played for her. For me. For everyone. We drove the song hard, Gray ending with a thrash of drums. Tanner waved me over.

"Do it now," he said.

"No, I can wait until the end."

"No, do it now, but it better be friggin' amazing," Tanner said.

Grayson nodded, taking a gulp from a water bottle. I switched guitars, pulling the strap of the acoustic over my head. I hadn't given much thought to how I was going to introduce the song. Only knew I wouldn't say her name. The rest I was winging.

"Gonna slow it down a little. This next one is a Yellow Number Five original. Kind of the world premiere."

"You suck!" someone yelled.

Was it a mistake doing it now that everyone was so pumped? Screw it.

"Thanks," I said, laughing. "This one's for, um . . . well, she knows who she is."

Brilliant, Jess.

I fumbled with the opening chord, my mind suddenly empty. Blowing it big was one thing, fucking up completely in front of a room full of people who could remind me on a daily basis was another. I stopped strumming, took a breath, and found Madison in the crowd. She smiled. It was all I needed.

I strummed, feeling the buildup to the opening verse.

You come in like a storm
A force strong and true
Eyes alight with fire
Powerless against you

I closed my eyes, lost myself in the words and the melody. I was in the meadow, under the stars, filling the space, my mind a montage of visions of her—her hands in my hair, her face at Fallingwater, that sketch in her room, the fight in my VW—as I sang. Everything. The good, the bad, the best. When I opened my eyes, I saw that Tanner had pulled up a lighter app on his phone, inspiring others to do the same.

Madison's eyes were riveted on mine, her head tilted slightly; she stood stock-still in the swaying mass. She knew the song was for her. The crowd broke into applause as I strummed the last notes. We had a moment, an exchange, the two of us alone in the crowd, before I had to dive into the rest of the set. I wished I could say I knew what she was thinking, that we had telepathically communicated our mutual desire, but when the moment was over, I was just as unsure as I'd been at the start. I switched guitars again, the worry of what she really thought of the song threatening to paralyze my ability to play. She liked it, that was sort of evident, but how did she really feel about it? I pushed it out of my head as I called out the next song.

The final two songs were a blur. We'd practiced so much they were automatic and we finally loosened up and acted crazy. Me and Tanner stalked each other across the stage, jumping now and then. Laughing, even. By the time we finished, we'd wrung out the gymnasium.

At least it felt that way.

The stage crew helped us break down our stuff and we loaded it into the 'burban just as the fourth band took the stage. The stress from before the show was gone. I was relieved—the set had gone well, we'd played our best. That was winning enough for me. I hoped Tanner and Gray felt the same. A new kind of anxiousness tightened my throat as we walked back into the gym. Had Madison liked the song?

The fourth band was in the middle of their set as we hit the gym floor. Wren spotted Gray first and waved him over. Jazz beamed at Tanner. Madison wasn't with them. My stomach took a free fall.

"You guys were awesome!" Wren screeched over the band. Gray pulled her in for a kiss. I looked at Jazz.

"Where's Madison?"

She leaned in toward me and cupped a hand around my ear. "She had to run home."

My playing high deflated in seconds. "What? Why?"

Jazz shrugged. "She just said something like, 'I have to go, call me if you go out after,' and then she was gone before we could stop her."

"Was she pissed off or anything?"

She shook her head as Tanner joined us.

"You were great," she said to him, punching his shoulder.

He pulled on his hat. "Works every time."

Had she hated the song that much?

The crowd suddenly felt thicker. I pulled on my collar, trying to cool down, looking around the gym on the off chance that Jazz maybe hadn't heard Madison right. That maybe she was just at the back of the gym, waiting for me.

"Hey, do you mind if I bail?" I asked Tanner. He crossed his arms.

"I'll try to make it back before they announce everything."

"No you won't. You sure you don't want to be here for the results?"

"Not really. In my mind, we won."

Tanner laughed. "I guess I can catch a ride with Gray. You better come out after. A plate of disco fries is the least of what you owe me for tonight."

"Tanner, thanks, man. For everything."

"Yeah, yeah, you better, like, name your first kid after me or something," he said.

I pushed my way through the crowd and out into the hallway, checking my messages hoping to find one from Madison. Nothing.

"Jess."

I spun around at my name.

Hannah stood behind a table of cupcakes. There were two other girls with her, in front of a sign that read: SUPPORT THE ARTS! $1 CUPCAKES! They stopped talking as I came over.

"Hey," I said.

"You guys were the best," one of the girls said.

"Thanks."

"There's still two more bands to go," Hannah said. "We're rooting for Plasma, remember?"

The girl shook her head and held out a cupcake to me. "You guys are still the best. Here, on the house."

"Nah, I'm good," I said.

"Do not refuse her cupcake," the other girl said, taking it from her and holding it up to my face. I laughed.

"Well, um, okay." I took it from her. "Thanks."

"Can I talk to you for a minute, Jess?" Hannah motioned for me to walk over to the side with her. I followed. We stopped in front of a bank of lockers. She leaned against one and smiled at me.

"I'm kind of in a rush," I said.

A crease formed between her brows. "You're leaving? You're not even going to watch Duncan?"

"No, I'm sure they'll be great."

"Guess you're not afraid of the competition, then."

I shrugged. "I don't know, not really thinking about it. I just . . . We played our best. It's not really a competition to me—doesn't matter who wins."

"Your song was beautiful, Jesse."

My mouth went dry as she reached up and ran her fingers under the lapel of my jacket. She had this sparkle in her eyes for a moment, but then pulled her hand away quickly, like she suddenly realized she shouldn't be touching me.

"Thanks, I really have to—"

"So did you write it the other night? Your notebook looked pretty blank, I was just wondering. It was so pretty, the way you introduced it," she said, looking down at her feet. "Are you really powerless against me?"

Holy crap.

She thought it was about her.

The kind thing might have been to ignore it, I guess, but I couldn't. I should have been happy, this was what I'd wanted for so long, for her to come back to me, but she'd been right about the breakup. Maybe I had a lot to do with it, but we'd both been a little too comfortable. It was time to move on. I could feel that now.

"Hannah, I . . . There's someone else. You know, that girl you met the night at Mugshot? Madison?"

The look on her face jabbed me in the gut.

"Oh. I . . . I'm sorry, Jess," she said.

I had no clue what to say to her. Whatever doubts she'd been having about Duncan were things she had to deal with on her own. As much as I still cared about her, I wasn't ready to dole out relationship advice. Still, I didn't want to leave it at that, without saying something upbeat. I didn't want her to feel like shit over any of it.

"The song Plasma is playing, the one Duncan wanted so bad . . . just, you know, listen to it. There was a reason he wanted it. You'll like it. I promise."

Her eyes brightened. "Thanks. Um, Madison seems really nice. I hope you guys are happy."

"Thanks. Me too."

"Banana girl, you're fraternizing with the enemy, come back!" the cupcake girls called to us.

"Bye, Jess." She walked to the stand without looking back.

This felt like good-bye.

I dashed out the door to find Madison, hoping the song hadn't scared her off. Sometimes you just had to have faith in grand gestures.

THE SONG WAS FOR ME. I KNEW THAT. AND I WASN'T running away—I hoped Wren and Jazz made sure Jesse knew that when they saw him after Yellow #5's set. I wanted to see him after the battle, and I would, but I had to do something first before it was too late.

Thankfully, the night was warm—winter finally giving way to spring—and it was pleasant walking across town. I stopped at the bakery. I'd made it just as they were about to close, buying the last of the good doughnuts, the one sure thing that Paul and I shared. Well, the second, I guess. We shared Mom, after all.

I wasn't about to let Paul get away with not saying good-bye to me. I wasn't an architect yet but I was the architect of my own life and this not-saying-good-bye crap set up a weak foundation.

Jesse's song—seeing him alone, vulnerable, voice and guitar—reminded me that being an open book, sharing what was inside, was an uncertain leap. Scary but necessary. I didn't quite understand what had come over me as I watched him. Or maybe it was something that had been gradually happening since I met him. Jesse poured out words that cut me straight to the core. I couldn't help but melt, my heart firmly and sappily on my sleeve. Maybe only Jazz and Wren knew the song was for me, but it felt like everyone in the Bergen Point gym had.

I climbed the stairs to my house two at a time, still harboring the tiniest hope that I'd burst in on Mom and Paul in a lip-lock, they'd profess their love to each other and me, and we'd be a family and live happily ever after just like my birthday wish.

No such luck.

"Madison, I thought you were out for the night," my mother said.

The two of them were in their usual spot in the dining room, each with a glass of wine, half-eaten pizza still in the box between them. I lifted up the grease-stained white bag for Paul to see. He grinned and raised his glass to me before taking a sip.

"Pizza and doughnuts, this is quite a send-off," he said.

"Were you really going to leave without saying good-bye to me?" I placed the bag on the table and pulled out a chair. Paul put his glass down. My mother rested her chin on her hands and waited expectantly for him to answer.

"And don't give me 'I'm not into good-byes.' I think that's

sort of Parenting 101—you say good-bye to the people you love when you leave. Especially your kids. Especially me."

He looked between my mother and me. "Okay, I can do that."

"There's something else," I said.

My mother gave me the same expectant look she'd given Paul.

No turning back now.

"I did some research about summer programs in California and I thought, well, maybe I'd apply someplace out there."

"The one at Cal Poly?" Paul asked.

"No, the one at Berk—wait, how do you know there's one at Cal Poly?" I looked at my mom, who was chuckling and shaking her head.

"After we spoke the other day, I looked into it, I thought I'd toss the idea out to your mom, see what she thought first. I know how important it is for you to earn your way."

"I'd have to earn my way into Berkeley. I think I still have time to get everything together." I stopped, looked at my mother. "Are you okay with this if I get in?"

She smiled. "I think it would be great, for the both of you. And I guess I would have to maybe fly out at some point. Ugh, a vacation out west, how awful would that be?"

"The three of us in the city by the bay again," Paul said, lifting up his wineglass. "That would be something."

The three of us.

It sounded weird but nice.

Not exactly what I'd wished for on my birthday but it was a start.

Going to diner. Need a ride?

I was about to answer Wren's text when I got another one.

never mind

What did that even mean? I hoped it meant what I thought it did. Moments later I heard footfalls on the front porch. My heart jumped into my throat and I sprung up from the table, crumbs from the doughnut I'd eaten falling to the floor.

"Wait, no good-bye peck on the cheek for your old man?"

I laughed. "Old man?"

"Yeah, I don't like it either."

"Let's stick to Paul."

I ran back and gave him a kiss on the cheek, Mom, too, just as someone knocked. "Don't wait up," I said, heading out, and right smack into Jesse.

"Hey."

He smiled, shrugging his shoulders up to his ears. "Hey."

His hair was all over the place from flipping it around as he played, but the disheveled look worked on him. I resisted the urge to run my fingers through it.

"What are you doing here? Is the battle over? Did you win?"

"Isn't it obvious?"

"That you won?"

"No, why I'm here."

I felt oddly shy remembering the song, the words, the way they made me feel.

"Come on." I led him down the stairs to the first landing, and motioned for him to sit.

"I came to see if you wanted to hang out," he said, perching on the concrete step. I eased onto his lap, eating up every moment of the surprise on his face.

"Yes, I do, but first . . . Jess, that song . . . you . . ." Every word I came up with sounded cheesy, or strange or horribly inadequate to describe how his song touched me. How it made me feel. How I felt about him.

"Thank you," I whispered. "Thank you for the song, for being here, for Fallingwater, for hot chocolate, for being kind even when I wasn't . . . for everything." I touched my lips to his. His mouth was soft and warm. I closed my eyes, letting myself drift into the feeling, that even if it was just for a moment, everything was the way it was supposed to be. This was right. He drew me closer to him, encircling me with his arms while I wrapped mine around his neck.

I never wanted to come up for air.

The diner was noisy and packed with people when we walked in. Jesse had his arm around my shoulders as we scoured the tables to see if we could find the other members of Yellow #5 who were supposedly somewhere in the crowd. I saw Wren and waved. They sat at a big circular table in the back, menus still spread out in front of them.

"Finally, you're here to share in our victory," Tanner said as we got closer.

Jesse stopped. "Victory? What do you mean?"

"Do you want to tell him or should I?" Tanner looked at Gray.

"I think you should be the one."

"Come on, one of you say something already!" Jazz said.

"We won." Tanner grinned, pulling the ear flaps of his hat down. "Lucky hat."

"What? How?" Jesse pulled out a chair for me, but I nudged him onto it and plopped down on his lap again. Wren wriggled her eyebrows at me. I wrapped my arms around Jesse's neck and smiled.

"I guess the judges didn't read the rules."

"And since Plasma came in second they are contesting it, so we can't claim we're the winners yet, but yeah, win or not, the crowd loved us," Gray said.

"Wait, why would they contest it?" I asked.

"I wasn't supposed to play the song solo. It was against the rules," Jesse said.

"So then why did you?"

He touched his head to mine. Everyone at the table was looking at us—in truth, I didn't care. The old me, the

PDA-loathing me, finally realized that maybe when it was right, being in public was irrelevant, because it felt like we were the only two in the room. Warmth rushed through me as his lips brushed my ear.

"Because I had to play it . . . for you."

"And you risked losing?"

He looked at me, his eyes so intense and steady, like all this time he knew something that he'd been waiting for me to understand. I pressed my lips to his, ignoring the clapping at our table, shutting out everything else but us, this moment. It was scary and sexy and fun.

And real.

ACKNOWLEDGMENTS

Thank you, dear reader, for spending some time in Madison and Jesse's world; I hope you enjoyed your stay! If you're the sort who turns to the acknowledgments first, you should know that this book in your hands would not have been possible without the following excellent people:

Tamar Rydzinski, agent extraordinaire, I'm so lucky to have you and Laura Dail Literary Agency in my corner, two words can hardly contain my gratitude.

Donna Bray, dream editor, you have the knack for saying the right words, just when I need to hear them. Thank you for helping me shape a rather unwieldy manuscript into this novel, and for believing that I was up to the task.

There are so many people at Balzer+Bray/HarperCollins who've toiled on behalf of my work—a million thanks for being such a brilliant and dedicated team, with special shout-outs to Viana Siniscalchi, you're simply the best; Erin Fitzsimmons, for another cover I want to hug; Caroline Sun, for your patience and mad publicity skills; Nellie Kurtzman, for your marketing prowess; and Bethany Reis and Brenna Franzitta, for the amazing copyedit.

Thank you to Meg Wiviott for fresh eyes and words of encouragement.

Thank you to the writers from the Montreat weekend, who laughed at all the funny bits—Kip, Patty, Lauren, Juliana, Jen, Mary Ann, and especially to Jro, for letting me crash your party in the first place. Great food, good wine, laughter—let's do it again soon.

Thank you to the stupendously talented One Fours, for wisdom and laughs and for sharing this wild, wonderful ride. I owe my sanity to you. Group hug. We made it!

At one time or another, the following individuals have offered honest critiques, gentle advice, shoulders to cry on, or are just plain awesome—so blessed to have crossed paths with Cindy Clemens, Laura Renegar, Judy Palermo, Janice Finnell, Brianna Caplan Sayres, Gale Sypher Jacob, Megan Miranda, Megan Shepherd, and Kasie West.

Thank you to my Gurls, for memories old and new and for your unwavering support, even during a blizzard.

Thank you to Mike, Jan, Dylan, and Grace for road-trippin' with me in the name of research. It's the journey, not the destination!

Thank you to my family for being a safe haven in an uncertain world, especially Mom, my number-one fan and unabashed book pimp.

And finally, a ginormous fireworks finale of a thank-you to Jim, for giving me the space to follow my dreams, for knowing when I need a break (sometimes better than I do), for making me laugh, every single day, and for just for being you. My heart is yours. Always.